Illirin Book One

Laura Maisano

*Gillian,
May the wind be to your back!*

Lake Dallas, TX
www.RayhaStudios.com

SCHISM
By Laura Maisano
© Copyright 2015 Laura Maisano

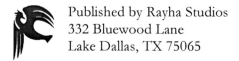

Published by Rayha Studios
332 Bluewood Lane
Lake Dallas, TX 75065

This book is a work of fiction. All characters, places, names, events are either a product of the author's imagination or are used fictitiously. Any likeness to any events, locations, or persons, alive or otherwise, is entirely coincidental.

All rights reserved, including the right to reproduce this book or portions thereof in any form. For inquiries and information, address Rayha Studios, 332 Bluewood Lane, Lake Dallas, TX 75065

First Rayha Studios paperback edition April 2015
Edited by Lisa Petrocelli
Cover by C. K. Volnek

ISBN 978-0-9860932-0-3
LCCN 2015931271

This book is licensed for your personal enjoyment only and remains the copyrighted property of the author. Please do not redistribute this book for either commercial or noncommercial use. If you enjoyed this book and would like to share it with another person, please encourage them to purchase their own copy. Thank you for respecting the hard work of this author.

~ For Tom, who believed in me no matter how crazy the dream,
and for Kahlan, whose love brings my imagination to life. ~

One

Her charcoal eyes stared back at Gabe from the page—almost alive. If only she lived, maybe she could help him remember, actually remember. Sure, Matt told him the facts, like a dossier on his life at the university, but you don't live a grocery list.

Gabe tightened his elastic hair band and flipped to the next page of the sketch pad. His hand flew across the paper, the vine charcoal making tiny squeaks as it left dark and light traces behind. She appeared again, wavy hair and soft freckles dotting her nose. *Heather*...only a name, but she should be so much more. If her image remained when the accident stole everything else, why didn't he know more about her...about anything?

At night, the empty studio became a cavern of cement that smelled of turpentine and sawdust. He didn't belong there. A lively class full of students wouldn't change that either. He felt out-of-phase with the others, floating by as witness instead of participant. Memory loss set him apart, but this feeling edged on instinct, something deeper.

Gabe studied his new sketch. He added a few touches, but as always, nothing came back. The school shrink told him to keep at the art therapy. *"The right side of the brain can unlock the subconscious,"* he'd said, along with some other crap. A lot of good Gabe's therapy was doing him now—another drawing, another failure.

He ripped the portrait off the easel and threw the crumpled sketch into the supply box.

Midnight came and went. Gabe packed up and headed back across the pebble walkways, rounded smooth by thousands of rubber soles. Without wind, the night transformed the campus into a snapshot, a world where nothing moved except him.

Clang! What in the…? Gabe followed the sound of scraping and intermittent little *tings* coming from the front of the Student Union.

Someone climbed the pole of the glass awning over the walkway by the Union, the entrance where the roof sloped down low. She threw her leg over the glass ceiling and stretched to reach the building. Her brown braid got caught in the strap of her tote bag as she contorted herself onto the roof.

That girl looked familiar. She adjusted her wire glasses, and bingo—Drawing 1500 on Mondays and Wednesdays. What was her name? The guys called her Looney Tunes. Well, scaling the Union in the middle of the night certainly fit right in with the crazy rumors.

Gabe walked up close to get a better look. Should he say something?

The girl pulled a gadget from her bag with a handle and a small screen. She waved whatever it was around like she belonged in one of his roommate's sci-fi flicks.

Three hazy lights appeared in the air behind her, fading in and out. They looked fuzzy, dancing behind a sheer curtain that wasn't there. A vibration ran across Gabe's skin, tingling.

The lights moved closer to the girl.

"Hey!" Gabe shouted, "Watch out!"

The girl snapped her head, her foot slipped, and she pinwheeled her arms in a failed attempt to catch her balance. Something big fell from her bag. She yelped and tumbled off the roof.

Oh crap! Gabe dove toward the wall, arms outstretched. Pain burst through his back, and her flailing body thrashed in the dense bushes that saved them both. The pain in his spine dulled into an ache. Apparently, he'd broken her fall with his back, and he'd have a nice bruise as a souvenir. Groaning, he yanked his arm free from the bush with only minor cuts.

Above the roof, the lights had vanished. The girl rolled out of the bushes and onto the cement, wincing. Her rapid breaths trembled, but when she caught his eye she calmed down. She took one deep breath. "Thanks."

Gabe rubbed his sore arm. "Are you insane?"

"I like 'eccentric.' Less hospitalized." She flashed a toothy grin.

"What the hell were you doing up there?"

She glanced around the sidewalk and behind her, looking for something. "Studying."

"Right."

On the bush, Gabe found what she was searching for, a three-ring binder with yellow sticky notes poking out from all the edges. He grabbed the binder with "ED Project" scrawled across the front in bold marker. What kind of project required students to use university buildings for climbing practice? The gym had a wall for that kind of thing, and it was safe, and you know, not crazy.

The girl clutched the bag still slung across her front. "Thanks for finding it." She reached out, but when she moved to stand, she gasped and fell back on her butt. She gingerly touched her ankle and gritted her teeth.

Gabe frowned and handed her the notebook. The girl got hurt pretty bad; he should be helping her, not harassing her.

"Here." Gabe reached for her hand. "The clinic's closed, but Bruce Hall's just up there." He nodded toward the main walkway. "They've got bandages and stuff at the front desk."

She searched until she found the handheld thing she dropped lying in the mulch. The plastic device had an old-style screen and grainy black text on a tan background. She shoved it in her bag with the binder before taking his hand.

Gabe helped her up and pulled her arm over his shoulder. "What's your name?" He adjusted his canvas portfolio on his other side.

"Lea Huckley." She closed the top of her bag in a tight fist. "I've seen you in Drawing. It's Gabe, right?"

"That's what the ID tells me," he said.

"So uh…not a nickname or short for Gabriel then?"

Oh God, not this conversation again. "No, it is." Gabe pulled her thin frame against him. It surprised him. She felt toned, way more substantial than she appeared. "Here, just hold on, and don't stand on your bad foot. I'm strong enough."

"All right, but that better not be a crack about my weight." Lea laughed and hopped on her good foot while holding him. "And…thanks for not thinking I was some terrorist or psycho and calling the cops on me."

Gabe stopped and dropped his jaw. He must be an idiot. What if she had been a school shooter? "It never even crossed my mind…"

Lea's grin broadened, and her nervous laughter brightened. "My lucky day."

They finished hobbling up the slope together, and Gabe swiped his ID to open the door to the dorm building. The student assistant at the desk gave him an Ace bandage, and a few more lopsided hops got them to a pair of open chairs with worn green upholstery.

Most of the lobby had emptied out. Only the resident "lobby lizards" took up the square of sofas in the back corner to give each other back rubs and complain about the banality of college life. The cafeteria closed at nine, but the smell of dorm cuisine permeated the fabrics. It was one of the less odious smells available.

Gabe unwrapped the bandage.

"I can do it." Lea reached for the bandage, and he pulled it back.

"It's okay. It'll be tighter if I wrap it from this angle." He carefully removed her sneaker and wound the bandage around her foot. He could draw it out and take his time. Now that they weren't outside in the open, maybe she'd tell him what she was doing on the roof. Remembering the translucent lights brought back that odd sensation, like déjà vu.

She flinched, putting her hand back over her bag that held her weird meter and the ED binder. The chair's ancient springs creaked every time Lea leaned or shifted, which she did often.

Gabe kept his eyes on his work. "So, who's ED? Must be important if he makes you risk your skin."

"What? Oh, that." She tapped her fingers on her bag. "ED is an acronym."

"What's it stand for, Erectile Dysfunction?" He smirked.

"Yes. I was testing the efficacy of Viagra at higher elevations."

Gabe snort-chuckled and wiped his face. *Now* he looked like an idiot. "No, really. What were you doing up there?" He attached the second clip to secure the bandage and rested her heel on the beat-up coffee table.

Lea attempted to wiggle her foot. "It doesn't matter." She threw on a smile again.

He wasn't gonna drop it. "Does it have anything to do with those floating lights?"

Like flipping a switch, Lea sprang to life. "You saw something? What did they look like? Where were they?" She put her bandaged foot back on the floor and edged up to the front of the chair.

"I'm not sure."

She spoke a hundred words a minute. "You said lights? How'd they appear, phasing in gradually or with an abrupt flash? How far up? Ten meters? Fifteen? Could you gauge a diameter?" She fluttered her fingers in the air as she thought. "Damn, right behind me? If only I hadn't fallen."

She poked her finger toward him. "Can you give me any details?"

"Why do you need to know?" Gabe leaned back further into his seat.

Lea pulled out the binder and gripped it like a life vest. "ED means Extra Dimensional. I'm gathering data to prove a theory. If you saw something, it means you may have an eye for this kind of thing." She huffed. "I'm so pissed I missed it."

Gabe eyed her bag. "What were you doing with that handheld thing?"

She put her hand over the bump in the tote. "Oh, the EMF reader?"

"Another acronym?" What was it with this girl and letter combos? Some military brat?

"It just measures electromagnetic fields." She shrugged like that was the most normal thing she could say.

"What were the lights then?"

Her mouth twisted in as she chewed her lip and inspected him under a dropped brow. Why was she looking at him like that? She was the one with sketchy self-preservation instincts, not him.

Lea flipped open the notebook and rifled through a few pages. She popped her face over the edge of the binder. "Fourth floor of the art building."

"What?"

"Meet me on the fourth floor of the art building, tomorrow at noon. I'll explain then." She stood carefully and walked out to the bowling alley-esque hallway.

"But there isn't a fourth floor…"

She grinned. "Tomorrow, noon." Lea hobbled past the front desk and back outside.

He didn't have to meet her the next day, but Gabe's curiosity burrowed into him. The strange vibration felt, well, not familiar…nothing felt familiar. Though talking with Lea kept him from obsessing about his memory for once. Anything that could manage that feat deserved attention.

Okay then, tomorrow. Noon.

Two

At the top of the stairs, Lea waited with her back pressed against the metal door. The final flight ended abruptly at a short wall of windows, which displayed a view of the gravel-coated roof. The school built this stairwell to the fourth floor of the art building, but ran out of money to finish the actual floor.

Thus Lea's test—Gabe had to push past his assumption a fourth floor didn't exist, and if he could, maybe he'd stretch that leap of faith. Curiosity wasn't enough. He had to want to know the truth. If she couldn't convince someone who *wanted* to believe her theory was law, how would she convince those who didn't? Baby steps.

She rested her head against the hard metal. At a shorter height than the rest of the building, the ceiling drooped and the space seemed to shrink. Cracks in the cement webbed around the corner, and she traced the delicate threads down each bend until the echo of footsteps shook her out of her daze.

Lea turned her gaze to the figure on the landing. *Gabe? He actually showed?*

Broad-shouldered and with perfect posture, Gabe didn't seem to match his physique. In class, he looked the part of a jock bent over an easel smoothing his dark-blonde hair in a neat ponytail. A brooding figure who rarely talked, an art student all the way…or was he?

You can't read a face like a formula, and if you could, you'd make a false conclusion. Life's fickle rules were good for nothing, so Lea tweaked 'em till they made sense. Number one, people want to believe what they see; show them anything. She tossed her mask back on. *Smile for the camera.*

Hands in his jeans, Gabe shook his head and half-chuckled. "Fourth floor, huh?"

Lea fixed her patented grin in place. "It's a tiny floor." She patted the small landing.

"I can see that." He leaned against the wooden railing and flinched when his arm made contact.

"Are you okay?" she asked.

"Yeah, just sore." He glanced at her ankle. "You?"

"It's only sprained, no biggie." She put weight on her good foot to stand. "Thanks again."

Gabe seemed to wait for her to speak. She let him. Come on, *want it.*

"Well?" He pulled his hands from his pockets.

She blinked. "Well, what?"

"You said you'd explain what happened last night. Is it something to do with this 'floor?'"

Lea chuckled. "Of course not."

His expression mimicked someone who stepped in dog poop. "Then why the he—"

"Because." She smacked her hand against the window. "Visual aid. This wall suddenly stops, but imagine there's a world beyond it. What you saw last night was something showing through from another dimension."

Any second he'd probably re-think his decision, run back down the stairs, and prove her experiment a failure. Why would he believe her? The story sounded unstable enough to the men with the white coats. Lea kept her doubts far from her face and waited to shout a goodbye.

But no. Gabe's stance shifted forward, not back. "What does that mean?"

He was still in the game. Lea yanked the ED Project binder from her tote and joined him on the landing. "I have theories detailing the existence of a fourth spatial dimension, which flows along the same time dimension as the third. You know, X, Y, and Z axes? Let's call the fourth one Bob. Bob is quadratic in nature and unseen from a three-dimensional perspective, so we can't interact with Bob. There are people who live in Bob, though we can't see them either since we're boring, three-dimensional beings. Their plane also rotates at calculated speeds around our own and intersects in different places I'm trying to pin down."

She took a breath. "I'm tracking paranormal phenomena to tighten my calculations." She opened the notebook to a page with a detailed graph overlaying a map of the city. Pencil-drawn equations sprawled over the opposite side. "Here, in about an hour, should be an interaction point. The parking garage of the mall downtown, not too far. We've got plenty of time."

"Wait...plenty of time for what?"

Lea clapped the notebook closed and stepped down three more stairs, just enough to make him wonder. "You coming?"

Gabe's over-loud sigh sounded more like a horse snorting. Cute. "Not unless you tell me why."

Lea turned halfway around. "You have no reason to believe me, but it's the truth. If I'm right, and we see evidence where I predicted, won't that show I'm onto something?"

He crossed his arms and took his chance to study her.

She dropped the smile, the act, and let him see that proving this meant everything. Lives depended on her.

"Okay." Gabe opened up again, hands relaxed by his sides, and he started down the stairs. "Let's go then."

"Wait," she said, "Thank you."

"For what?"

She watched his confusion wrinkle his forehead. "For showing up." Before he had a chance to reply, she turned and continued down the remaining flight of stairs.

"My car!" she called back up to Gabe with a wink.

Lea parked in the middle of a wide, open area of the garage. Dim florescent light strained her eyes; the garage was practically a cave after driving in the midday sun. She got out of the car to smell leaked oil mixing with the food court fare.

She set the notebook on the roof. This interaction might be close enough to touch. Anxious signals shot through her nerves, like electricity crackling along the pathways to her extremities. She reached high above her head to release the frustrated energy into the air.

"So…uh…what are we finding again?" Gabe looked around at the oh-so-ordinary garage, tossing cursory glances right and left, up and down.

"Imagine someone or something is partially showing through from the fourth dimension. We're looking for evidence." She thought a moment and shook her finger, pointing at nothing in particular. "Think of those ghost shows, what do they always see? Weird lights like last night, or shadows, or even something moving by itself."

"Okay then…basically anything."

"Congratulations! You've caught on." She noticed his glance back at the car. She hoped he'd give her a chance. Let the evidence speak, just wait for it.

Lea grabbed her binder off of the car and started her search. She walked a bit, peeked under cars, moved forward and backward, all the while checking her watch again and again. At last, the calculated time window approached. Where was it? She looked anywhere that made sense, but nada. Her heart thumped faster. If nothing happened…what if she'd calculated wrong?

Another minute passed. Lea checked her watch again and flung open her notebook. She absorbed the basic layout of the garage before closing her eyes. Feeling the air brush her skin, the tiny hairs on the back of her neck tingled. A whisper of silence. They were searching in the wrong place. She didn't know how, but they were. They had to go to the other side of the store. Now!

She slammed the notebook closed and glanced at Gabe who was messing around near a car a few rows over.

"Over here!" She waved for him to follow as she went around the corner. She stopped halfway down the length of the garage. Over the tops of the now numerous cars in the lot, some of the air seemed lighter than usual. No time to waste.

With the interaction happening aboveground, she needed to get higher. The SUV next to her had one of those short ladders on the back. She climbed on top and walked carefully across the cars toward the end of the garage. The roofs popped under her feet, echoing like an enormous bag of microwave popcorn.

"What are you doing?" Gabe followed on the ground.

"Can't you see?" She ignored the dull ache in her ankle as she crossed the cars.

"No. Get down!"

An alarm blared from a black Escalade.

"Look." Lea reached out. Her hand passed a point and the temperature dropped like a miniature cold front. The little hairs all over her body stood on end. Inside the space something moved, ethereal—beyond reach.

Gabe gasped. "What was that?" He ran toward her.

She fumbled for her thermometer and GPS, never looking away from the interaction. There was movement, real movement. It was like she could almost see through!

She took notes, eyes fixed open, until the area returned to the same temperature as the rest of the air, and all interesting activity ceased. She got out her laser measure and pencil, jotted down a few more numbers, and only when she gasped did she realize she had been holding her breath.

"You gonna get off the top of that car now?" Gabe waved her to come down.

"Oh, yeah." Her hands still shook, but she scooted over so he could help her to the ground. "Did you see? You saw it, didn't you!"

Gabe nodded and checked back toward the car blaring the alarm.

"It was amazing!" She clapped. "It was the clearest I've seen. I need to make some adjustments—"

Gabe yanked on her arm, pulling the sore tendon in her shoulder. He pointed to the golf cart with flashing blue lights rushing toward them. The car alarm obviously caught the parking guard's attention.

"Let's go." He pulled harder on her arm, and she followed after him with a wince.

Her ankle throbbed.

"Hey you!" The parking guard caught sight of them, now fleeing and not simply loitering. Maybe they should have just played dumb. Too late, and she couldn't run any faster.

"My foot…"

"Am I gonna have to carry you *all* the time now?" He picked her up like a child, one arm under her knees, the other around her back. "Don't get used to it." A smirk hid in the corner of his lips while he ran the rest of the way to the car.

The golf cart pulled close as they got in, and Lea peeled away leaving some rubber on the garage floor. The small motor in the cart was no match for her full-sized engine.

Once back on the road, Lea let out a breath. That was close. Maybe she had a hidden love for adrenaline, because running from the scene made the whole thing more thrilling, and that was hard to do. She got a ton of useful information *and* got to see a prime interaction.

She turned the radio to the traffic station and nodded to the passenger seat. "Thanks for being my legs."

"I didn't want to answer that rent-a-cop's awkward questions anymore than you did."

"Still, thanks." Now it was time to ask. "So…you saw it then?"

He rubbed his neck. "I saw something…sorta…move."

She tried, and failed, to keep her voice a normal volume. "I know! I haven't seen such clear evidence like that before. The visual interactions are always too far away, and the ones close up just move things."

"Whatever that was then, it was in another world?"

At the stoplight, she took a moment to study Gabe. His tone and his eyes had changed, and that layer of skepticism had vanished.

"Yes." Lea gripped the steering wheel, slick under her palms from sweat. She did it. With more evidence, she could prove it to them. Maybe she had a real chance to save her parents.

Gabe adjusted the air conditioner vent. The air blew wisps of blonde hair around his face. "You get what you needed?"

She found way more than he realized. Hope. "I got some awesome measurements. This'll help a lot."

"Good, I'm glad."

She concentrated as she merged onto the highway heading back toward campus. "So, hero, you saved me from the evil parking guy. I say that calls for a reward of non dorm-related food. I'll treat. Do you like Chinese?"

He shrugged. "I don't know."

"Wow, you've never had Chinese before?"

"Don't know."

"You *don't know* if you've ever had Chinese?" She tried to see his face, but he was staring out the window.

"I don't remember," he replied without turning around. "I have amnesia. I was in a car wreck nine months ago."

"Oh no! That's awful." She bit her lip. "You haven't remembered anything?"

"No."

Lea tried to keep her attention on the road, suddenly very aware she was driving on the highway. What could he be thinking? She almost cut that guy off when she got on, did he notice? She intentionally drove safer and slower, in the middle lane. He'd think that was considerate, right? Or would he interpret that as pity?

Her internal monologue became an outward silence. Great, now he probably thought she was making up weird theories about him, or worse. She got someone to listen to her, to understand what she was trying to prove, and now she was about to blow it because she wasn't the only one with issues. The awkwardness was gonna make her brain explode. She had to say something, anything! "Gabe?"

"I'm okay. I wasn't mad, just thinking," he said.

"I understand." She turned off the radio. The monotone news guy wasn't helping any. "It must be hard, not remembering anything."

He faced forward, but his eyes shifted in her direction. "Yeah?"

"You don't have to talk about it if you don't want to."

He sank further into the gray fabric of the seat. "That's the problem. There's *nothing* to talk about. I don't know anything."

"Yes, you do."

He finally turned. "That so? What exactly am I supposed to know?"

She tapped her finger on the steering wheel and looked out the windshield for an example. A bus passed on the left. She pointed. "There. What's that?"

"A bus." He raised his eyebrows.

"And did you learn that neat fact in the last nine months?"

Gabe sighed and rolled his head. "I know 'stuff' stuff, but nothing that happened in my life. You can't compare the two."

"Better than 'nothing' nothing, right? I mean, that could've happened."

A pause and then he laughed hard, causing Lea to almost miss their exit. He slapped his hand on his knee. "*That* is how you plan to cheer me up? At least I'm not a vegetable?"

She steered onto campus and slowed to the requisite snail-like speed. "Worked, didn't it?"

"Still lame," he said through a leftover chuckle.

The car rolled into the packed lot where she pulled into an aisle and idled. Now that Gabe believed her theory, maybe he could help her find hard proof. Getting one person to listen without blowing her off took a miracle, a leap of faith. She had a chance to do the same. At the very least, she'd suggest it.

"I've got an idea. Help me prove the existence of the extra-dimensional beings, and I'll do everything I can to jog your memories. Deal?"

He pulled his navy jacket back on before opening the door. "Thanks."

She beamed. "It's only fair."

Lea watched him trot across the street to his dorm building. Adding him, four people knew about the world just beyond their reach. Well, those four recognized the beings were real and not delusional ramblings of the neuro-atypical trapped in a mental institution. Two inside, two on the outside—those were much better odds.

Three

That night, Gabe dreamed again. Wind tightened the skin against his face, fueling the indefinable freedom of flight. The ground so far below, it blurred into swathes of color like thick streaks of paint on the canvas of the world. He dove into a barrel roll and pulled up, flying higher into an endless blue.

A blinding light threw off his balance and he plummeted to the ground.

Gabe bolted upright, and hard breaths pained his lungs. He often flew in his dreams, but he'd never crashed before. He tried to ignore the tightness in his throat and checked the clock, quarter to seven. Might as well get ready.

A few minutes later, he heard a rapid knock on the door.

Matt grumbled, "Who the hell is here now?" He sat up on the top bunk wearing his jeans and sweatshirt from the day before. Matt was either an insomniac or intent on reading the entire Internet night after night.

"One sec." Gabe finished combing his hair into the tight ponytail. He opened the door to find Lea, bright-eyed and unconsciously bouncing on her heels. "Morning." He yawned and motioned for her to come in. Matt must be glad he didn't change before bed now.

"Good morning!" Lea waved at his zombie roommate. "Matt, right? I'm Lea."

He nodded. "Yeah, Gabe's mentioned you. Nice to…uh…meet you." He ran his fingers through his short, black hair, but the one side remained squished flat against the side of his head.

"You're here early." Gabe stifled another yawn. He kicked Matt's RPG sourcebooks under the bunk to give her room to stand amongst the mess.

"I couldn't wait, sorry. I texted I was on my way," Lea said.

"It's okay, I left my phone on silent. Want some coffee?"

"Sure."

In the overcrowded kitchen corner, Matt had the genius idea to duct tape the coffeemaker to the wall. Space-saving, but not exactly user-friendly. Gabe yanked the pot free and filled two insulated travel mugs. He turned to hand Lea one, but she occupied herself by looking through some of the pictures in his canvas portfolio.

She flipped past another page. "Wow. These are beautiful. Who's your model?"

Oh crap, no. He opened his mouth to answer but nothing came out.

"He doesn't have one." Matt disentangled himself from the black comforter and jumped to the floor. "Well, not currently anyway."

"What?" Lea pulled the portrait free from the portfolio. The thin paper crinkled in her hands as she flattened out the picture.

Gabe tried to stop him. "Matt—"

"She's dead. Gabe's fiancée Heather. She was killed in the car wreck where he lost his memory."

"It doesn't matter." Gabe finished his sentence.

Lea traced her fingers over the drawing and returned it to its home. "You remember her? You *do* have some memories. That's great!"

Damn it, Matt, you had to drag it up, didn't you. He handed her the mug and sat back on his bunk. "No, just her face. I wouldn't even think she was important, except that her image is the only thing I remember."

"Hey, I told you what I knew." Matt squeezed into the microwave corner and got a box of cereal out of a set of plastic drawers.

"I appreciate it, really." Gabe smiled and blew across the surface of the coffee, making little ripples lap at the edges.

Holding her mug tight with both hands, Lea took a long sip. "Don't your parents have any pictures that might trigger something?"

Gabe sighed. "No parents. Matt's the closest I have to family and he's just my roommate."

"Sorry." Lea flinched. Her eyes darted around, landing on anything but him. She bit her lips together and breathed out her nose. "I don't give up easily. I said I'd help you remember, so…you'll remember."

If only he could believe her. "Yeah."

"Come on, we'll talk on the way." Lea poked Gabe to prompt him to leave.

"Where're you guys going so early?" Matt rummaged in the box for a couple pieces of dry cereal.

"Well, there's this—"

"Gabe's helping me with a school project. We need to drive pretty far." Lea opened the door.

What was she talking about? He gave her a knowing nod before she nudged him out of the room.

They were already halfway down the hall when Lea said, "I don't want to tell Matt or anyone else. Easier to avoid explaining." She scrunched her nose, an innocent little bunny without the innocent part.

"Gotcha."

The interaction they went to study that day ended up a bust as far as Lea's data was concerned. Her mark was off, and if anything happened, it would have done so underground. Though a failure, the trip started the first of many. Most of their excursions gave Lea something useful—she said so anyway. That stuff was still way above his head.

Several weeks passed, and The ED Project became more than a casual thing. Gabe honestly wanted to help prove Lea's theory. His idle thoughts drifted to their plans. What would they find there? Could the beings see them? The black wall in his mind seemed to shrink, or at least it didn't bother him as much. He had ED to thank for that.

Noon—maybe those lazy boys would be awake by now. Lea knocked on the dorm room door. Along with Gabe, she'd tracked a bunch of interactions, so many that her near-perfect formula could predict an interaction zone down to the size of a room. But that progress came with a price, and she hadn't kept up her end of the bargain.

She hefted the backpack on her shoulder. It was her turn to do something for him.

Matt answered the door, still looking like he just woke up. "Oh hey, come on in."

Gabe spun on his desk chair, a knot wrinkled above his brow. "Sure was a cryptic text you sent. *Time for payback. I'm on my way*'—if I didn't know you, I'd be scared for my life."

She swung the backpack onto the floor. "Today, we're gonna work on jogging your memory." She pointed. "Matt agreed to help since he knows more about what you guys already tried."

"It's been awhile so maybe it'll work now." Matt scratched the back of his head.

After a pause, Gabe got down on the rug. "Sure. What's the worst that can happen?"

"That's the spirit." Lea squinted. "Sort of."

She sat down on the cheap rug and opened up her bag. "Let's get started!" She set her notebook and trusty mechanical pencil to the side and pulled out a handful of tiny blue bottles.

Gabe picked up a bottle and shook it, the liquid splashing inside the indigo glass. "What kind of experiment is this? I didn't sign any waivers."

"Aromatherapy." She unscrewed one. "These are concentrated scents and essential oils designed to evoke emotions based on memories you might associate with them. For example, this scent combines pine, baked goods, and some other essences most people smell near Christmas. If you have any memories related to these scents, maybe they'll come forward."

"I thought you were some kind of math major, what's with the hippie voodoo?" Matt unlocked his phone and Googled aromatherapy.

"General Studies is essentially three minors instead of a major. I've changed the minors multiple times, so I've studied a bit of everything." Yeah, she nearly had enough credits to double major in physics and mathematics, but they didn't need to know that. If she declared a real major and graduated, she'd lose her opportunity to hop schools and finish her research.

She waved the bottle under Gabe's nose. "Anything?"

He closed his eyes to concentrate on the scent. He sneezed and rubbed his nose with his fist. "Nothing, guess pine doesn't do it for me."

Matt slid his thumb across the screen, reading the web page. "The site suggests we're all connected to local smells. What about the wildflowers we get around here?"

"Nice thinking." Lea looked through the bottles until she found a sampling of floral scents. "Here's bluebonnet, Indian paintbrush, and buttercup." She waved it under Gabe's nose.

He sneezed again. "Woah, strong!" Another sneeze, and he backed away from the bottle. Lea pushed it toward him again.

"Sniff lightly," she prodded.

Gabe squeezed his eyes shut and actually spent a minute with the sample. Was he getting something? His brows furrowed as he concentrated.

Lea tensed and rocked back on her knees.

He opened his eyes and shook his head. "That's enough."

Lea picked up another bottle. "But we still—"

"Leave it, we're done," he said. "Nothing's coming back, and nothing's gonna come. I'm done with this now." He stood and went to his desk, sitting hard enough that a book fell off the edge, the loud thud standing out in the quiet.

"Gabe..." She frowned and returned the bottles to the backpack. What did she do wrong?

Matt slid the phone in his back pocket and reached to help Lea to her feet. "It's not you."

Gabe released a sigh. "I'm tired of being a science experiment, and all this therapy crap has done nothing. I'm beginning to think if my memory is gonna come back, it'll be...I don't know."

He had been so positive before. She likely approached his problem the wrong way. Controlled experiments—that's what she was good at, not people problems. Would he even want her to stick around now?

Gabe rested his hand on the keyboard, facing the monitor but not really looking at anything.

What was he thinking? The experiment didn't piss him off that much, so what was the real problem?

She glanced back at Matt. He wasn't giving her any clues to whatever was swirling around in Gabe's head either. She chewed the tip of her fingernail. Just play happy, brighten the mood back up. That's what usually worked.

She threw on her smile and clasped her hands in front. "Okay, so colossal failure. Let's forget about it, order some Chinese, and put on a movie. Sound good?"

Gabe stared at her, like he was trying to read her, and of course he'd fail. He did a slow head nod. "O…K."

"Or…" Matt flashed a wicked grin. "You're my new challenger for video game night."

She laughed. "When did I agree to that?"

"When you came in here the first time. It's an invitation for a challenge, didn't I warn you?" Some of the tension in Gabe's face relaxed.

"No, leave me to find out the hard way." They included her. They wanted her to stay, to play, and be with them.

Matt thrust a controller into her hands. "Bring it on." He smiled for a second and then went to put the disc in the PS3.

Matt's idea of a challenge was trouncing both of them in a *Street Fighter* tourney. When the pity wins were no longer enough to keep them playing, Matt subjected them to a lengthy *Farscape* marathon. Luckily, Lea ended up liking the show, but more than that, she enjoyed the company.

Through the window, the black night became a picture tacked onto the wall, something fake compared to the energy flowing through the room. Matt's serious possession of the controller, Gabe's unrestrained laughter, and even the smell of long-gone takeout, Lea soaked it all in till her smile cut through the mask.

Fun lasting this long had consequences. Her stomach started to grumble.

Lea jumped to her feet behind the boys. "Kolachies!"

"Gesundheit." Gabe twisted away from the screen to look at her.

"I'm starving, and they sound really, *really* good. If we leave now, we can get them fresh out of the oven with the first batch of the day."

Matt paused the DVD. "It's four a.m."

She giggled. "It's a three-hour round-trip to West. I've got a meat-filled-bread craving, and I want the best. Come on, where's your sense of excitement?"

Gabe stared at her a moment before he laughed too. It was the same tired laugh she had, where you've been awake so long that even televised golf is funny.

Matt grabbed his keys from the desk. "Gabe's warned me about your driving, so we're taking my truck."

She gave Gabe an exaggerated glare before accepting a chuckle. "Fine, so he's right, but I call shotgun."

The trio embarked on the long trek south to the tiny, gas-station town of world-famous pastries. Two hours later on the return drive, Lea sat in the passenger seat of Matt's truck with a full stomach, and her prized pink box loaded with sausage and fruit kolachies. Unfortunately, more than just her stomach was full. The three cans of pop from earlier in the evening were trying to force their way out of her bladder.

"Guys, we need to find a gas station. I've really got to go."

Matt searched the signage on the road. "We're outta luck. There's nothing for miles."

"Keep an eye out. We'll find something," Gabe said from the tiny backseat of the extended cab.

"There has to be something!" Lea crossed her legs tighter. Further on the highway to the right, some bright light peeked above the trees. It had to be a gas station, and gas stations had bathrooms. "I see lights, that means pee!"

The guys laughed and then she did too—big mistake. She bit the inside of her cheek to keep the floodgates closed.

They exited toward the lights and veered to the right to see nothing but a well-lit billboard for On the Border. The halogen bulbs made the queso in the ad look delicious, but it wasn't a bathroom.

"No!" Lea cried. She couldn't hold it anymore. What was she going to do?

"Go behind the bushes by the billboard, we won't look." Matt choked on a cough, or a laugh. "Really. You're dying, please just go."

Gabe leaned forward between the seats. "I'll cover his eyes to be sure, okay?"

She opened the door and jumped down. "If either of you watch, you die." Her cheeks blazed.

She ran off the side of the road and behind the small bush below the solar flare of a sign. Squatting into the grass, she hid as much of herself as possible. After relaxing enough, she went and glanced back to see the blonde and black heads bobbing in laughter. She yanked up her jeans, stomped to the truck, and threw open the door.

"You two are witnesses to my deepest, most embarrassing moment, and if you *dare* tell a soul about this I'll…I'll…" She stopped. "Brain dead. You think of an adequate threat, and that's it. That's what I'll do to you!" Her face burned, and though she tried to play if off with humor, she was mortified.

The driver's door opened, and Matt jumped down. He hiked toward the billboard.

As if he read Matt's mind, Gabe squeezed out of the truck and followed him. Both boys stood with their backs to Lea and unzipped to mark their territory at the bottom of the queso sign. When they finished, they marched back grinning.

"Now it's not only you, we've all peed on the Mexican food." Matt put his hand in his pocket.

"The three amigos." Gabe mimicked a Spanish accent.

Lea's blush disappeared, replaced with a welcome smile, and they reloaded themselves in the truck to head back. Though she should be exhausted enough to sleep, she was more awake than ever. Something renewed her, and she wanted more of whatever it was, even if Gabe's rain cloud continued to follow their little group.

Four

Lea drank a breath of the humid air. "Today," she spoke out loud. "Today I get my evidence."

The weather began to warm to the perfect in-between jacket and tank top temperature. On a Saturday, the university seemed an echo of its weekday life. Lea had spent the morning strolling through the empty campus listening to the sounds of her sanctuary, noisy trees filled with stubborn grackles and fearless squirrels. So she walked alone, as usual. She lived alone and studied by herself. She could always trust herself.

Although used to solitude, she enjoyed working on ED with Gabe. She never thought about bringing someone in before, and it was the best thing she could've stumbled upon. But something about him puzzled her—the way he carried himself, as if his body betrayed his lack of knowledge and showed he had a self-confidence the destruction of his memories couldn't erase.

Gabe's puzzle would have to wait. Lea predicted a prime interaction point for the seven o'clock hour. She spent every night of the previous week perfecting her hypothesis. If at the right moment enough friction contacted the interaction point, it could open. She would open the point, and then cross into the other dimension. There, she'd finally see what she knew she'd find. Those monsters, those things that stole so much from her and her family, she could prove they were real.

Her campus stroll ended at Gabe's dorm room door. She knocked *shave and a haircut*. No answer.

"Gabe? Matt?" Maybe they didn't hear her knock. She glanced at her watch again, four o'clock. She told Gabe they didn't need to leave till five. Oh well, too early again. No worries, she could wait.

Downstairs near the lobby sat a room dubbed The Red Room, though painted a delightful pale blue. She'd pass the time in the lounge till Gabe returned from whatever he was doing. She plopped herself comfortably on the least worn of the four sofas. No one around. Good, she had complete control of the television. She grabbed the remote and flipped through the channels to watch only ten minutes of each show, because everything on Saturdays was crap.

From outside the side door to the lounge, a female voice whispered, "Did you see who's in there?"

Another unfamiliar voice said, "Why, do you know her?"

Lea stared forward, pretending to care about the lion advertising the *Animal Planet*.

"That Huckley girl, you haven't heard? My boyfriend had an astronomy class with her last semester and he found out some things about her family."

"Like what?"

"They're legally insane, at least her parents are. They're in a mental institution, and you know that girl, she's not normal either. I think she needs to be locked away too."

"Oh my goodness! Really?"

Lea clenched her fists tight, and her nails bit into her palms. If it hurt, she didn't care. How dare they spread that gossip! Let them talk about this.

She jumped to her feet, which startled the girls into silence. She plastered on her one-of-a-kind smile and stomped to the wall nearest the door. Without even a hint of anger, she shoved everything off the top of the bookshelf in one giant push. Magazines and a potted cactus crashed onto the floor, scattering dirt and torn, glossy pages across the threshold.

The girls gasped, giving Lea mild satisfaction. She pivoted on her heel and marched out of the room through the front door.

How dare they! They didn't know her, and they didn't know her parents. Everyone assumed they were lunatics, being locked away like that. Those monsters did this to them. The longer it took to prove it, the longer they'd remain imprisoned. It wasn't fair.

"Lea?" Gabe surprised her; she almost ran into him.

She didn't stop, choosing to head toward his room. "Oh, hi! I've been waiting for you. Guess I'm a tad anxious to get going." She pranced up the stairs and down the hall.

Gabe caught up and opened the door. "Lea?"

She jumped to tap the doorframe with both hands before walking inside. "What?" She went to the kitchen corner and found a granola bar in the plastic drawers. "Can I have one?"

He nodded permission and watched her with that sad look on his face, the one he wore when he got too introspective. "What's wrong?"

She cocked her head, still grinning. He'd never know anything happened, not with her happy self. "Nothing. In fact I'm keyed up for tonight."

Gabe stood motionless and stared right through her smile. "What's wrong?"

"Nothing, I'm fine."

"No, you're not. What is it?" He came closer, his eyes turned down at the corners.

Why was he worried? How could he tell? No one could ever tell. They only saw the expression she chose. They never saw her.

But Gabe kept looking at her, right through her.

Lea's face fell, her mask broken. She cradled her cheeks, and the loose frown felt unfamiliar in her hands. The muscles were accustomed to the tight lines of mania—they didn't know how to relax either.

"How?" she said to herself. "How did you see it...how could you tell?"

He replied, "You're upset." Hesitant hands touched her shoulders, another caring gesture.

"But I didn't *show* it." Her voice cracked. "I...no one can *ever* see it, they haven't, not ever."

"I knew something's been on your mind. What happened? Are you okay?"

Lea couldn't respond. Her eyes welled with once-hidden tears, and she slumped to her knees. Her shins stung where they hit the thin rug laid over unforgiving tile.

Gabe held on and knelt also to keep her upright.

Grabbing onto Gabe's shirt, she buried her face into the fabric and cried ugly sobs into his chest. The jersey knit was soft and then wet against her cheek. Underneath, he smelled like morning after a rain. His arms curved around her shoulders and back, protective like a cocoon where the caterpillar hides until she's ready.

She cried for a long time on the dorm room floor. What made her so upset? The small aggravation from earlier had faded into a memory. Her tears came from something else, from never being herself. If everyone was going to think she was insane, it would be on her terms. Gabe saw through her façade, the only one who ever had.

She wiped her wet cheeks with the sleeves of her hoodie, and though blurry, she saw Gabe's frown.

"Thank you," she whispered.

The anxious wrinkles on Gabe's forehead smoothed away. "No problem."

A silent exchange cleared the fog and made what could have been awkward into something else. Somehow he understood what she needed, and that was all he wanted to give her. How did he do it? Without knowing anything about himself, he found a way to know her—more than she did it appeared. Yet another mystery surrounded Gabe, though maybe one she couldn't solve.

On the drive, Gabe didn't quite know what to say to Lea, and she didn't seem to mind the silence. He pretended to be interested in the music. *The Beatles—Blackbird* scrolled across the XM radio display.

Lea chewed her lip pretty hard with furtive glances in his direction "Um," she said. "I know you wanted me to drop the amnesia thing, but I did say I'd help. Is it safe to ask you something?"

"Sure." He pulled on the lever, letting his seat move back a few inches. They made compacts for short people.

"When did you remember what Heather looked like?" she asked.

"Pretty soon after I recovered."

She steered the car onto the freeway, nearly clipping a passing sedan.

Gabe winced. Maybe she didn't notice.

"Oops, heh." She slowed her speed with the rest of traffic. "So you haven't remembered anything since then?"

He flicked the zipper of his jacket and pulled it back and forth an inch. "Like I said, nothing before the accident." Talking about it brought the black wall into his thoughts. An empty past, nothing to make him anything more than a shell. He watched the traffic fly past the window.

"Well, you do remember Heather's face, so everything else is probably locked away in there somewhere. You can get it back."

He glanced at Lea. In her mind she had stated a fact. People weren't like that, not that he'd met anyway. He didn't agree or disagree with her silver lining, but instead returned to staring out the window. Oh gee, another billboard for the retirement community. Old people have all the fun.

The radio took over as the prominent sound for several minutes. Lea had some weird tastes. He pressed the button on the dash, and the station scrolled across, *Oldies—1960-1980*.

Lea nudged the volume down. "My grandma listened to nothing but oldies when she drove me around, so they stuck with me."

"Ahh."

Looking out the windshield, she returned her voice to a normal level. "You know what I think?"

He lifted his eyebrow.

"You don't have any baggage," she said.

"What?" He turned to her.

She still faced forward, dutifully driving the car. "And that's not a *bad* thing. You don't remember anything, so you don't have any hang-ups either. No childhood traumas, no broken hearts, and no issues." She clicked her tongue. "Minus the memory loss of course, but you see what I mean."

"I don't know…"

She glanced at him and turned back to the road. "Listen. I'm not saying this to make you feel better. Just imagine. You can choose to be the kind of person you want to be. You can choose to be anything…maybe even the kind of guy who randomly helps a girl, who may or may not be a lunatic, prove something, which may or may not be real." She gave him a double-eyebrow raise like a bad actress in a low-budget film.

He chuckled. "Is psychiatry one of your minors?"

"No." She quickly added, "And I'm not saying you give up or anything. We'll still try to get your memory back. But I thought you should try seeing your situation a different way."

Was it really that simple, starting over? Nine months of his "new life" passed, and what was he now? A student who spent all his time in therapy or thinking about everything he didn't have to think about. Anyone else would say he was obsessed and probably a little weird. That wasn't who he wanted to be.

Gabe repositioned himself in the seat, stretching his legs under the dash. "Okay, you win. I'll play your game."

"You'll see, it'll be worth it."

He couldn't keep the grin away. Lea had a strange way of doing things. All his meetings with the school shrink didn't do as much good as one conversation with her. Between Lea and her ED Project, maybe he'd find a way to build a new version of himself—a fresh start.

Lea packed light. Other than her phone's GPS and a flashlight, she kept a small notepad, her lucky pencil, and the thermometer in her cargo pocket. She didn't need to find data; now she needed proof.

She led the way down the alley where skyscrapers blocked the glowing moon and the lamps from the highway. Yellowed fixtures above each back entrance threw faint cones of light onto the cement, like holes in Swiss cheese.

Lea checked the coordinates on her phone while she walked, and the little red arrow crept closer to the flag icon she placed to mark the interaction point.

Gabe spent his time surveying the area for anything that might be a danger. He kept fidgeting behind her and turning around every few seconds, a twitchy meerkat on patrol.

"We're only between buildings. It's not the end of the world." Lea checked her phone again to make sure they were headed in the right direction.

He glanced over his shoulder. "I still don't like it. It's night, people do get mugged, you know."

"The statistics of that are so low. We're really not in any danger, considering the population and how many times that sorta thing happens."

He shifted uneasily behind her. "Whatever, we're raising the chances by being out here at night."

Lea rolled her eyes. "I'm not missing this opportunity."

"I know that. Neither am I."

"Good."

They came to a cross section behind two major offices where the loading docks and dumpsters sat for both of them. A stream of water trickled down the concave cement into the large sewer grate. Old garbage left a fume hanging around, and the humidity only made it worse.

Lea double- and triple-checked her coordinates, cross-checking with her notes. "This is it. Within I'd say, a fifteen foot diameter, low to the ground." She shoved the phone in her cargo pocket. "Perfect."

"How long?"

"Roughly ten minutes."

Ten minutes may as well have been six hours. She paced back and forth, her sneakers scuffing the gritty pavement.

Gabe continued to keep a watchful eye out for muggers or vagrants. What a dork.

She snickered quietly. For someone who didn't know his own experiences, he sure seemed paranoid. She watched him standing straight, darting his eyes to the entrance and even up to the windows above them. Watch out bad guys, Gabe's on to you. She smiled and turned to see what looked like heat waves rising from the cold cement. Crap. The interaction had already started.

"Gabe..." She waved him over next to the loading dock.

This interaction provided no shining lights or obvious movement. Not much stood out visually, but her digital thermometer found the coldest point.

"Here," she whispered, not wanting anyone or anything on the other side to hear. She stretched her arms forward, and Gabe did likewise.

"On the count of three." She waited for him to nod. "One…two…three."

They both reached *through* the interaction point and grabbed at the thicker air. Nothing. They tried again, pulling, grasping, and making any sort of motion to trigger a rip. Gabe leaned in and pulled out at just the right angle, because the light tore across like a jagged line. Lea grabbed the edge of it and tugged, opening the tear wider until they both fell through.

Five

Lea rubbed her head where she banged it on the ground. Her right temple throbbed and moving at all sent her reeling. She waited to let the dizziness pass, and after a minute, opened her eyes. Piercing light forced her to squint. She pawed through the scratchy grass, and as her eyes adjusted some, she saw her blurry hands digging through green fuzz. Where the heck were her glasses?

"Here, let me help you up." Gabe's voice came from beside her.

Turning around, his hand reached for her, though it wasn't his hand. She traced the glistening cobalt-tinted arm up to the body that owned it. Her mouth dropped open, and she froze. What the hell? Was that even him?

Gabe stood beside her, but his skin shimmered a silvery-blue and his hair had turned bright white. Stranger still—enormous wings made of translucent slats stemmed from his back. He wore the same caring expression on his face, his bluish face. He reached to help her, unaware of his appearance, or that giant wings ripped up the back of his T-shirt.

"Lea?" He gently took her wrist. He tried to pull her to her feet, but she couldn't move. Was she losing her mind?

It was then Gabe noticed something was wrong. He looked at his hand holding onto her arm. He let go and stepped back.

"What...?" He studied his hands, opening and closing them like he was making sure they were, in fact, attached to his own body. He stumbled back another step. He glanced to the ground near Lea where her glasses reflected an image of his changed face, pointed ears, hair, wings. "No." He shook his head violently. *"No!"*

Lea couldn't say anything. She only watched as he tried to understand what happened and failed. He clutched his head and yelled. His eyes rolled back and he fainted, a marionette with cut strings collapsed on the ground.

"Gabe!" She snapped out of her shock and ran over to him. She lifted his upper body against her, but he was unconscious. "Gabe? Gabe! Wake up."

She started breathing hard, like she'd maneuvered someone ten times his size. She gasped and tried to fill her lungs, but it wasn't enough, never enough. The thin air lacked sufficient oxygen. She was drowning on land—impossible.

Using the strength she had, she pushed Gabe into a sitting position. Come on, wake up. It didn't matter what he was or what happened. She'd worry about that later.

"Get—" she gasped. "Up—" Out of the corner of her eye, two silhouettes approached against a blinding sky. She couldn't make out anything more. Not that it mattered, because the lack of oxygen began to affect her motor functions. She blinked at the figures through heavy eyelids right before she passed out.

"No, nothing. Physically, he looks fine."

"I'll check the vitals one more time before we make the call. You're sure it's him?"

"Yes, positive. I saw him with his father at the last Council celebration."

Lea pretended to remain asleep while the voices talked over her. Voices speaking in English—in the other dimension? Why? How? The curse of the scientist, every answer added more questions.

"All right, everything looks good. We can call it in."

Lea opened her eyes a smidge. She was lying on a hospital bench surrounded by a plastic box with a tube in the side connected to a gas canister. She glanced to her right. Gabe, still blue and unconscious, lay on the medical table next to her. His pulse beeped rhythmically on a monitor.

A female with rosy-orange skin pressed a button on an intercom. "He is unharmed, but unconscious. Get a message to Councilman Ilat and tell him his son Makai is here." Her long monkey-like tail swayed behind her. An orange tuft of fur feathered over the end of the tail.

"Isn't it strange? I thought he had been killed," said the man. He had a grey-green tinge to his skin and the same slatted wings as Gabe. Both wore white coats, like the kind human doctors would wear. They *were* human in appearance, mostly. The strange colors and extra appendages were the only things differentiating them.

"We all thought the Winged Councilman's son was dead. It's what they said on the news." She took off her latex-ish gloves and threw them away in the bin next to the counter.

"I'm sure Councilman Ilat will be ecstatic to find out he's all right. Well, just about all right. I still can't tell why he fainted."

"He should wake up in a couple of hours, regardless." The woman flicked her tail and picked up a folder of papers from the counter. "Come on, we need to inform the supervisor about the human girl."

Lea shut her eyes.

Footsteps clicked against the tile floor, and a pair of hinges squeaked. "Yes. I didn't know they could even *get* here," the man replied.

"They can't."

After that, the door shut behind them. Footsteps and voices gone, Lea opened her eyes. The room was now empty except for her and the unconscious Gabe. She tightened her abs to sit up but stopped. If she opened the box, the concentrated oxygen would dissipate, and she'd only have a few minutes to do anything before passing out again. How would she have the time to get anywhere when she could hardly breathe?

She wiggled her phone out of the pocket and brought it to her face. She pressed the button, but the screen stayed black. The battery had a full charge. Something about this plane kept it from working. What luck.

The cold air from the tank filled her nose with a clinical smell of plastic. She sighed. There wasn't enough time. The doctors could come back at any moment, and she didn't have any maps or theories to find an interaction point on this side. Focus. She needed a plan.

Maybe she could take the oxygen tank with her? No, she had to haul Gabe, and she couldn't carry both. Could she reverse the tracking algorithm? That was a shot in the dark, and she didn't have their coordinates anyway. Damn it.

Frustrated, she emptied her mind and listened to her surroundings. A buzzing noise and some clicking behind her, and the air pumped into the box with a wheeze by a loose connection. Then she felt it again, that hunch, that tug in her gut that an interaction point was close by.

She twisted herself to see behind to the door. Just through that door, the interaction was there. The little hairs on the back of her neck prickled. She didn't know how, she just felt it. It had to be there.

Lea inhaled so deep the breath hurt like a rock inside her chest. She lifted the top of the plastic box and crept out quickly but quietly. Step one done. Step two, grant the miracle of carrying Gabe. Compared to her, the guy was a giant. That might be a hyperbole, but he had at least forty pounds on her.

She rolled him onto his stomach and ducked below the bench to grab his arm. The sensor slipped off his finger, and the beeping stopped. She slid him off the table to drape him over her back. Blue-boy better be grateful. She was gonna strain something lugging him around.

Her held breath burned her lungs. She blew out the pain, and then drew in as much of the oxygen-poor air as possible. With her elbow, she propped the door open. No one there. That was a plus.

Then, right through the doorway she could see Earth through a foggy, rounded area. It showed grass, trees, and a building with a Wells Fargo sign.

She peeked around the edge of the door. Someone was pushing a cart down the hall away from them. She ducked her head back in, heart racing. Gabe's dead weight pulled hard on her shoulders and she breathed, gasped again. No time to double-check. She hoisted Gabe on her back and made a run for the thin spot between dimensions. It didn't provide a lot of resistance, and they fell through with no problem.

Kneeling, she moved Gabe onto the cement. She blinked. What happened?

He was back to normal. The wings, the strange hair and skin color, they all disappeared. His lips had drooped open with a little bead of drool.

How'd he change? What was he? Who were those others? How'd they know him? Questions, hundreds of questions, but she couldn't get her answers. More importantly, she had to find him help.

"I assure you, he's absolutely fine. He only fainted." The doctor squeezed Lea's shoulder before leaving the room. Exactly what the other doctors said, he just fainted. Gabe must have overloaded his brain to find out that he wasn't human. It made sense. He had no idea who he was, but the only thing he knew for sure was that he was human, and even that wasn't true.

Gabe stirred on the cot, wrinkles appearing in the flat white sheet over him. Lea sat in the folding chair next to him. "You okay?"

He blinked and squeezed his eyelids a few times. "Huh?" He looked around and started hyperventilating.

Oh, no. Last time he woke up in a clinic must have been after the accident. "Gabe?"

Wide-eyed and breathing fast, he turned to her. "Lea?" He swallowed and his breathing slowed. "My name is Gabriel Jones. I met you when you fell from the Union. I remember…" He sighed.

She gripped the rail on the bed, wrapping her fingers all the way around the metal tube. "What?"

He squirmed his way into a sitting position and leaned forward to grab his head. "I was afraid I'd lost what little memory I have. But no, I'm good. Nothing less than before." He cradled the side of his head. "Did I get a concussion? The light must have knocked me to the pavement."

Lea shook her head. "No, you're okay. We can leave whenever." She held her breath. He had to know what happened. She needed him to know. "You don't remember?"

"No, but I didn't lose anything more. That's good, right." Gabe smiled and pulled the sheet off of his legs. "I had the weirdest dream. I turned blue, like I dunno, one of Matt's video game characters."

He swung his feet over the edge of the bed and paused, probably waiting for a headache to wane. "Next time I ask, 'you think this is safe to eat?' tell me no. If the pizza's not in the fridge, I'm not touching it." He grabbed the rail and put unsteady feet on the ground.

Lea held his hand for support. "So you really don't—"

No. If he didn't remember what happened, maybe she shouldn't say anything.

"Don't what?" He let go of her hand and took a few steps.

"Nothing. Just worried about you walking like a drunk." He couldn't handle it when he saw it himself. His mind made the transformation a dream for him, to protect him. His amnesia might be partially psychological, and she shouldn't mess with that.

"Ha ha." Gabe rolled his shoulders back into his perfect posture, supporting wings they couldn't see. "Headache's going away. I'm fine."

Lea watched him, his reassuring smile and his carefree ignorance. He was one of them, one of those beings, and didn't even know it. How could she be mad at him for that? The same look flashed in his eyes, the look that helped her, the one that was there for her. But even though she cared about him, a ball of anger tore through her stomach like an ulcer. She tried to ignore it, but it gnawed her raw.

He didn't know what he was, so she couldn't explain why she was mad. More annoying than that, she couldn't hide her feelings from him either. He'd see through her, just as he had in the dorm when the girls pissed her off.

She said, "Good, I'll take you back to your dorm. I have to make a trip home after that."

"Home?"

"I'll tell you later."

Six

Heten Nor straightened his shoulders and walked through the double doors of his private chamber. The dark interiors of the compound cooled the dry, desert air, but couldn't prevent it from leeching the moisture from his body. He ran his fingertips along the wall, and sand fell to the floor. Nothing stopped it, that damned sand got everywhere. He hated it all—the sand, the heat, even the acclaimed play of light the spring sunsets "blessed" the desert with. The wasteland of their ancestors was just that, the refuse of Illirin. The scraps no one else wanted, thrown to the scavengers.

Heten brushed his palms together, but the dust clung like a second layer of skin. Why did the Seers deserve to be cast off like garbage? Of the five traits, theirs was the least prominent, but that wasn't a real reason. Their ancestors lost some wars, so he was supposed to accept his place? No, not anymore. The other traits didn't have to deal with such humiliating conditions. They didn't survive on dried fruit and salted meats, because the fresh food took too long to arrive. It wasn't any matter. He would leave the wasteland of their ancestors soon and finally have the respect he deserved.

He paused to smooth the wrinkles from his shirt before opening the carved wooden doors. The balcony overlooked the grand hall, meticulously decorated in comforting sandy tones, which complimented the environment. Hanging from each pillar, mosaic lanterns of crimson glass cast a welcoming light on the people assembled below. A few Tailed and one Legged counted among the throng of Seers gathered on the marble floor. He didn't expect any Finned, too insular to care about his cause, but the one Legged surprised him. Those four-legged freaks usually sided with the Winged.

Heten forced a passive smile to squelch the nerves. He surveyed the crowd. So many men, young and strong—they were enough to complete his army. Now, he needed to woo them. It wouldn't matter if he got all the riddles and found his prize without a substantial force to make use of it. Worse than that, if he didn't at least earn their support, those who disagreed could spread rumors of his intentions and ruin everything.

He scanned the audience to see the faces of his constituents. As the Seer Councilman, his position could manipulate better than his words alone. He inhaled, dry air cracking his nostrils.

"Seers!" Heten's voice resonated. "What do you think of when you hear the name of our trait? Do you think of prosperity? Do you think of glory? Do you ponder any future of ease or happiness? No? Well, you should…and you will."

The audience applauded, and the echoes amplified the noise to multiply the number in attendance. The acoustics helped to bolster the supporters into believing they were part of something great.

"I am the Seer Councilman, Heten Nor, and I've been working with the Council to move toward their goal of equality. Years I have worked with these leaders, *years*. Ask me, 'Nor, haven't we made progress?' Ask me, 'Nor, aren't we equal now?' And I could spout the sweet lies of the Council, paint you a picture of a unified Illirin where the others greet our eyes with respect, but I won't. I won't lie to you. You want and deserve the truth! We all know their *equality* is a fable."

He opened his hands, using well-worn pathos to draw them in. "Traitism runs rampant despite their efforts, and as we, the Seers, were placed at the bottom of the ancient hierarchy…we still receive the most ridicule for nothing more than a less-apparent trait. Snickers and insults continue to follow us; some even dare say 'traitless.'"

Heten held his hand over the crowd, and the applause stopped. "Yes, traitism is alive and will not simply vanish as the others hope it will. The caste system is gone, but we suffer still. The other traits tell us times have changed, but have they? No! Low-paying jobs and manual labor for those of us in the *integrated* cities, and for the rest of us? We live in a desert, *still* in the wasteland of our ancestors! How are we better than where we were? The answer, my friends, is that we're not!" He straightened his shoulders and swung his arms over the balcony.

"The Council failed to create the unity we deserve. They preach equality, but practice a system of separation, divided by our traits. Under our broken system we will never have anything but an illusion of peace, as long as the traits remain sovereign. For real unity, we must join together under *one* leader, *one* trait!" He paused, waiting for the cheers of agreement to quell.

"Who is the one to bring us together? Who is this one man to unite Illirin?"

A few of his men within the crowd began the chant, and soon the masses shouted in unison, *"Nor! Nor! Nor!"*

His name filled the corners of the grand hall, reverberating off the majestic ceiling as an auditory addition to the emotion in the air. Heten let the smile spread as victory closed in, and his outward charm could only earn more loyalty.

Thunderous applause followed Heten's speech. He waved for the people, playing his role as the trustworthy leader. Those unwitting sheep followed anyone who promised what they wanted. They were going to help him conquer Illirin as its emperor, and they had no idea what that meant. Only he could bring about a new age, his perfect vision.

He waved a few more times before retreating back into the shadows inside. Metal walls and utilitarian lighting felt more natural than the ostentatious design of the grand hall.

He turned the corner to see a messenger totting toward him.

"Councilman Nor, I have news." The messenger failed to hide his trembling jaw.

Heten's Seer eyes narrowed. "What is it? Now."

The messenger bowed before continuing. "Councilman Ilat's son has been found in Illirin. He disappeared soon after, so it may be a rumor, but the informant sent the message with utmost importance."

"What!" Heten banged his fist on the metal wall, deafening the nervous messenger. "Where? How!"

He stammered. "Uh…from Getha, he's in Getha."

"Winged territory," Heten grumbled. He dismissed the messenger, who darted back down the hall.

If Makai returned to Illirin on his own, had he regained his memories? He needed to ensure Makai was out of the way. Dangerous as it was to let him live, he could still prove useful. Heten required all of the parts of the riddle to find his prize, and the boy might end up being valuable for that end.

He doubled his pace back to his chambers. He had to contact the wizard, his so-called ally, and prepare him that they might have to begin sooner than they anticipated. It was time to meet him face to face. Time for action.

The flight to upstate New York felt like the travel equivalent of the watched pot phenomenon. At least it gave Lea plenty of time to think. The ulcer-like twist in her gut went away, and she fixated on her initial reactions. She couldn't stay mad at Gabe, not for something beyond his control. He didn't even know what he was. Still, the questions buzzed around her like nagging mosquitoes. Was he one of them? Could he have been with those attacking her parents?

He couldn't have. It wasn't possible; he was too kind. Whatever his past or what his memories held, his true character rose above it all. She had faith in him, and after taking long enough to realize, she also trusted him.

Lea gripped the armrests. Her knuckles turned white as the cabin tilted forward. Landings sucked—sudden noises, the plane pitching to the side. The tin can could hit the ground and break in half like the one in Taiwan last month. What if the landing gears failed?

The plane approached the runway, toy houses whizzing by the window to mock her fear. Her stomach opened into a pit. Don't throw up.

The tires touched ground with a jolt, and they landed smoothly without incident. She checked off another blank chamber in her mental version of Russian roulette and made a hasty retreat from the cabin to go find a taxi.

About six months had passed since Lea visited her parents. Usually, she'd go every couple of months, but the last few were quite productive for her research. Spending time with Gabe and Matt took several of her weekends as well.

Her absence hadn't erased her familiarity of the routine, and going through security to enter the institution was as automatic as ever. She wore her sandals, easy to slip off, freed her bag of metal objects, and never brought a large coat, even in the midst of a New York blizzard. Nearly all the entry guards knew her, so that made the process of getting inside less of a hassle.

Strolling through the familiar corridors, she had forgotten how her sandals scuffed the tile floors, sending dusty-sounding echoes into the alcoves. The facility looked pleasant enough, almost homey, but she detested every inch of it. The framed artwork of flowered vases, the outdated wallpaper, and even the long hallway of windows grated on her. She never wanted to see that stupid vase of wildflowers again.

The guard accompanied her down to the rooms where her parents stayed, not lived. Only temporary, she would get them out.

The guard opened the door and announced, "Mrs. Huckley, you have a guest."

Her mom put down the piece of paper she was writing on. She smiled, though dark bags lingered under her eyes, and her hair never seemed quite combed all the way.

"Oh, Lea!" She leapt from her chair to embrace her.

Lea hugged her back with a tight squeeze. "Mom." She let go a bit so they could look at each other. "How have you been?"

Her mother's smile seemed forced. She gripped Lea's hand and brought her over to the bed where they both sat down "Fine, dear, fine. I've had more time with your father, which is always nice."

"That's wonderful." The springs creaked in the thin mattress when Lea moved to get comfortable.

"Oh yes, they've even opened the window between our rooms again. We can talk to each other all the time."

"Lea, honey? Have you come to visit?" Dad's voice came through the opening in the side of the room.

"Yes Dad, I'll be over soon."

He chuckled. "Don't worry sweetie, take your time with your mother."

Lea squeezed her mom's hand. "So, it's been awhile then…since the last time?"

She nodded. "Yes, yes." She lowered her voice to a whisper. "*They've* not come in a while, and as long as the doctors don't think your father and I are harming each other, we can be together." She frowned and fidgeted with her cotton pants at the knee. "I'm always afraid they'll come back and ruin it all again."

"Don't worry, Mom, you'll be out of here before then." Lea clutched her mom as if her hug could force her words into reality. She had only to get evidence now, but she didn't want to give her mother unintentional false hope. Whatever happened, she had to save them. She'd keep her promise.

Mom didn't reply right away. She swallowed hard, which put a crook in her smile. "I…I…" She took a breath. "A couple months ago, I nearly said we made it up again, just for a chance. Maybe they'd let us leave then."

Lea gasped. "Don't say that, Mom. It didn't work before, and it'd just make them come back."

"Ssshhh, not so loud."

She stood up, everything about to burst out. She pressed her arms against her sides, vibrating on a subatomic level. "I'm so close, *so* close to proving it's true."

Why did her mom have to be shut away like some criminal? She couldn't stand it. She'd show the institution her parents weren't insane. The picture popped into her head, Gabe with his shining wings. He was the proof. Proof she couldn't use. The spot in her gut that hurt before from anger warped into something else.

She wanted nothing, *nothing*, other than to save her parents, and the evidence she needed hung just out of reach. She couldn't trade him for them. Who knew what they'd do to Gabe if they knew his true form. And he thought he was treated like a science experiment before? They'd lock him up or worse. She wouldn't do that, not to him, even if it meant freeing her parents.

Her stomach bubbled. She turned to the white wall, away from her mom's face. If only her mom knew they were a betrayal away from freedom. A move Lea couldn't make, but the temptation made her sick.

Mom took Lea's hand and rubbed her thumb, soothing her. "It's all right, sweetheart, I know you're trying."

Her hand shot to her face to hide the rivers beginning to creep down. Her parents were so patient, so wonderful. All that they went through because of this horrible situation could end, but because she cared about Gabe, she was just as far from freeing them as before.

She felt thin arms pull her into an embrace, fingers smoothing her hair. She let herself drift back to memories of her childhood, sitting on her mother's lap, curled into a ball, the yellowed light from the reading lamp—*safe*.

"It's okay, it's okay. Your father and I are fine. We have much more freedom. It's not so bad."

"I'm sorry, Mom, I'm sorry. I'll come back soon, and next time I do… next time, you and Dad will walk out of here."

"Of course." Her mom untwisted Lea's braid and combed her fingers through her hair. She should be the one comforting her mother, not the other way around.

The clock ticked in the quiet, time slipping away. Lea wiped her eyes. "Do you think they'd allow us all to play a game together?"

Her mother let go enough to look at her, worry lines exaggerated from a smile instead of their namesake. "Of course." She walked over to the door where she pressed the intercom. "Bill? My husband and I would like to go to the rec room with our daughter."

Static fuzzed through the com. "Yes, Mrs. Huckley, I'll send someone right away."

Through the window in the room, Dad chuckled. "Let's play *Monopoly*."

"My favorite!" Lea snickered, catching his clue. *Monopoly* took eons to finish, so her dad made sure they had the most time together. They would have more time together soon. On her next visit, she'd get them out of there. She'd find some other way to prove the extra-dimensional people existed. She'd protect Gabe and save her parents. She had to find a way.

Lea was in a better mood when she returned to the university than when she left. So that crossover didn't give her proof, yet. She learned several details that could help on the next trip. She'd have to gather a little more data, but her parents' days imprisoned were numbered.

While driving back to campus, she made some mental observations to add to her notebook later. For now, she wanted to see Gabe and Matt. Though exhausted, spending time with her friends seemed a better plan than working her mind over those formulas for another zillion times in one evening. She had friends to return to, people to talk to. Almost like a normal girl for once. She giggled silently. Maybe she shouldn't get used to that.

Lea knocked on their door.

"Who is it?" Matt called from inside.

"Candy-Gram!" Lea sang.

She heard Gabe's confused, "What?"

Matt answered, "Get it, will ya? You know it's Lea."

Gabe opened the door. "We didn't order any." He waved her inside. "How was your trip?"

She popped her shoulders and cracked her neck. "Good, but I don't want to talk about that now. I'd rather just relax."

"Then why'd you come over? We don't sleep here." Matt dismounted the bunk bed and landed with a thud.

She plucked the game controller from his hand. "Exactly. I said relax, not sleep." She stuck out her tongue and took a seat on the bottom bunk. Matt blinked at his now controller-less hand.

Gabe chuckled and moved his desk chair over by the bed, closer to the TV. "Where's my candy and my telegram?"

Lea rolled her eyes and continued beating down the computer opponent in Matt's fighting game. "The giant land-shark ate it and ran away before I could deliver my message."

"Damn land-sharks." He picked up the second player controller and replaced the computer opponent.

"Hey guys, my game!" Matt sat on the rug and leaned against the bed next to Lea. "I play the winner."

They began an impromptu tournament, playing each other over and over. Lea beat Gabe by mashing buttons randomly, but lost easily to Matt. He used special combo moves to push the opponent in the corner and stun them so they had no way to run—dirty but effective. Button-mashing had no chance against that type of skill.

She lay down on her side and started to doze in and out of consciousness, while Gabe and Matt went two out of three, or five of seven, or till they got bored. She gazed at Gabe, Matt, the screen, and then to Gabe again. She never really noticed it before, but staring at the back of his head, she could see it. His back always stayed so straight. Now she knew it was from the weight and musculature of his wings, not good breeding. He couldn't feel them, couldn't see them, but they were there even now affecting how he walked and how he sat.

She sensed before that Gabe was different somehow, but had no idea it was so connected to her goal. Though, it was more than that. Gabe's origin didn't account for the feeling he gave off. There was something special about him, but just like everything else, she couldn't place it. She mused over his mystery for a bit, and after a few minutes the grunting of video game characters faded, and Lea fell asleep on the bed.

Seven

Heten Nor eyed the man waiting in *his* private chambers. "I was under the impression that humans couldn't survive in Illirin's unique atmosphere. There was something about an insufficient amount of oxygen, or so I heard." He raised his brow. "Why aren't you dead?"

The man was not colored as any Illirin. He had peach skin and wore a thin black cloak. Not thin like silk, but a coarse fabric with no lining to add opacity or weight. Cheap.

The man smirked. "For someone working to restore a historic age, you really should read more. Even I know once a human wizard connects to the magic in Illirin's aether, he can live in its unique atmosphere. Hence, my failure to die." He inclined his head, and Heten took his seat on the other side of the wooden desk. Scrollwork designs carved intricate details around the edges and on the corners.

"Thank you, wizard, for bringing me up to speed." Heten waved his hand. "Please sit. We are equals, as you are a representative as well."

"We can cut the niceties now, Nor. We've talked before. Just because it hasn't been in person doesn't mean we're not on the same page. We both want the same thing, and if you help me, I'll help you. It's as simple as that." The wizard relaxed into the chair

Heten laughed politely and lifted a metal pitcher to pour two glasses of water. "You are right as always. I was only so surprised by your presence, I almost forgot what we needed to discuss."

The wizard leaned in. "What have you learned? You've made progress toward acquiring the Stand of Unity?"

Heten shook his head. "I cannot be too hasty with such a delicate process. No, the news I have is related to Earth, actually. Maybe you can shed some light for me."

The wizard straightened.

"Two doctors spotted Makai Ilat—here in Illirin." He waited for an explanation. "Do you know how this happened?" He searched the wizard for any sign of guilt, but he only stared back poker-faced, twisting his ring around. "Did you neglect to tell me he's regained his memory? How did he break the Schism?"

The wizard sighed, tapping his finger rhythmically on the armrest. He took one of the glasses and sipped some water. "No, of course he hasn't regained his memory. If he came here, it must have been by accident, but if he returns we may not be so lucky. I suggest you hurry getting the information you need from the Winged Councilman. The sooner we no longer have to babysit Makai, the better."

Heten inhaled through his nose and stifled a sneer. He didn't need to take suggestions from that human brat. The pawn had no concept of the terrain Heten played in. But, to use him, he had to play along. "I've already begun working on a plan." He lifted the small receiver built into the desk. "Send in my daughter."

"Using family, hrm? Interesting method."

"Family I can trust with the most important tasks." Smiling, Heten gestured with an open hand. "I think of you as family, of course."

"You've proven your trustworthiness to my family, I agree. But don't be offended that I can't return the sentiment. Our family is very proud, very close." The wizard twisted the old signet ring again.

"I'm not asking to be adopted." Heten took a sip from his own glass. "I want you to assure me I can count on you to fulfill your bargains. Your family reached out to me, and I took care of the descendant for you.

You will be unopposed by another sorcerer in the upcoming conflict. You must swear loyalty to me, that you will use this opportunity for both of us."

"I'm hurt by your lack of trust." He held his hand over his heart and feigned an injury. "I'll keep my promises and those of my mother, too. You have me honor-bound by the house of Morgana."

Heten replied, "Thank you for your confirmation. I meant no disrespect by asking, of course. These are unstable times, and I must be sure of my allies."

"I expect the same."

A soft knock on the door interrupted the serious conversation. Heten grinned. "Come in, Vermillia." The door swung open. "We have much to discuss."

All day, Gabe's mind wandered. He couldn't concentrate on calculus, not surprising, but ignoring Politics of the Twentieth Century was weird because he usually hoped something there might jog is memory. Why did Lea suddenly go home for the weekend? They had attempted that crossover, and even though they failed, they still had more to do for the ED Project. Didn't they?

He looked up from the back of the blue plastic chair he'd been staring past. It hit him. He had something to focus on, and that something had pushed the black wall in his mind so far back, he forgot it was there. The time he spent with his friends and working with Lea developed a new part of himself. Now, he was more than nothing. His bank of experience was a fraction of a lifetime, but it was a beginning. If he never remembered, maybe he really could start over.

Toward the end of his government class, Gabe's cheerful thoughts drifted downward again. Start over? But then he'd never know who he was before. He didn't want to be someone else, he wanted what he lost.

Before he knew it, everyone stood up and shuffled out of the room. Caught in a wave of repetition, his body gathered his books and followed the mob out the door. His autopilot set to guide him to the dorm, but derailed when he nearly ran into someone on the sidewalk.

"Oh, sorry," he muttered and stumbled back over the curb. Regaining his footing, he looked up from the pair of black leather boots to the face of the girl who wore them. An intimately familiar sight greeted him. A relieved expression sat on the face he had drawn hundreds of times over the past few months.

"Heather?" he said on an exhaled breath. She had the same freckled nose, strawberry-blonde hair, and even the touch of pink lip gloss.

"Gabe!" Her oval face stretched with surprise, and little tears beaded in her skylit eyes as she lunged forward. She reached behind his shoulders, pulling him down to her.

He wrapped his arms around her, seizing the ghost. No, not a ghost, a warm, solid presence. A million things ran through his mind. Feelings, images, sounds, thoughts, and even smells flew into his brain. Memories, short and jumbled, came rushing in, an overload of sensations in a single moment.

He whispered, "Heather," pushing his face against her neck into her hair...lavender shampoo. "You're alive."

How? It didn't matter. He felt her and the times they spent together. Slowly now, his mind began to set pieces into place. There wasn't much, but he remembered some of his past—their past.

They sat on the stone table at the park with the sun setting just over the roofs of the neighborhood houses. She whispered something about the sky glowing the same color as her favorite sherbet, Citrus Swirl.

He laughed out loud at the theatre when the guy in front shouted at the screen. She agreed with a straight face, which made him snort and turned the eyes of the audience to him instead.

They ran inside the dorm, dripping wet from the sudden downpour. He dried her face with his T-shirt; it was his fault they didn't make it back before the storm broke.

"Thank God I found you!" Heather pressed her bony wrists into his back. "I thought I'd never see you again."

"How, when, where?" He squeezed her close, afraid to let go of her. She might vanish into the air, all of it a dream.

"It's a long story. Let me just be with you here for a second." She balled up handfuls of the back of his shirt in her fists.

Gabe took a deep breath. She was tangible, alive, and far more than a memory. "Of course." The world vanished while he held her and remembered fragile slivers of their life together before the accident.

Heather loosened her grip, and he reluctantly followed suit. She brushed a stray lock of hair behind his ear. "I'm back."

"Welcome home." His heart pounded, making him a little dizzy. Don't be a dream.

She hunched her shoulders and glanced around. "People are starting to stare. Are you still in the same room?"

He nodded. "There's so much I want to ask you."

She took his hand and gripped him just as hard. His quick walk home from class turned into an eternity, and he would be more than happy to leave it that way.

Matt wasn't home, to Gabe's relief. He needed some time with Heather alone. He wanted to be the first to hear her story and just be there with her, soaking up her presence along with the feelings and memories she revived.

"I just…you're here." His mouth parted a little, and he compared her to his drawings. Pearl studs, he would never forget that again.

Heather clicked the door closed behind them. "I'm so sorry you were alone, Gabe." She took a seat on the bottom bunk, so light that even the old mattress barely moved under her weight.

He cradled her hand between his and sat down next to her. "No, no, you don't have to apologize. Being here now is enough."

"But you thought I was dead, that's awful. It must have hurt so much."

"Don't worry about it. The accident, I—" How should he word it? "I got a serious concussion and lost my memory. I still have amnesia, but now you've brought back so many glimpses."

She leaned against him and rested her head on his shoulder. "How horrible, I can't imagine what you've gone through."

"I've been dealing with it." He put his arm around her shoulders and laid his head on top of hers. "It's better now that I remember you."

"I missed you enough for the both of us."

"So what *did* happen? How come it took you so long to get back? Why did the doctors tell me you died?"

She sighed. "You'll never believe me. It sounds insane."

Gabe squeezed her arm, his head still leaning on hers. "Try me."

"After the accident I woke up someplace else. It wasn't normal there, not...it's hard to explain. It felt different, and I couldn't see well. At first I thought it was just the headache, but it never got any better."

Gabe rubbed her shoulder. She could tell him anything, and he wouldn't judge. Some truths were beyond weird—he'd be the one to know.

Heather paused for a minute, glancing down at the dingy carpet.

"Go on," he said.

She took a breath. "I was taken by these...aliens. I don't know what they wanted, but I was never awake very long at one time. The kept putting me out." She waited for him to respond, facing away, like she was afraid to look him in the eye.

"Are you okay? They didn't hurt you, did they?"

"Yes and no." She turned and blinked at him. "You don't think I'm crazy?"

He laughed, which only made her stare wider. He tapped her chin to close her jaw. "They probably weren't aliens like you see in movies, but yeah, I believe you. They must be some of those people from the adjacent dimension."

"Huh?"

"That would take a long, long time to explain. Short version, I know you're telling the truth."

She hugged onto him. "How do you do it?"

"Do what?" He pulled his other arm around her.

"Make me love you even more." A small smile spread across her shiny, pink lips.

"I don't know, but you've learned the trick, too." He put his forehead against hers. Her nose speckled with freckles, the real thing was incomparable to his drawings. He'd never have to substitute a picture for flesh and blood again.

Heather's sweet giggle filled his ears. "I must have learned from the master." She closed her eyes, tilting her chin up, and he leaned in for a long-forgotten kiss.

Gabe bent over to put his charcoal in the supply box and felt a tap on the shoulder.

"Hey Lea," he said sitting up.

Lea looked at his easel and back at him with her jaw hung open. Instead of a portrait, his pad showed a crisp sketch of the still life piled in the center of the room. "You did the assignment today." She then smiled. "What happened? Something happened."

He grabbed the pad of paper and slid it into the portfolio. He slung it over his shoulder and started on his way out the door, nodding for Lea to follow. "You're right, and it's amazing."

"Cut it with the suspense, I'm dying here!" She hefted her own supplies and had to double-step to keep up with him on the treacherous pebble walkways.

He paused a second for effect. "Heather's alive, and I've gotten a bunch of my memories back." He was bursting, and only social convention kept him from jumping in circles. "I didn't even know how much I missed her. I remembered moments, smells, feelings, and even some bits of things that happened. And now I don't need to miss her because she's *alive* and she's *here!*"

Why was Lea staring at him like that? She should be happy for him, excited even. But she only nodded.

"Really? Wow…that's good…" She paused again. "Are you sure it's her?"

Gabe stopped mid-step. "Yes, I am. Her face has been the *only* thing in my head for almost a year. Yeah, I'm sure. And also, she's brought back memories. She's Heather."

"That could happen even if she were an impostor."

"Why the hell would someone pretend to be my dead fiancée? And more so, get plastic surgery to pull it off. You should be happy for me, but instead you're accusing her of being a fake?"

"No, no, I didn't mean it like that, I…" She inhaled slowly, buying time to reply. "I would be happy for you if I thought it was her. It just doesn't make any sense. She was gone so long, and ya know, after a wreck, wouldn't the doctors know if she were alive?"

"And you think someone pretending to be my dead fiancée makes more sense? You of all people should believe her."

She looked like she was about to say something else, but she bit the inside of her cheek. "Why is that, Gabe?"

"She was captured by those people, those beings from the other dimension. You know they exist. It's her, she's real."

She gazed down at her feet, twisting her sneaker, which squeaked against the stones. "I just think you should be more careful."

"I am being careful. You can trust me."

"All right." She didn't say anything more until they reached his dorm. A couple guys walked past them in the hallway, and then they stood alone in front of Gabe's door.

Lea readjusted the portfolio strap on her shoulder. "Can I stash my stuff in your room? We need to make it about eighty miles south by two o'clock. There's construction on the way, and I think a building site in the spot I calculated, so it might take longer."

Gabe dropped his things in the hall to retrieve his key. "Are you serious? Not today. She came back only yesterday. I need to see Heather."

"Fine, back out on me. I'll go by myself." She turned and started to walk away, but Gabe grabbed her portfolio.

"Didn't you say construction site? That's dangerous, you can't go by yourself. Remember falling off the roof?"

"Then come with," she said.

"I told you I can't. This is important."

Lea gripped her portfolio and yanked it free from his hand. "So is this! I'm going with or without you. I'm losing time, and I need to leave."

He smacked his hand on the side of his face. She didn't need to be a brat. "You have a lot of data. You can miss this one time. It's not that big of a deal."

"It *is* a big deal!" Her taut arms wavered, and she had a scary, tight grip on her portfolio strap. "Every day without proof is another long day. Do you know why I got so mad at those girls in your dorm? Do you know why I broke down?"

He shook his head.

"They were making fun of the fact my parents are locked in a mental institution. My parents were imprisoned for hurting each other when it was really those people from the other dimension. When they claimed aliens attacked them, they were put away for 'their own good.' They didn't know then what it was. I *need* that evidence. I need it to get them out of there. Every day I waste, they're still trapped."

Holy cow, was that true? He took a breath and asked calmly, "When did it happen?"

"Twelve years ago. My grandmother raised me till I left for an early college program in high school."

"I didn't have any idea."

Lea looked away and muttered, "There's no easy way to work it in conversation, ya know."

"Yeah…"

She hitched the strap up on her shoulder. "I've gotta go."

"You won't do anything risky, will you?" He noticed her intentionally avoid his eyes when she turned around.

"Somehow I survived before I met you."

He didn't deserve a sarcastic quip like that. "Lea, come on."

She sighed, and her braid slid over her shoulder blade as she gave him her profile. "If I'm right, the interaction should arrive too high for me to do anything 'crazy,' don't worry. I have to confirm I'm one hundred percent right, so I can find a good spot to actually get evidence. I'll be careful." She twisted enough to look at him, though only for a moment. "Okay?"

"Okay."

She hurried off down the hall, and Gabe couldn't shake the feeling that he didn't know the whole story. Yeah, his refusal to go should annoy her, but she seemed more than a little miffed. He'd ask her about it later. For now, he needed to concentrate on Heather. He finally had her back, and with any luck, he'd remember even more.

Gabe spent the rest of the afternoon going around town with Heather. They talked about the places they went and tried to urge parts of Gabe's memory to return. The café by campus, the bookstore, and then they stopped by Beth Marie's for ice cream sundaes. He didn't remember anything new. They talked a lot about the last year and what happened while she was gone. She seemed more interested in the here and now than in the past. She had a good point. Of course thinking about the future was more productive, but he hoped more glimpses would come back to flesh out their history together.

After a while, they ended up at the table in the park, just like in that memory. He ran his hands over the gritty stone and let the cold soak into his skin. "It feels good here."

"Yes, it does." She leaned her head against him.

The soft sent of lavender mingled with damp grass carried on the breeze. The gentle wind brushed over his skin, wisps of Heather's hair tickling his cheek. Gabe drifted off.

"I lost it around here somewhere." Heather's voice echoed in his right ear.

"I'm looking as fast as I can." He crawled under the table, fingers combing the velvet grass. Her earring had to be around there somewhere. They only went to the park and the bookstore before she found it missing.

He heard a worried sigh. "Those were my grandmother's. Oh, I hope I find it."

"Don't worry, I've got the eye of an eagle." He caught a glint of light sparkling near the base of the oak. Pinching the tiny earring between his fingers, he said, "I found it!"

He started to stand but banged his head into the table.

"Are you all right?" She knelt and picked up his head from the ground.

"Ow." He puffed out his bottom lip.

She leaned down and put her forehead against his. "I think you're gonna survive, goober." With his head in her lap, she bent over to kiss him. "Thanks for finding my earring."

The memory revived as clear as if it happened moments ago. Once Gabe remembered, it felt like he never forgot. Why couldn't he remember before when it was now so vivid in his mind?

Disjointed images drifted into his thoughts. A grey sky with a white sun above, and below, an aerial view of mountain peaks next to verdant valleys stretched into the distance. He snatched a glimpse of Heather holding a package, his name on the tag. Heather…she led him into another memory.

"Here, I had it made for you the last time you left." Heather handed him the package. Inside were some papers and a plastic card, a school ID—his ID.

"How? I thought you had to work for—"

"I have some friends who did it for me. I pulled in a bunch of favors just for you." She winked.

He stood there staring at it, astonished. It was perfect, a real ID. It showed his picture all right, and the card had the magnetic strip and everything. "It's really mine?" He raised his eyebrow. "Gabriel Jones?"

"Just like the angel that brought Mary her joyous news. You make me happy. I thought it fit." She reached over and brushed her hand on his cheek. "Besides, I've always loved the name Gabe."

He clutched the ID tight with both hands. "Gabe it is. From now on, I'll wear the name you gave me."

That didn't make any sense, why would she name him? Why would she need to have his ID forged? He was always Gabe, wasn't he?

A sharp pain pierced his forehead. He grabbed the front of his face, pressing against the stabbing in his skull. Hundreds of flashes rushed through his mind, making his head pound through his temples.

"Argh, no." *Stop. It hurts.* The images sped up, flicking by so fast he couldn't pick anything out.

Heather grabbed his shoulders, her fingertips digging in. "Gabe! Gabe, snap out of it!" She shook him.

His racing mind halted, but a lingering headache remained—a dull throbbing with no more memory to show for it. He put both hands behind him on the table to steady himself. "Thanks."

"Are you okay?" She cupped his cheek in her hand.

"Am now." He let himself return to the present. He forgot about the glimpses for the moment, and let Heather take him to dreams of the future. As long as she sat beside him, the pain went away and so did the onslaught of images. She was right, tomorrow was far more important than yesterday.

Eight

Heten paced throughout his chambers. The thick soles of his boots echoed on the metal floors and made soft thuds when he crossed the decorative rug. He hated being in the dark about his own projects. Vermillia hadn't come yet to give her progress report, and he couldn't count on the Wizard to keep him up to date. This plan had made him nervous from the beginning, and it would take so little for it to backfire. If it worked, they'd be in the clear for a good while. If she failed, they'd have to progress faster than he anticipated on the search for the Stand.

"Councilman Nor." The voice sounded over the speakers in the corner. "Your daughter has arrived at the complex. She should be near your chambers soon."

He hurried over to his desk and picked up the receiver. "Good, unlock the doors." The remote locking system clicked in the wall next to the door. He released a breath, and the doors opened soon after. Vermillia strolled inside.

"Hello Father." She tossed her pale, orange-red hair over her shoulder, the short pieces in front framing her Seer eyes. In her, the cross-shaped pupils of their trait were a vision of beauty and not a symbol to be detested. She would help him change that view for everyone.

"Welcome Vermillia." He put his hand behind her shoulders and guided her to the tufted leather chair. "I hope you're doing well."

"Don't worry Father, I've good news." Her smile broadened. "The Ilat boy has fallen for it. The idiot couldn't be more gullible, I swear. A slight nudge of magic and he throws himself at my suggestions. I can easily keep him from remembering himself. All he thinks about is me." She shook her head to rearrange her hair.

Heten laughed, thrilled with her progress. She certainly took her mission faithfully. "I always knew you had it in you."

"I told you I was better than those flunkies of yours."

"Indeed, my darling daughter." He smiled. As long as she kept Makai occupied, he shouldn't have anything to worry about. That wasn't going to make him lax on his backup plans. He wasn't a fool. For now the plan assured him time to work, and that was worth the effort.

"You do know what to do in case he…looks away from you?"

She nodded. "Who do you think I am? I said I was better than your flunkies."

"Only if absolutely necessary. If things go wrong here, he might be the only way to retrieve the Winged riddle."

"I'm not a moron."

Heten let his triumphant smile return. "Always knew you were special."

Vermillia gave a cursory bow. "I need to return, or the love-struck idiot will be missing me." She left as gracefully as she had entered.

She wasn't as young as she used to be, and her usefulness only increased with her age and experience. As a child, he easily trusted her, always eager to please her father. But, he'd need to ensure she was true to her word now. He wouldn't be tricked simply because she was his blood. She seemed dedicated, although she could be working more for herself. Because as his daughter, she had a great deal to gain with him in charge. He'd trust her greed at the very least.

No matter the direction, the sidewalk to the dorm tilted so Lea walked uphill, and with her hurried pace she was getting a bit winded. She had to catch Gabe before he left with Heather, or she wouldn't see him at all. Though she didn't really need him to help go over her plans, the company would be nice.

On her way to the building, she caught sight of a girl walking in the same direction with almost as much purpose. She did a double-take—wavy long hair, small nose, all the same as his drawings. She must be Heather.

"Hey!" Lea called.

Heather walked a little closer to her. "Hello? You're talking to me?"

Lea nodded emphatically. "Yes. Heather, right? I'm Gabe and Matt's friend, Lea." She held her hand out.

"Oh, well, it's nice to meet you." She loosely took Lea's hand for a quick shake.

Lea let go and rubbed her fingers together.

"So…uh, you heading over there today? Have plans?" Lea used her practiced mask to stay pleasant, but underneath she felt frigid, like coolant rose up through her esophagus.

"Yes, Gabe and I are spending the whole day together." Heather was truly gorgeous. The drawings weren't an exaggeration built from Gabe's mind. She really was that pretty.

"Wow, that sounds great."

"What about you?" Heather asked, "Did you have plans today?"

The innocent question felt loaded. She replied, "I was just gonna hang with Matt."

What was she doing here? Why did she come back *now*? Where has she been all this time? She couldn't ask. Her distrust of the girl would only hurt Gabe.

Heather giggled. "Do you play those Dungeon Monster games too? I know Matt spends a lot of time playing with his group."

"Nawh, we just play video games sometimes." She shoved her hands in her jeans.

"Sounds like you guys are pretty close." Heather slid her fingers down the strap of her purse, a little frilly thing of quilted fabric patches. "Are you really just friends?"

Lea coughed and had to clear her throat. "What? No…no no no no. Friends, we're just friends…*really*."

"Oh, okay, I was only asking."

Lea's throat dried up, and she felt even guiltier for having a bad vibe, if that's even what it was. It wasn't. She knew better. The icy pit was jealousy. She had no right to envy Heather; she was Gabe's fiancée after all. She should be happy for him, but she couldn't. Maybe that made her a horrible person.

Lea fought through the small talk until they reached the dorm room. She leaned forward to knock when Heather paraded inside like…like she belonged there.

"Gabe!" Heather gave him a bear hug and snuggled her face against his shoulder.

Lea stood outside the door like an unnecessary annoyance. The three inside the room all fit together, they belonged. They had more in common with "golden girl" than the weirdo with the nutty parents.

Gabe saw her through the door. She sighed. Now she felt more out of place waiting in the hall, so she went in as well.

"Do you want to go to the aquarium first or get lunch?" Heather tugged Gabe's arm and pulled him toward the door.

"Whatever you want to do, Love," he replied and glanced at the texts he obviously ignored before now. "Hey," he asked Lea. "What are you up to today?"

Lea added a wink to her trained grin. "Just hanging out. Thought I'd try to add some skill to my button mashing in *Street Fighter*."

Matt stood up from his computer chair. "Challenge accepted."

"Have fun then." Gabe said, Heather still squeezing his arm.

"Later guys." Heather waved and closed the door behind them.

Did they need to rush out so fast? Now it felt weird. She didn't really want to stick around, but after coming over, she had to. Hopefully, the weird vibe would go away soon enough.

She felt a controller planted into her hands.

"I'm not going easy on you." Matt plopped himself down on the rug, and Lea did likewise.

She rolled her eyes at his goofy grin. "I wouldn't want you to. I can mash my way to victory!"

They started playing, Lea mashing buttons as promised and Matt thoroughly crushing her in a few rounds. She wasn't very good but continued playing anyway. She didn't want to be alone with her thoughts, and Matt made good company.

"Just because you've beaten me six times in a row doesn't mean you'll beat me again!" Lea cackled. "I can last at least three minutes. Watch in amazement as I run down the clock."

Matt snickered. "Okay, okay, if you want, or I can let you keep some dignity, and we can end now. My movie binder awaits."

"Why not?" She set the controller on a stack of books and leaned against the rail of the bottom bunk. Matt put the disc in the machine and sat on the bed, his legs dangling down next to her right arm. The trumpets blared over the logo as they watched the opening.

She liked the cozy atmosphere of the dorm room. So much stuff crammed into a tiny space revealed how utterly "boy" the room was. Not that all guys were messy, but in general, yeah, they were. The room might appear less cluttered if they hadn't left books and pop cans scattered all over the floor, but that was part of the charm. Even some of Gabe's stuff took residence on the ground.

Gabe. He was out with Heather. Why couldn't she be happy for him? She wished that dumb, jealous feeling would go away. She had no right.

"Wands, potions, and fake Latin." Matt kicked his leg against the rail with a little *clank*. "Do you really think magic works like that?"

"Why not? It can work any way the author decides it can, right."

He pointed to the screen. "It's silly like this. I meant, what if it was real. How do you think magic would work?"

Lea shrugged. "Who knows. You're the D&D guy, not me."

"Yeah, I guess so."

Another few minutes of weirdness followed, coated in silence.

Matt took an unusually deep breath, loud too. "You don't seem that interested in the movie."

Lea said, "Naw, just have a lot on my mind."

"Copper piece for your thoughts?" He casually smoothed the bit of black hair spiking up in the back.

"That is so dumb."

"Got you to smile."

She laughed at him and then puffed a soft sigh through her nose. What could she tell him? She didn't want to air her suspicion of Heather, especially because it might be completely unfounded. He was trying to be nice, but to be honest, she didn't feel like talking about it at all. She'd sound stupid.

She looked at him and let another genuine smile lift the corners of her lips. "Don't worry about it. But thanks for caring. That helps enough."

"Of course I care," he replied quickly, "We're…friends."

Lea leaned her head back on the bed, the springs of the top bunk weaving above in a pattern of coil and dingy mattress. "Yeah, I'm glad I met you and Gabe."

Next to her, Matt sighed.

"Matt?" She twisted her head on the bed, and Matt appeared sideways.

"I'm sorry. I know Heather's sudden reappearance has to be hard on you."

She sat up and spun around. "What? Why? Why would you say that?"

"I'm not blind, ya know. It's obvious you like him, and now she's here and you're on the back burner. Anyone would feel bad about that." Matt scratched the back of his head.

"I…I never meant to make it seem like—"

"Don't worry, I won't tell."

Lea's jaw hung open. "There's nothing *to* tell!"

"I'm not accusing you of anything." He tapped his finger on his knee and shifted around like he couldn't get comfortable. He glanced toward at his computer, the TV, and then the floor. "I just, I just wanted to say that…I don't know what I was gonna say. Damn it."

"We're only friends." And as she said it, her conscience screamed *Liar!* Stupid jealousy. Why'd she have to feel like this? She did like Gabe, who wouldn't? He was thoughtful, smart, and if you weren't blind, exceptionally hot. She never imagined she'd go for the long hair, but since it was attached to him, she fell for it too. He wasn't even human and that should make her pull away. Instead, she wanted to know more about him.

It didn't matter. Her feelings wouldn't change anything. He was engaged and in love with someone else. She'd be a good friend, just like she said.

"Fine, whatever." The tops of Matt's cheeks darkened. A heavy pause allowed the dialogue from the movie to join in with their conversation, which was worse than real silence.

He cleared his throat. "Umm…well…I…"

"What?"

"Dunno…just…" He drew in a long breath before continuing, "I'm here for you."

Lea let some of the tension in her shoulders relax. Her eyes softened as she looked at his blushing face. "Thanks, Matt. I needed that. You're a good friend."

He sighed again, fingers raking his hair. "Yeah, you're a good friend, too." His smile tilted half to the side.

Lea knew that look. If he wanted to hide something, she didn't need to probe.

"That actress from the BBC show." She pointed to the screen. "What was her name again?"

Matt nodded and looked up at the television. "I can't remember either. I'll Google it." He stood to fish his phone from his back pocket and took a new seat on the far side of the bed. They watched the rest of the movie, pretending that nothing happened. Matt and the distractions kept her from thinking about Gabe for a while. Part of her hoped she was wrong about Heather, and that Gabe could be happy. But the jealous, and surprisingly the rational, parts of her agreed that something was wrong with the whole picture. He didn't know who he was, but that didn't mean no one else did.

Nine

Gabe spent another glorious day with Heather. They went out to a movie, ate lunch at The Greenhouse, and found themselves sitting at the stone table again like he felt they had many times in the past. Was he dreaming? The weight he carried with him for so long had lifted, making him light and airy. It couldn't be real.

Heather's smooth fingers laced between his. Solid. She was real. He pulled her against him and squeezed.

She giggled in his ear. "Sweetheart, I'm not going to drift into the air like a helium balloon."

Gabe startled before kissing the side of her head. "I didn't even realize I was doing it. I guess I'm subconsciously afraid you'll disappear."

"Oh, I think you're pretty conscious of that paranoia. I'm fine, don't worry. I'm not going anywhere without you, squished up or not." She poked him in the side.

"I'm holding you to that, missy."

"Yes, sir!" She pressed her lips tight like she was serious, and then erupted in a fit of laughter, the musicality of her voice filling Gabe's senses. Her nose wrinkled her cute freckles. A gust of wind blew her hair into her face, and she fought to push it out of her eyes.

He fixed every moment to his memory, snapshots and videos in his head. It all seemed so familiar, and he began to feel as if he were watching Heather through a cloudy window from far away.

"Then why are you doing this?" A deep voice echoed in his mind. *"Of all things, breaking the Schism, my son. Makai, don't you see how wrong this is?"*

He felt himself reply, *But I love her. She loves me, too!* The sight of Heather through the thinning floated in the background.

The vision faded to black, and a sudden pain crashed into Gabe's skull. He grabbed the sides of his head.

"Gabe?"

He heard Heather's worried voice, and felt her holding his shoulders. But he was still far away in his own mind, seeing another image of the mountains moving swiftly below him. He flew fast, wind rushing against his ears. Searing pain burst in his head, pushing the memories away again.

Heather called to him, pulling him back from inside himself. "Gabe? Gabe, are you okay? I'm right here, focus on me. Please look at me," she repeated over and over.

The pain faded, and he blinked his eyes open. "Makai?" he muttered to himself. He looked at Heather. "Does that mean anything to you?"

"Why are you trying so hard to remember? It doesn't matter." She didn't seem right, her expression hard to read.

"It does matter."

"I'm here. We're together. We have a future, that's what matters. Forget the past, there's nothing there that'll change anything."

Gabe tried focusing on her. "But *I* care. I want to know. Don't you want to help me remember?"

She held his hands, her wide eyes staring into his. "We're together. I care about our future together. Don't you?"

He wanted to agree with whatever she said. She was right, she had to be. He needed to forget and stop trying to remember. But, he had searched for his past so long. Everything in him needed to break down that wall. Just let it go? No, never. A shiver ran through his body. Something wasn't right. He could feel her pushing these thoughts onto him, thoughts that did not belong to him.

He shook his head and stared back at her. The loving blue eyes he had drawn so many times vanished. They became a light orange, pupils shaped like a rounded cross. He gasped and an unresolved anger filled his chest.

"Seer…" He breathed. Where did such rage came from? It grew stronger the longer he watched her.

Heather's sweet smile turned to a cold scowl. "It was for your own good, you damned idiot. You couldn't stay blissfully ignorant; you just had to make my job harder."

"What the hell is going on?"

Heather gritted her teeth and drew her hands together. Light pulsed from between her hands, and the space around them glowed. Blinded, Gabe felt her shove him backward to the ground.

His eyes only began to adjust when his intuition made him roll to the side. A streak of pain sliced across his stomach. He grabbed at the cut; blood smeared his hand. He got up and searched for his attacker.

The woman who used to be Heather stood to his left, crouched in an offensive position. She held a long, three-pronged dagger in her right hand, a tri-blade. Once strawberry-blonde hair flowed around her head like a mane of saffron fire, and her orange skin glistened with a metallic sheen. She shifted her weight from her back leg, and lunged toward him blade first.

He dodged her attack like his body knew what to do.

"Who the hell are you!" he shouted.

She remained silent, focused on making her blade find its mark. She came at him again, grunting with the effort. Her blade cut his arm at the shoulder. Gabe cried out, clutching the wound, and stumbled a few feet away from her.

"What's going on?"

She snarled. "He won't punish me because you're an idiot, Makai!" She ran forward, and Gabe spun around to flee. She wasn't going to stop; she was trying to kill him. He had to get away, find a thinning, and jump through. No thinking, just run.

She ran as fast as he did, faster now that the pain in his abdomen and arm slowed him. A tongue of fire flew past his face, and pain shot through him somewhere new.

He ground his teeth and glanced back to see his left wing scorched down the outer frond. *His wing?* His skin was that same silvery blue as in the dream. Not a dream, a memory. He was one of them. Distracted, he caught his toe on a rock. He stumbled but got his footing again to keep running.

Oh no, too late. The girl swept her leg behind his knee, and he tumbled to the ground.

Gabe watched in slow motion. The tri-blade came down toward his chest, paralyzed even from breathing. He was going to die.

Move! Instinct shouted. He rolled to the left.

Her blade stuck in the ground where he had been lying. That was too close. As she struggled to free it, he got up. He kicked her hunched form and fled, chest pounding. Searing pain ran through his wing, and he chewed his cheek. It didn't help.

Just ahead, a small lake pooled at the bottom of the hill, and there, a thinning sat right near the shore. Anyplace was better than here. He checked back, and she had gotten to her feet, already in pursuit.

Almost out of breath, Gabe dashed to the thinning and leapt through. He landed on hard concrete, and the impact on his slashed-up stomach made him yelp. The open wound gathered the gritty dirt like glitter on glue, which made it itch wildly.

He clenched his teeth and got up. She could jump through and come after him. He needed to get away from there fast.

Sidewalks ran on either side of the street, and parking lots stretched between him and some retail outlets. He crossed back over to Earth somewhere on a city block. The thinnings could spit you out anywhere, not just where you went in. It depended on the movement of the dimension, Illirin.

He took a deep breath and hobbled as fast as he could down the street and around two corners before he found a bus stop. He recognized the city, not too far from the University, thank goodness. He watched the sidewalk as the bus approached, and he didn't see her. Maybe he was safe for now. He boarded the bus, hiding his injuries with crossed arms, and started the long trip back toward campus.

The bus stopped on a street a block from Lea's apartment. Gabe had gone there with her only a couple times to pick up supplies, but he remembered where it was. He knocked on the door and waited a minute or so, hearing Lea check the peephole before she answered.

"Gabe? What are you doing here?"

"Oh, just in the—" He winced, holding his stomach over the crimson-soaked shirt. Blood trickled down his arm.

Lea's gaze traced his injuries and her mouth gaped. "What the hell happened to you?"

"Neighborhood."

She pulled him inside. "Never mind, don't talk. Come here." She ushered him to the bathroom of the tiny apartment. Without a pause, she grabbed the tear in his T-shirt and ripped it wide open.

"I—"

"Sssshhhh, sit here." She sat him on the toilet facing the tub, and then darted out of the room to return with an enormous box of medical supplies. "Let me take a look." She moved his hands from the abdominal wound, and he gritted his teeth.

She frowned. "Could you have gotten more dirt in there? Move to the edge of the tub." He was about to reply but then moaned when she aimed the handheld shower at his stomach. She worked swiftly, and her careful hands showed she knew what she was doing.

"Now…" She held up the hydrogen peroxide. "This will hurt."

"But—" And he yelled as the liquid made contact. *"OOOOwwwwwwwww."*

Was she pouring acid on him? He hoped she'd go easy, maybe not do the other wounds? No such luck. He screeched like a girl two more times before she started bandaging him up. The laceration on his stomach was wide enough to need the medical glue.

The box of supplies had a bit of everything—gauze, the liquid stitches, splints, and real sutures. "You sure are prepared." Gabe gripped the side of the tub to stop himself from scratching his cuts.

"Before we met, I took more risks doing my research." She rifled through the box and pulled out the stuff she needed. "Grabbed a few things from the ER the last time to avoid going back."

"Glad you haven't needed to." Maybe his tagging along had made a difference, at least...until now.

Lea unrolled some gauze and leaned forward to wrap it around his waist. "So, what happened?"

He exhaled slowly. He didn't want to have this conversation, but even though she might hate him, she deserved to know. Nothing good came from hiding the truth.

"You were right." He paused. She kept wrapping. "She wasn't Heather. She's from the other dimension, and she tried to kill me."

"Holy crap! Thank goodness you're okay," she said, "relatively speaking."

"Yeah..."

She sighed. "I didn't want to be right. I'm sorry."

"Me too." Gabe looked past her to a tear in the wallpaper by the floor.

"Any idea why?" She wrapped the bandage around his shoulder and sat back on her heels to roll up the remainder of the gauze.

He tried to say it again. "I'm sorry too. I...I..." He stopped and glanced toward her. She sat there waiting for him. She raised her eyebrow, and he looked down at his feet. "Me too, I'm one too. I'm one of your monsters."

He looked up and frantically tried to keep her from interrupting. "But I didn't know! I'm so sorry, I had no idea, and I still don't really, not really. I'd never—"

"It's okay. I know, and it's fine." Lea snapped the box closed.

He took a breath to continue explaining, and it registered. What did she say? "Wait," he grasped the tub harder, "What do you mean 'I know?'"

"That dream you had when we crossed over wasn't a dream. You just couldn't handle it at the time." She shrugged.

His eyes widened. "You've known since then? You knew I wasn't even human and you didn't tell me?" He raised his voice. "You could have helped me remember, and you didn't? How could you?"

Lea stood up with her teeth clenched. She threw the bloody washcloth into the tub and it thudded hard against the fiberglass.

She shouted back, "How? Well, number one…" She bent down her index finger. "Your damaged psyche couldn't handle it, and you already have amnesia. I didn't want to break your brain!" She inhaled and bent her second finger. "Number two, think how I feel. There you are, proof, *right there*, and I can't use it. I can't trade you to be some Area Fifty-One experiment for my parents, so they stay locked up and I get the joy of knowing I still don't have a way to get them out. And three, you can get off your high horse for just a minute to see I've been protecting you!"

She huffed, grabbed the medical box, and left the bathroom. Gabe sat perched on the edge of the tub, his righteous indignation gone in a simple count of three. Maybe he deserved to be the scolded child.

He stumbled out to the living room. She waited for him on her garbage-picked sofa, a plaid thing with wooden armrests. The only decor in the room sat on the mantle above the fireplace—a framed picture of him, Lea, and Matt, a vanilla jar candle, and a small leather journal. The rest of the room remained the blank eggshell color seemingly used in every apartment building in the country. Lea's lack of decoration wasn't very feminine, but it showed that she didn't waste a moment on anything but her quest to free her parents.

Now Gabe understood what she meant, and she was right to be angry. After all, he just found out about his origin, but she knew for weeks, and that was more time her parents lived incarcerated.

He avoided looking at her as he rounded the room. He clipped the mantel with his hurt shoulder, knocking the journal onto the floor. While holding his stomach, he bent to retrieve the worn book. It looked like a diary with a plain metal clasp locking the side, though it lacked the keyhole he'd seen on the ones in the store.

"It's an heirloom," Lea said. "My grandmother gave it to me. Be careful, please."

He returned the journal to the mantel and eased his way onto the sofa before saying a meek, "I'm sorry. I didn't think."

Her stern jaw softened. "Apology accepted."

A moment of silence passed before Gabe spoke. "I didn't want you to hate me."

She scratched her finger on the plaid, fabric cushion. "I could never hate you. It shocked me back then." A wry smirk edged her lips.

"Well, I didn't faint, so I've got one up on you. But don't worry about it. I'm pretty sure you aren't personally responsible for my parents, so no harm done, okay."

"Okay," he replied, though he still felt guilty. He had helped her look for the extra-dimensional people for so long, it felt like a betrayal to find out *he* was one. They had attacked her parents, which took them from her at such a young age. He didn't want to be anything like them.

He felt an odd twinge above his shoulder, both connected to and apart from him. "My...uh ...my wing hurts. Where she burned me, I can feel it. I can't feel anything else. It's weird." He leaned forward and rubbed his forearms against his knees, uncomfortable in his own skin.

"Sorry, I can't really bandage a four-dimensional appendage." Her joke fell flat. She asked, "So, what do you remember?"

"That girl, when she was Heather, I recalled a bunch of random things about being with her. I remember. I know what I've lost now. Everything else is still a blank, my only memories surround her, and she's gone."

Lea picked at the seam in the sofa some more. "I'm sorry. About Heather I mean—I'm sorry for your loss."

"Thanks." He added, "That means a lot."

She leaned over her knees so she could see his face. "What happened when you found out she was an impostor?"

"When she crossed us over to Illirin, I saw myself and realized what was happening. I crossed back through and escaped. I don't remember anything new. I only know I'm Illirin because of how I looked. Seriously, a few months ago I thought I couldn't be more lost, but now...yeah."

"Illirin?" she asked.

"That's the name of the other dimension."

"How do you know that?"

How *did* he know that? He just did. In fact, he knew a lot more than he realized. "You're right. I guess I do remember some things. Like facts. It's weird; it's just like after the accident. I couldn't remember my own history, but I knew who was president, stuff like that. I've remembered that stuff from Illirin, just stuff."

She reached out to "hit" him on the arm, but Gabe leaned back to avoid the strike. She blushed. "Woops, forgot. Anyway, you remembered something! Maybe if you go over some of it, you'll remember more."

Gabe scratched his head. "Like what?"

"Tell me about Illirin."

"Those interaction points or thin spots are called thinnings." He looked to her for a hint. She seemed interested so he continued, "Um, all the Illirins have traits. I'm Winged. There's Legged, Finned, Tailed, and like the girl who attacked me, Seer." The last word came out like a hiss between closed teeth.

"Any idea why she wanted to kill you?"

"Wish I knew." He closed his eyes a moment. It all felt so futile. Even with more glimpses and more information, he was almost as puzzled as when he first woke up. Instead of a blank mind, he swirled in a fog of confusion—not much of an improvement. He might not remember a ton about himself, but something had changed. A pressure filled him from inside like his memory had a physical presence, something strong or something heavy. It was hard to tell.

Lea put her hand on his knee and squeezed. "Well, you *do* know more now. Don't be discouraged."

Did she read his mind? At least someone should know what's going on in there.

She said, "You know your name now, right? Makai. That's what the doctors said on the other side."

"That is what the Seer called me too."

"They said you were the Councilman's son. Does that bring back anything?"

It sounded important, but Gabe still couldn't dredge up any relation to himself. "Not really, but it might be connected to her assassination attempt."

"As good a guess as any," she agreed. She had a twinkle in her eyes. "Don't worry, my equations are almost perfect now. We'll make a plan, cross over, and get your memories back. I'm already prepared." She gestured to a canister of compressed oxygen for scuba diving in the corner of the room.

An oxygen tank? That's right, the thinner atmosphere would pose a problem, but other than that she'd be okay if they crossed over. He already waited nearly a year to get his memory back, a few more days wouldn't hurt. On the other hand, they could go right now and get the proof she needed to free her parents. What in Illirin would convince…who? A doctor or director of course, but who were they? How did Lea know she could trust them?

In his head, Heather's sweet face melted into that orange Seer's glare once again.

Gabe stood, startling Lea on the sofa. "At the institution, who do you need the proof for?"

"What thought train were you riding, and did it derail somewhere?"

His slashed-up stomach smarted. "Heather fooled me. She was Illirin. How do we know there's not someone like her at the institution keeping tabs on your folks? I don't think we can get them out by flashing the sanity card."

Lea sank back into the too-soft cushion behind her. "I don't know what else to do. The thought crossed my mind, but after weighing my options, I didn't see any other way than to take that chance."

"We've got another way." Gabe put his hand on her shoulder. "I have an idea."

"Gabe…" She bit her lip. "Thank you."

"You can thank me when we succeed. For now, let's get ready and head to New York."

Ten

The taxi dropped Gabe and Lea off outside the Days Inn, and Gabe gave in to yet another jaw-popping yawn. The trust Lea's grandmother officiated for her had a sizable balance, but that didn't mean she could spring for the nonstop flight, which left them with a late-night arrival and subpar sleep onboard.

Gabe hung back by the dust-covered ficus while Lea buzzed for the overnight clerk to check in. The hotel was her usual, so she handled all the arrangements.

By the front of the lobby, he took in the ambiance, or lack thereof. Lea must have seen that faded carpet and those stock paintings many times before. Would she see things differently now that it was the last time?

With no small talk, the desk clerk passed the key cards across the counter and slipped back into the office where he could nap in peace.

Lea stifled her own yawn. "All set." She picked up her duffel bag from the floor by his feet. "Hey, is Matt gonna wonder where you are?"

He hoisted one backpack over his shoulder and lifted the other in his right hand. "I left a message saying I'd be out of town for the weekend. No problem."

They walked down the hallway lined with a dingy floral carpet. Though freshly vacuumed, the layer of dirt had muted the colors of the fibers themselves, so old it could never come clean.

Turning the corner, Gabe heard a *click, click, click* to his side.

Lea was flicking the key card with her fingers. She caught him looking at her and stopped. "I was thinking. What are you going to tell him about Heather?"

He hadn't thought about Heather—well really, that impostor who tried to kill him—since they started planning the trip. Matt probably assumed he was spending all his time with her, that she really was Heather.

He sighed. "I don't know. I didn't think about it."

"You'll have to tell him something." She tapped the card against her leg. This must have been bothering her.

"You're right, and the truth probably isn't it." What could he tell Matt? There was way too much to explain. Matt might freak out on him. They had more pressing things to think about anyway.

"I'll worry about it on the flight home. For now, let's get ready for tomorrow."

"Good deal." Lea slid the key card into the slot and opened the door. She gasped, and dropped her bag on the floor.

The room contained a single, queen-sized bed, not a double as he expected.

She shook her head. "Oh no! They gave me my regular room. I didn't think." Her cheeks flared.

"Don't worry about it." Gabe replied evenly, he hoped. Please don't sound weird. "I'll take the floor. It's cool." He walked in further and set the backpacks on the table.

Lea leapt over her duffel and hurried toward the phone on the nightstand. "I can call the manager, get the room switched."

"It's late. We don't need to bother anyone. One night on the floor won't kill me. Promise." He smiled, and she seemed to calm down some.

"Okay…" She grabbed her bag and put it on the bed. "Sorry. I've never come here with anyone before. It didn't cross my mind."

Gabe pulled out his phone. "Besides, it's more important to make sure we're ready for tomorrow. Can you save the location for me?" He tossed Lea the phone. "How far is the thinning from the front doors?"

"About four hundred yards or so." She compared the GPS against hers and the notepad she brought with her longhand calculations. "I'm pretty sure the thinning will show somewhere aboveground, and it may be hard to reach. Google maps can only give me an aerial view of the park."

"Don't worry. We'll see it in person in the morning," Gabe said.

"Don't worry?" She shook her head. "In the morning, tomorrow. The day we're doing this, and only twenty minutes or so beforehand. That's not planning, that's winging it." She tapped the phone against her chest. "*I* plan."

He sat down by the desk and rested one foot against the turbine engine of an air-conditioning unit under the window. "So, because you don't have an eighty-five column spreadsheet and reconnaissance photos, it's not a plan?"

Lea narrowed her gaze. "Are you making fun of me?"

He held up his hands. "Me? No, no, no." He smirked. "Yes."

She locked the phone and tossed it at him, grazing his knuckles. He fumbled to catch it before it hit the floor, and the sudden bending made him wince with the thin pain on his stomach.

"Sorry." Lea cringed. She rummaged through her bag and walked over to put her small first aid box on the table. "Okay, let's see the damage. I need to re-dress the bandage."

Gabe did as he was told and lifted his shirt so she could inspect the cut across his abdomen. She took off the old bandage and wiped his stomach with an alcohol pad. She carefully taped a new patch of gauze across his front. After that, she placed a new smaller bandage on the wound on his shoulder.

Lea said, "They're healing nicely, no infection. I can't promise the big one won't scar, though."

He frowned. "My career as a swimsuit model over before it began."

Laughing, she closed the box and tossed it back onto the bed. "Scars might be the next big thing. Don't lose hope!"

He chuckled and straightened his sleeve over the bandage. "Thanks for patching me up. You did a great job."

"Practice, practice, practice." She winked.

"No offense, but I don't plan to give you any more chances to practice."

"I'm holding you to that," she said pointing her finger at him. She glanced at the bathroom door. "It's late, but do you mind if I shower?"

"Take your time. We've got cable and…" He picked up the plastic table advertisement and read, "Free *HBO* and *Showtime!*"

"Have fun." Lea grabbed her things and disappeared into the bathroom.

Gabe turned on the TV and opened the folding closet doors. Where was it? Ah, top shelf. He reached above the ironing board and grabbed the extra blanket and pillow. Between the bed and the wall, he spread out the blanket for a cozy little "bed." She'd crashed in their room before; this wasn't any different.

His ears started to burn hot through the sides of his head. Why did he feel so awkward about the single-bed thing? Lea's embarrassment was predictable, but it wasn't until that moment he even thought about them together as a couple. It was too natural, too quick for him to think that, especially so soon after losing Heather again. He just remembered her. He *just* lost his fiancée. It wasn't right to think about another girl that way. Right?

The door handle rattled, and a wave of steam poofed through the crack. Lea exited the bathroom, her damp hair brushed straight, and the natural waves framed her face. She didn't have on her glasses, cutesy smiling moons speckling her pajama pants. She dressed down in plain, ordinary nightwear…but she was beautiful.

Gabe blushed and turned his head, pretending to arrange his bedding. She usually looked nice, but now something made her different. What changed?

He worked to hide the heat building in his face, and elsewhere. She was extremely important to him, but that didn't mean he liked her *that* way. He must be reading into things. He couldn't disgrace Heather's memory like that. Thinking of losing Heather was as good as a cold shower, better even.

Lea clicked on the lamp next to the bed. "Reality TV. You?"

"You don't watch *Cast Iron Smackdown*?" Gabe faced the television. The glow would cover his flush. "Former wrestlers face off in a culinary showdown. Who wouldn't love that?" He chuckled to push back his reaction to her coming into the room. He was her true friend, a best friend. He let his rationalization stand as a lie to himself.

She laughed. "I'll have to trust you then, won't I?" She jumped onto the bed and bounced a couple times before lifting the bedspread to squirm under the covers. "Let's get to sleep. Big day tomorrow."

He tried to calm her nerves. "It'll work out."

"Can you promise that?" The amusement she wore like a garment slipped away, leaving her vulnerable, and the apprehension that took its place fit her wrong.

He'd make sure she'd get her smile back, and this time for real. No more shadows to haunt her. They'd free her parents. They had to.

"Yeah, I promise."

With the backpacks tucked between the overgrown roots of a large tree, Lea led Gabe from the park toward the looming doors of the institution. She tapped the GPS on her phone one last time to see how their little red arrow inched away from the pinned location.

"You got it right, you know that. The thinning will show up there." Gabe's solid hand gripped her shoulder.

She flinched, the touch triggering the tension she held high in her back and down her arms like a rubber band stretched beyond its limits. "We've got a fifteen-minute window after visiting hours start, and that's assuming everything is exact. What if I calculated wrong?" She shoved the phone in her pocket.

He chuckled. "You didn't."

His thumb moved in smooth circles on the back of her shoulder, and that shaky feeling morphed into a tingle of a different sort. She breathed in and out. Her worry eased away with Gabe's certainty, and now she could focus. She had a promise to keep.

They arrived at the institution, Lea making small talk with the security guard as they went inside. She pocketed her belongings, waited for Gabe to do the same, and they headed down the hall the way she had a million times before. Lea listened for the scuffs of her sandals, but their tiny echoes were cut short by the louder thud of Gabe's shoes. He walked beside her, and his presence made all the difference. This was the last visit she'd ever make, no matter the outcome.

When they reached the pair of rooms housing Anna and Jonathan Huckley, the escort waited by the wall and nodded for them to enter.

The door opened, and Mom brightened, a wilted plant getting some water at last. She stood up from the folding chair and wrapped her arms around her daughter.

Lea squeezed her tight. "Hi, Mom."

"It's so good to see you." Mom hugged her and jumped a little as she let go. "Who's this?"

Gabe waved from just inside the open door. "Gabe. It's nice to meet you, Mrs. Huckley."

"Oh." Mom covered a ridiculous grin with an act of surprise. "Oh Jonathan, Lea's brought a boy to meet us."

Dad's startled cough came through the window between the rooms. "What?"

"No, no. He's a friend from my art class." Lea felt her heart skip. Was there some hole she could hide in, a ditch maybe? He just lost his fiancée, and she wouldn't risk their friendship by insinuating anything. After the single-bed fiasco, he'd think she was intentionally coming on to him.

"Oh, yeah?" Mom clasped her hands and glanced between them.

Gabe swallowed and nodded along. "Yeah, college buddies."

Like they had time for this circus anyway. Lea leaned out the door to get their escort's attention. "Hey, can you let my dad out? We're all gonna walk to the rec room if that's okay."

"Sure." He turned to open the other door.

Lea ducked back inside and grabbed Mom's hand. "We're gonna run," she whispered. "To the park, north of the front doors. If we fall behind, you and Dad keep going."

Mom gasped. "You aren't serious."

Gabe threw on a smile and ushered Mom out the door, laughing like an idiot. "I love that game. You really have it here?" Good thing they only had to get out the door. His acting was in serious need of help, or more accurately, life support.

In the hall, Lea gave her dad a hug and fell in next to him as they walked in pairs behind the escort. Lea glanced at Gabe, who had her mom's hand gripped tight. They approached the intersection in the hall, to the left the rec room, to the right, the way to the front doors.

He nodded and mouthed, "On three."

One, two…three.

"Now!" Gabe sprinted past the escort with Mom in tow.

Lea grabbed Dad's wrist and yanked. "Run!" She followed, tripping the escort on their way. A loud *bang* echoed behind them as he hit the tile floor, and when she checked back, he had curled into a fetal position cradling his head.

Dad slowed her down, looking all around for an explanation. "What—?"

"Keep up, we're leaving." Lea pulled harder and he finally picked up the pace. They turned the corner where Gabe and Mom had reached the end of the hall.

Woo-woo-woo! The alarm blared in concert with the strobe lights on the ceiling. The deafening siren and flashing lights disoriented Lea. Did she lose track of something important? She shielded her eyes with her free hand. She had stopped for only a second when Dad changed his grip to guide her.

He yanked her behind the corner and pushed her to the floor.

"Aagh," Gabe grunted from ahead.

Two security guards had their guns aimed at him. Mom pressed her back against the wall out of the way. The one guard kept his eye on her, but his gun on Gabe.

"Hands behind your head. On your knees, now!"

Gabe held up his hands, one closed in a fist around something big.

A guard pointed with his chin. "Drop it!"

Opening his hand a little, Gabe positioned the wad of heavy key rings in his palm. He hurled it at the guards and ducked. The key rings hit one of the guns, sending the bullet he fired into the ceiling. The other shot hit the wall.

Instead of retreating, Gabe dashed forward in a crouch. With his forearm, he swiped the guard's knees out from under him, and he dropped onto his back like a hundred pound bag of rice. The other guard spun to Gabe, repositioning his gun.

Lea's vision tunneled, focusing on only Gabe and the guard over him. Her breath caught, and she yelped something unintelligible.

The guard glanced at her.

From the belt of the prone officer, Gabe grabbed his baton and brought it down against the guard's head. He pitched forward, and Mom jumped out of the way. Her mouth hung half-open between wanting to yell and knowing not to.

The tile under Lea's hands thumped the percussive rhythm of someone running. The siren drowned out the noise, but someone was coming their way.

Dad's grip tightened on her elbow, and when she stood, he came with her. She pulled him. "Come on, run."

"Mrs. Huckley, over here." Breathing heavy, Gabe waved her toward the front doors. Both guards were now unconscious at his feet, and he gripped the baton firm in his right hand like it belonged there. Maybe not a baton, but a weapon of some kind.

Mom and Dad stopped just short of the security area, and Gabe pushed forward all the way to the front. The alarm had locked the doors down, so they probably couldn't force them open. Gabe tried anyway. He yanked on the handle of the glass door, but it didn't budge.

"Move out of the way." Lea bent and took the gun from a sleeping officer. Gabe stepped back, and she squeezed off a round into the door. The recoil wrenched her wrist. The gun slipped from her grip and bounced into the guard's torso. Her hands shook, and a speeding heart made it harder to breathe. Her rational brain shouted, *Stop freaking out, they need you!*

The bullet had pierced the glass, and cracks radiated from the hole like the web surrounding a spider. Gabe threw his shoulder into the center. The entire sheet crackled against the frame, thin webs exploding outward. He ran into the door again, more cracks, but the glass held firm.

"Someone's coming." Mom pointed in the direction Lea had felt before. An orderly wearing ivory scrubs sprinted toward them.

Gabe crashed into the door again, and the glass rained over the cement outside. "Now, go!" He grabbed Mom and shoved her through the door. Dad jumped over the broken glass and took Mom's hand, guiding her away.

Gabe waited like a moron.

"Go!" Lea yelled.

He ran through the door after her parents, and a second later she passed the threshold. Her parents had a good lead, and Gabe wasn't too far ahead. She could catch up, if she could breathe at all.

Lea sped through the parking lot and crossed onto the grass embankment. A heavy weight pounded into her shoulders. Reflexes forced her hands to take the brunt of the impact, but she hit the ground with the side of her face. The stinging pain wrapped around her jaw. Her glasses dug into nose.

Lifting her head, she saw the orderly get up. He grabbed her upper arm.

She twisted to get out of his grip. Her neck tingled with the familiar rush of her sixth sense, and a sudden fear held her still. He was Illirin—a spy.

A flurry of motion came from overhead. Gabe charged into the man, knocking him back and away from Lea.

"Get them to the thinning." Gabe had him on the ground, but the man kneed him in the stomach. Lea couldn't tell who was winning.

"Go!" Gabe barked through gritted teeth.

Lea scraped her knees into the dirt trying to hurry to her feet. Her gut wanted to help Gabe, but she listened to him anyway, running full out until her lungs burned. It wasn't false bravery; Gabe bought her the time to get to her parents.

They waited for her in the open part of the park. Lea caught up fast and checked behind her. Gabe was getting up off the ground, but the other man didn't. Half-bent over, Gabe sprinted their direction with that guard's baton still in his hand.

"Come on." Lea waved her parents to follow her to the large oak where she stashed the backpacks. She grabbed hers and put it on.

Dad caught his breath. "What are we doing here? I'm sure they've called the police by now. They'll be here soon."

"We'll be gone. There's a thinni—interaction point up in this tree. We've only got a few minutes to get though it anyway. Put this on." Lea handed the other pack to her father.

He stuttered. "The areas you studied? You mean where *they* come out?"

Mom shook her head. "No, you can't mean that. We can't go—"

"We are. There's no other choice now." Lea laced her fingers together and squatted wide. "Step in my hands, now climb." She made eye contact. "Please, Mom."

The cardboard sole of the hospital shoe felt flimsy against Lea's fingers. She used her knees to lift Mom high enough to grab onto the branch. The weight in her palms vanished, and she helped Dad up next.

Labored breathing announced Gabe's arrival at the tree. He dropped the baton and took hold of Lea's waist. He lifted Lea up till she got her grip, and the three of them helped him climb after. They all found places to perch on a few different branches, Gabe on the lowest. He groaned, leaning into the trunk.

"You're bleeding!" Mom gasped.

Dark splotches dotted the middle of Gabe's heather-gray T-shirt. "The wound popped. It's okay. I'm okay."

None of them would be okay if they didn't get out of there. Now where was the blasted thinning? Lea couldn't see any visible interaction, but that didn't mean it wasn't there. It only meant nothing moved near it on the other side. She closed her eyes and felt that tug she felt before.

"Just over that branch." Lea pointed above Mom's shoulder.

Gabe grabbed hold and tore his hand across the air, bright light following where his fingers touched like the trail on a sparkler. He backed out of the way. The rip opened wider, and Mom and Dad's faces reflected recognition and fear.

"Ladies first," Gabe said.

Dad stared. "It's just like when—"

"They'd come. It was always behind them." Mom shook her head.

"I'll explain more later. Let's go." Lea took her mom's hand; the shaking didn't stop. "It'll be okay. I swear." She took her mom through the thinning with her.

It better be okay.

Eleven

Lea plunged downward, the ticklish feeling from a roller coaster turned to a body-wide terror. Mom wrapped her bony arms around Lea to take an unknown impact for her little girl.

Inertia halted, playing that sick trick where Lea kept moving, but her body had stopped. Sharp branches and little twigs scraped her legs. Nothing else hurt though. A pained breath blew hot in her ear. Mom!

"Mom, are you okay?" Lea wriggled out of her mother's tight hold and rolled out of the bush onto the ground. She sprang to her feet and held her mom's face.

Mom smiled and flinched. "I don't think I broke anything." She had fallen into the bushes on her back. It took a struggle to get up from the tangles of thin sticks, and aside from the clusters of leaves sticking out of her hair and pricking through her cotton clothes, she looked no worse for wear.

A shout came from above—the thinning.

Lea yanked Mom away, and Dad fell right where they had. He groaned. Another victim of the sharp bush, though at least none of them got too hurt. They missed slamming into an enormous tree by only a couple of feet, and any other number of trees similar to live oaks. The density of the forest meant luck had played on their side. Hopefully it would hold out.

A light-headed rush came over Lea, the dizziness making her queasy. Duh, air. She got the mouthpiece from her backpack and turned the spout to release the oxygen. Just like on the airplane, put your mask on first and then help the others. Of course, Gabe had the other backpack with the rescue breathers for her parents. He'd be through next.

At the base of the tree, Dad had contorted himself free from the foliage when Gabe emerged through the thinning. Gabe's cobalt wings spread wide like a parachute, and his knees buckled as he still smacked hard into the ground.

Lea stepped toward him and got whiplashed when she was yanked backward by her arm, the pull almost popping her shoulder with force. Her dad's grip on her forearm tightened.

Mom screamed, and Dad shielded her with his body as he tried to guide Lea behind him.

Gabe rubbed his leg and took his time getting up. The shorter strands of white hair fell over his eyes, blue like his skin, though without the silvery sheen. His wings slid into place behind him, and he paused to stare at his hands. He seemed uncomfortable. At least he didn't faint this time.

"He's one of *them*." Dad stared. His stiff stance only betrayed by hyperventilation.

Mom shouted, "Stay back!" She panted hard afterward. They both needed the rescue breathers in Gabe's backpack, and soon.

Lea spat out her mouthpiece. "Wait." She pried Dad's fingers off her arm. "It's fine. He's my friend."

"What do you want with us?" Mom strained; her voice gave way to a gasp.

"The air's too thin here. You need oxygen, and Gabe's pack has a couple rescue tanks we can use till we find another thinning and get you guys out of here." Lea walked between her parents and Gabe.

Dad reached for her. "Lea, no, he'll hurt you."

"I'd never." Gabe slid the backpack from his shoulder and let it drop. He panted, grabbing at his waist where the blood soaked through even more.

Lea took a breath from her mouthpiece. "He's not the same as them. We don't have time for this. You're running out of air." They both breathed harder by the second. She grunted in frustration and stomped back to her parents. "Mom, take a breath." She pressed the mouthpiece to her mom's lips, and she breathed in and out. Dad took a turn next.

Gabe unzipped the pack and pulled out the one-liter tanks. They each fit in one hand and had a rubber nozzle at the top to breathe from. "Lea, catch."

He tossed her the tanks, and she handed them to her parents. "We have to get away from here." He waited to catch Lea's eye. "That last guy, I think he's Illirin, and if he comes looking for a nearby thinning…"

"I got that vibe, too," Lea said.

Dad sipped a breath from his tank, though he didn't look away from Gabe for an instant. "I don't understand. If you're one of them, why are you helping us? Why did your people attack us?" He grabbed Mom's hand. The hand gripping the tank shook, not with fear, but with anger. "Why!"

"I don't know." Gabe threw up his hands, and his wings seemed to spread on their own. "I swear, I'm not one of the Illirins who attacked you. Probably…anyway."

"Gabe! Ungh." Lea sighed. That idiot took this moment to second guess himself. Impeccable timing. "The dumbass over there has amnesia, and I know he didn't hurt you. I trust him. We need to find another thinning."

She looked at Gabe. "Anything coming back to you? Know where we are?"

He shook his head. The smirk from her annoyance with him lingered in place.

Lea nudged her mother's shoulder. "Let's go then."

Mom didn't budge, also caught staring at Gabe. Frankly, it was embarrassing the way they acted.

Then Mom pointed at Gabe. "He's *not* one of them. Jonathan, look at his eyes."

"You're right. He's not," Dad said.

Gabe seemed to press his arm harder against his stomach. He exhaled heavily and walked over to Lea. Her parents stopped freaking out—finally.

"Where to?" he asked.

"What?" Lea popped the mouthpiece back in.

"Other than 'in a forest,' I've got no idea where we are either. You've always had a knack for finding thinnings, even without your notes." He tapped her forehead. "That sixth sense of yours."

Her neck tingled as if to answer him. She closed her eyes and concentrated on the feeling. The breeze tickled her cheeks and moved her braid against her back, the nudge in her gut starting to pull her in the same direction. She raised her arm to point and opened her eyes to find her finger guiding them into the denser part of the forest. Like in those cartoons with the fork in the road, they had to go down the path toward gangly trees with scary glowing eyes and not the land of sunshine and singing bluebirds.

"All right then, let's get out of here." Dad took a breath from his tank and nodded to Gabe, Mom at his side.

Gabe set out the direction Lea had pointed, and the three of them fell in line behind him in a strange case of the blind leading the visually impaired. Gabe went in front, both to clear a path through the underbrush and to protect the others. So he didn't know where they were anymore than Lea, but if they ran into someone, at least he had a shot of blending in.

As they traveled, the space between trees widened only because the trunks grew in size to match. The forest towered over them like the redwoods in California, where Lea had run a short stint at a university. The overlapping branches created a deciduous canopy, blocking out the sun. Why didn't they go the other way? Oh yeah, the stupid nudge. Lea rubbed the back of her neck; it better be right.

Five feet ahead of Lea and her parents, Gabe stomped down some vines and pushed the bushes out of the way. A flurry of movement made him jump back. Someone found them?

With all her weight, Lea shoved her parents to the ground behind the bushes.

"Wha—"

She clasped her hand over Mom's mouth and shook her head. If someone saw Gabe alone, maybe he could talk them into leaving. Hyperventilating into a scuba tank was a bad idea. She needed to calm down.

A shadow fell over her. She held her breath. Nothing, and then a snicker. She sat up on her knees and turned her head.

Gabe stood behind her with a grin across his cobalt face. "Those squirrels weren't out to get you. I swear."

Lea pulled out her mouthpiece. "Oh, shut up. You jumped first." She got up and gave her parents room to do the same.

"There's a thinning right ahead. Let's get out of here before someone actually finds us." Gabe reached for her mother who struggled to free her arm from the branches. "Mrs. Huckley, here, let me help you up."

Mom glanced at Dad, in a not-so-subtle hesitation, and took Gabe's blue hand. "Th-thank you."

"This way." Gabe's wings folded as he turned.

They followed him to the thinning, which was easy to recognize from this side. An oval area about five feet wide floated above the ground, and instead of a view of tree roots, the space showed a backyard fence and a swing set. Though it wasn't clear, the thinning swirled like fog over glass—insubstantial and simultaneously impenetrable.

Like the appearance of the dark forest, reality bent far from perception, and they crossed through the thinning with no more effort than pushing back a weighted curtain. The thinning dropped them in someone's yard, who knows where.

Right after they arrived, Gabe gave Lea's parents the clothes they stashed in his pack. Lea guessed her clothes would fit Mom, but Gabe's T-shirt might be a bit big on Dad. Following Gabe's advice, they hopped the fence and called a cab from his cell.

Everything that followed blurred together in a surreal montage. Lea observed the scene flow before her, Gabe issuing instructions and giving her parents new IDs. Her parents played fugitives, while he acted as some kind of authority on running from the law. More so, Gabe oozed confidence in a situation that inspired uncertainty in any normal person. He was a natural leader, and even with all the hang-ups her parents had with his origins, they took every word to heart. He guided them on ideas of where to hide, and how to stay off the radar. What the heck did those memories hold?

The least real part of the whole situation came at the end when Lea hugged them both goodbye. They squeezed together in a tight circle outside of the cab—free.

Only a few hours had passed, but Lea's life was unrecognizable. On the way to the airport, she watched Gabe gaze out the taxi window at the blossoming trees. They didn't talk about anything, and she was at a loss for what to say to him anyway. She had one goal, one, and now because of him, she succeeded in fulfilling that wish. How could she possibly thank him enough? It seemed so paltry to say it, that she stopped herself every time she opened her mouth to try.

Even if she managed to help him recover his memory, it couldn't live up to what he risked for her, and for her parents whom he didn't even know. He could've been captured, experimented on, arrested, or killed. What would some aromatherapy or an inter-dimensional trip mean compared to that? And further, what did he get out of it? Nothing. He changed her and her parents' lives with no benefit to himself. He was amazing, and she wanted to tell him. She wanted to let him know that he was the most incredible person she'd ever met. When she thought about it, the buzz of static electricity tingled all over her arms and legs. Was that love?

She tried to push it back, but the warmth spread outward. It was stupid. What was she to him? Oh yeah, a college buddy. She was the loud, weird chick in the art class, not exactly his type. His type was Heather. Heather the beauty, the girl who seemed to sweat strawberries from her teeny-tiny pores. Lea couldn't compare to her alive, and now—a ghost was perfect. She could never live up to a ghost.

She leaned back in the hammock-style chair that made up the waiting areas in the terminal. When she shifted, the whole row of vinyl chairs moved on the rusty bolts that affixed them to the floors. The carpet might have once been blue, but turned more slate gray from the passage of time. At least the planes were newer, right? She readied her mental checklist, hoping this wouldn't be the flight that did her in.

Now wearing a new Buffalo Bills T-shirt, Gabe handed her a latte in a paper cup. He cringed as he attempted to achieve comfort in the squeaky chair.

"Sorry," Lea said. "Some gauze and an ace bandage were all I had. I'll fix you up with my real supplies when we get home."

"I'm sure it'll be fine." He slipped his left arm over his waist again.

Gabe had ripped open his wound fighting those guards and that Illirin spy who chased after them. They had planned to get the heck out of that building and pray they did it fast enough. What was the plan if they got caught? Yeah, "plan," they improvised whole thing. If she had known Gabe could fight like that, maybe she'd have been less nervous. His newfound skills did beg the question—*how*. How'd he know how to fight? Why'd he need to learn?

"Your parents seem nice," he said.

"They are." She sighed. "Except that they accused you of assault and freaked."

He took a sip of his coffee. "I don't blame them. I'd probably do the same in their place."

"I'm sorry, though," she said, still gripping the cup where he had placed it in her hands.

"It's okay."

"No, I mean for me. I reacted just as badly when I saw you that first time. I was mad, and it wasn't right. I'm sorry."

Leaning back, he tilted his head, looking at her in a funny way. What did that mean? Was he upset with her?

He chuckled. "So is this 'be brutally honest with Gabe' day? It's fine, really. I don't think you're still mad at me for being Illirin?" He did a double eyebrow raise.

She almost dropped her cup, but caught it in the tips of her fingers. "No, no! Are you serious?"

He laughed and jerked back, banging his elbow into the metal armrest. "Ow ow ow." He grabbed his funny bone.

"Serves you right! I'm feeling bad here, and you're laughing at me." Lea huffed.

He rubbed his elbow, trying to earn sympathy from her. It wasn't working. "Just wanted you to see how ridiculous you're being. Now who's laughing at my pain?" He pouted.

She rolled her eyes and took another sip of her latte. He was such a dork, but maybe that was why she liked him. She watched him rearrange himself in the little seat, and that fuzzy static crept all around her body again. If she couldn't tell him how she felt, at least she could say thank you.

"Gabe," she whispered.

"Yeah?"

She looked him in the eyes, his kind eyes. "Thank you for—"

"No problem, I'm glad I could help."

"No listen, I..." She twisted the cardboard sleeve around the outside of her cup. "This is so dumb. You say thank you to someone who gives you coffee. It's not enough, nothing is. You don't know how much it means to me."

He smiled that half-smile he sometimes did when he wasn't sure how to respond. "I think I do. And as I said, I'm happy I could help. You'd do the same for me."

She snorted. "In spirit, yeah, but I'm sure I couldn't fight someone like that."

His smile faded a bit, and he kept her in the corner of his eye. "I wasn't going to let you go back there again. I didn't like what it did to you."

She tried to catch his gaze, but he looked away. What did he mean by that? He went from goofing off to saying something like that. So serious. "I don't—"

"And also, Illirins put them in there. It felt wrong. I needed to fix it, to make it right." He turned to her. "You know?"

She nodded, and then bent to put her coffee on the floor. He changed the subject, saving her from saying something dumb, but now she couldn't ask what he meant. Was he just being protective?

Like always, he probably had a point. She drew a long breath. "I've been wondering about that since my dad asked. I feel like an idiot never even asking myself why they chose my parents or why they did what they did."

"How could you have found out? It's incredible you figured out all that you did. So you're not omniscient, big surprise there."

She sank back into the vinyl. "What if they're still in danger because I can't figure it out?"

Gabe's strong hand covered hers over the armrest between them. The touch sent a shock through her, like it really was static.

He gripped her fingers. "We will. I don't know how, but after I get my memory back, maybe I'll know something then that can help."

She stiffened and pulled her hand back into her lap. "I'll help you, I will. I'll help you remember. I promised."

He smiled. "I know, but don't think it's payback. I would've helped you anyway, you know that."

"You're too nice." She smiled outwardly as she felt her heart sink just a little. If he wasn't so sweet, she wouldn't feel jealous of a dead girl. Oh boy, was she a winner or what.

He shrugged. "I'm not so sure, but thanks."

"Why do you say that?"

"Dunno, just a feeling."

She nudged him in the side. "You've risked your life for strangers, and you've never been anything but kind to me. I think that's better evidence than some lame feeling you've got."

He laughed. "Okay, fine, I'm nice."

Twelve

Gabe had the whole plane flight and drive back to the dorm to think about what he should tell Matt about Heather. Standing in front of his door, keys in hand, he still didn't know. Maybe he should just tell Matt the truth. He'd never believe, but if he did, then what other problems would that cause? Though, Matt was the sci-fi guy, so he could handle it.

Okay then. He'd bite the bullet and tell Matt a short approximation of the truth, claim exhaustion as an excuse, and go to bed. He took a breath and turned the key.

Lights off inside, Matt wasn't home. He let out a sigh of relief. Walking over to his computer, he noticed something wasn't quite right. Aside from the note taped to his monitor, the top bunk bed was bare, and the microwave had vanished along with all of Matt's other stuff.

Gabe pulled the note off the monitor.

Hey, sorry to bail without calling, but it's kind of an emergency. My mom is sick, and I had to leave. She'll be out of the hospital in a couple days, but she'll need me at home for the rest of the semester to help out. I'll be commuting for the rest of my classes.

I'll request the same room, so if you do, too, I'll see ya in the fall, as long as you don't get hitched over the summer or something. Let me know if that's the case, hope I'm invited. Anyway, you got my cell.

Later,

Matt

Well, that made things easier. He now had time to think of what he actually wanted to say. Besides, tomorrow he and Lea were going to Illirin to see if his memories would return. If he did remember, maybe he'd have something else to tell Matt. Who knows, they still had a few months till the fall semester, anything could happen.

Old cigarette smoke assaulted Gabe's nose upon cracking open the door to the college bar. He coughed a few times and tried to clear the crap from his nostrils. Even before noon, Cool Beans already had a few smokers up by the bar. He went through the archway to the back area where he saw Lea occupying a booth, notepads spread all over the table, and a bowl of tortilla chips teetering on the edge.

"I didn't know we were bringing the library with us." Gabe scooted into the booth.

"I'm Type A, if you haven't figured that out." She lifted the backpack next to her. "Just bringing this. It's got my oxy tank, and I hooked up the nose tube so I don't look like a moron going dry-land scuba diving. Packed some basics in a pack for you—a flashlight, Swiss army knife, protein shakes, and bottles of water. Can you think of anything else we'd need there specifically?"

"Sounds like you're the one who knows more about what we— *you*—need then." The last time they were in Illirin flew by in a rush. It didn't seem real. For her, this was a trip to a different plane, but for him, he was going *home*. He dipped a chip in the salsa and tried to shake the weird feeling about the whole thing.

"Yeah, I guess so. I just want to be prepared." She slid some of the papers around and closed one of the folders. "I don't want to end up stuck without a plan. You know, a real plan." She picked up a stack and tapped them together, keeping her hands busy. She must be nervous, too.

"I think you've prepared more than a med student before the MCAT." He leaned back in the wooden booth. "So, Miss Type A, what's this 'real' plan?"

She perked up and opened the infamous ED Project binder. Tracing her fingers over the campus map, she said, "You likely frequented a thinning on campus, so if we cross over here, then we should be close to something you'd recognize." She tapped on the auditorium building. "Two thinnings pass through often, one on most afternoons and another overnight. My bet is on afternoon. What do you think?"

Gabe dipped his chip and took a bite. "That makes sense, and it's a good to place to start. But…" He paused. "What if I don't get any ideas once we're over there?"

"Explore!" Lea flashed that crazy smile for old time's sake, and then softened into her normal expression. "Come on, I need you to be positive. If you don't get something immediately, we'll keep looking. We'll go back again and again. You'll know someone, or someone will know you, and I'm certain you'll remember."

"I'll let you have the confidence. You wear it so well."

She rolled her eyes. "Fine, give me a chance to say 'I told you so.'"

He smirked. "I'll let you cherish the moment and everything. We can take pictures to commemorate the event."

She laughed and tossed a tortilla chip at him, narrowly missing his face.

"Who's the violent one now?" He ducked as another chip sailed over his head.

"Anyway." She pointedly ignored him and looked through her notes. "I've been thinking about something. What should we do if anyone sees me? I know we'll try to stay out of sight, but that might not be possible."

Gabe hadn't thought about it. She would stick out, and it wasn't exactly common for humans to be walking around Illirin. He imagined himself there, the wide wings stretching from his back. "You can walk behind me. I'll try to keep you covered with my wings." He paused. "That really sounds weird when I say it."

"With any luck it'll be normal to you by this evening."

He looked up from the bowl of chips to see Lea's positive smile. She was doing everything she could to help, the eternal optimist. Even if he couldn't jump on her happy train, he was glad she tried to pull him along anyway.

"Right." He ate another chip and continued, "So not to be intentionally negative, but nothing busted into my mind the last time we went. What're we gonna do? Go up to the first stranger we see and say, 'Why, hello there. I don't know who I am, and this is my human friend helping me out, do you know me?'" He leaned his head over the back of the booth to stare up at the tar-stained ceiling. "Yeah, this isn't gonna work."

"So if we get nothing this time, we'll go back. Eventually you'll get another flash of something."

He could feel her staring at him, though he didn't move his eyes from the patterns of stains above him. He waited for her to continue, to keep cheering him on. When all he heard was silence, he looked back to see her glaring at him.

"What?" he asked.

"You need to stop it."

"Stop what?"

She crossed her arms and straightened her spine. "Self-fulfilling prophecy is a real thing. If you go into this thinking nothing's gonna change, than that's what you'll get. The only way you're getting your memories back is if you believe you can. So you need to suck it up and have some faith."

Gabe blinked at her. Self-fulfilling prophecy? She could be right. Maybe all this time he had been sabotaging himself, forcing himself to stay in the dark. He didn't even realize it until it came out of his mouth. "Fine, okay. Maybe it's too real now. It can really happen, and now I'm freaking out. All I ever did was complain that I couldn't remember, and now that I'm facing it, I'm nervous, and that makes me a total jackass."

Lea leaned over the table, resting her chin on her wrists. "It's hard to face your dreams. People think it's sunshine and double rainbows, but really it's not. You think, 'What if it goes wrong? What if it's not what I saw in my head? What if I fail?'" The corner of her lips turned up. "All the work and the scary…it's worth it."

He slid his hand over to gather a stack of her papers and then winked in return. "I guess you'd know."

"You stood by me, and I'll be right there with you too, no matter what happens." She sat back up and snapped her lime-green mechanical pencil back in the ED Project binder. "So, don't wuss out on me now."

"Never!" Acting in the classic Lea style, he banged his hand on the table. Idiot! He looked like an idiot.

Lea doubled over in the booth laughing. She clutched her stomach to try to help her breathe, and Gabe ducked to hide himself from the students murmuring in their direction.

After her belly laughing died down, he whispered, "I'm not cut out for the spotlight like you."

She sat up and her grin stretched wide. "I love it. Do it again!"

He failed at forcing a straight face. "Not even if you paid me."

"Boo, you're no fun."

He chuckled and ate a few more chips. He glanced at the clock on the wall. They needed to get back to business. "What time does the thinning show?"

She checked her watch. "About one o'clock. We should head over now."

The thinning would appear across the street in the auditorium building. Lea seemed to know exactly where to go, so Gabe followed close behind. When she opened the inside glass door, the eerie pipe organ echoed through the halls.

"It always sounds creepy in here. The organ is so horror movie-esque. *Mary Had a Little Lamb* would sound disturbing." Lea rubbed her arms like the music gave her the shivers.

Gabe listened for a moment. "Scales…ooohhhhhooohhhh, how frightening." He checked the hallway to see nobody around. "Classes are still going, that's good. So where is it?"

"Should be on the second floor on this side of the building."

They made their way up the stairwell and into the hall. As they approached the area, the temperature dropped a few degrees, and Lea's telltale smile appeared on cue. Her calculations were perfect yet again. "You ready?"

She nodded. At the same time, they both reached for the thinning the way they had before. Gabe made contact with the barrier between their worlds, and he tore it open. With the light blinding them, he squeezed Lea's hand hard enough to cut off blood to her fingers. He wasn't going to let her go, both for her safety and his piece of mind. He stepped through, making sure she followed close behind.

They tumbled down onto the grass, the thinning hovering a foot above the ground behind them.

Gabe stood and looked around. They arrived in a large grassy field near the edge of a forest, where the smell of moist dirt and flowers filled his nose. He couldn't name the scent, but he knew it well.

He glanced back over to Lea, her new self-darkening lenses already changed to compensate for the brighter sun.

"You okay?" He held his shimmering, cobalt hand to help her up as he had the first time.

She grabbed his wrist, and he pulled her to her feet. After brushing the dirt off her knees, she opened the top of her backpack and retrieved the tube to plug in her nose. "Ready and raring!" She laughed a bit as she eyed him. "Déjà vu, but better without you fainting on me."

"And I'm sure you'll have a nicer visit without passing out too." He reached into the pack for the pocket mirror Lea brought and studied his reflection. His face looked exactly the same, except blue and with a hint of a metallic, silvery sheen. His ears came to an elfish point, and his hair turned stark white down to the tip of his ponytail.

"I still don't see *me*." He clicked the mirror closed and put it in his back pocket. "Ya know?"

"Yeah, but it's temporary I'm sure."

Gabe watched her face for a moment. To himself, he looked weird, but what did she feel about it? He wasn't human. Did it bother her? Her expression gave nothing away, but she could hide her reactions if she wanted.

He hesitated. "Do I freak you out?"

She actually laughed. "No, you dork. First time shocked me, but hey, blue's your color. And who doesn't like an angel?"

"These aren't feathery white." He slid the slats of his wings together against his back. "And I'm not an angel."

"Fine, maybe you'll recall your sense of humor along with your memories." She studied the area. "Where should we start?"

Gabe looked around the unremarkable spot where they arrived. Illirin didn't appear very different than Earth, and nothing special caught his attention, just the forest edge and then across the meadow, a dirt road. He walked over to the road, being sure to keep an eye out for any passersby. He knelt down and touched it, smooth and hard. Unlike a regular dirt road, it seemed finished as if it were pavement. The ground was compacted and without a single rock marring the surface. The odd road was just a bit off normal, hardly noticeable.

Lea joined him but kept her head up. "Doesn't seem like a busy location. Nothing's around here."

"Yeah." He stood and glanced both ways down the road. To the right he could make out the silhouettes of some tall buildings in the distance. "Looks like the closest city is that way."

"And your gut says?"

"Go that way." He took a few steps and glanced back at Lea. She waved him forward, forcing him to lead. He wanted to follow her, to let someone else make the decisions, but it was up to him. It felt annoyingly natural. He didn't like it, but for some reason he always ended up in front.

Once they reached the city, Illirins milled about everywhere, and Lea ducked behind Gabe's wings to hide. Most were Winged, like Gabe, but had varying skin colors that ranged the spectrum. Some walked the streets, some traveled in what looked like very small cars, and a few flew from the top of one skyscraper to another. The tall buildings had doors and balconies at higher floors to accommodate the Winged trait.

The city appeared both familiar and foreign. In so many ways it looked just like any place on Earth, except for minor features like the dirt roads and random doors. The buildings were primarily constructed of granite and marble instead of concrete. That simply made them look European, not alien.

Gabe led them through alleyways between a couple of shorter buildings. Lea opened her mouth, probably to ask 'where to,' but she didn't get the chance. He shut off his brain and went on without thinking.

His body guided them through some back alleys, down a few side streets, and then to a road leading to a residential neighborhood.

They stopped in front of a three-story house at the end of a cul-de-sac with two vacant lots on either side. Gabe stood silent, staring at the house. Marble columns straddled the front porch, and the slate door held a cut-glass window. The dimmed porch light called to him…familiar.

Lea grabbed his wrist and dragged him to the side of the house out of sight. "Do you remember something?" She breathed in and out through the tube in her nose.

"No. I uh…I stopped thinking and here we are."

"Muscle memory. Good idea." She nodded and slipped her thumb under the shoulder strap of the heavy backpack.

"What?"

"Muscle memory. If you do something enough times, your muscles remember the actions and can do it again. That's how gymnasts and ice skaters get so good at doing their stunts—repetition."

He studied the house, hoping something would click. "What you're saying is that I've taken that back road to and from the thinning to this house many, many times."

"That's my guess." She squeezed his hand.

Gabe let out a breath. "Thanks." He took his gaze from the house and looked at Lea. He wouldn't even be there without her encouraging him. He needed someone…no, he needed *her* by his side. Only her persistence could make him face the unknown, an unknown he wanted revealed, but that didn't make it any less frightening. He closed his fingers around hers, and let her grip strengthen his resolve. "Let's go on in then."

They walked around to the back of the house where they found a sliding glass door. Gabe jiggled the door a few times, and the locking bar fell, clanking against the glass. He pressed his fingers against the handle and slid the door an inch. Something shocked him, and he flinched his hand away. Tentatively, he touched the metal handle again but nothing happened. He needed to stop dragging his feet, too much static. He stepped through the door into the kitchen, Lea closing it behind her.

A shadow, leaving no evidence of his presence, Gabe tiptoed around the kitchen. He traced his fingers across the cold granite counter, rounded edges and a small chip by the sink. The layout came to him, and he knew where things were. He opened a drawer, and just as he expected, the flatware. He closed his eyes and imagined himself in the space. When he opened them, he saw a hint of something, someone else standing by the stove. It lasted only an instant, but a memory tried to surface. He breathed shallow as if the movement of his chest rising would frighten the memories away.

He walked through the doorway into the living area, and another flash hit him. He saw an older Winged man his same color sitting on the sofa. He blinked and the image vanished. He tried standing in different places, sitting on the chair, or walking toward the door to get more glimpses to come. Sometimes it worked. He saw a lavender-tinted woman in the chair by the lamp, and at a different time, the same man looking through a stack of papers on the coffee table.

"It's my house," Gabe whispered. "Nothing really clear, but I keep seeing flashes."

Lea barely nodded. When he didn't move, she nudged him in the small of his back.

He took her hint and walked up the stairs one at a time, fixing the details in his head—white plaster walls, iron railing, and a painted mountain landscape. His feet took him forward again, like they knew where to go. He found himself in the room at the end of the hallway. Posters lined the light gray walls showcasing Winged and Legged musicians. The largest poster was in fact a tattered campaign sign reading "Jeken Ilat—Councilman," its colors faded by years hanging in the sun. A blue, striped quilt neatly covered the loft bed, and the desk below appeared pristine from going unused.

Gabe sat down at the desk—his desk. He picked up a framed photo of the man he glimpsed downstairs, but a lot younger, and standing with a boy about seven years old, himself. They stood in front of a larger version of the campaign poster, confetti falling around them. Gabe's head began to throb.

Makai ran into the campaign headquarters. He panted, having come all the way from the park. He jumped up to get his father's attention, but with so much going on, his father didn't even notice. He flitted his wings enough to rise above the commotion. Finally, his father came through the crowd.

"What's wrong?" His father bent to his level.

"Hawlk says that if you're the Winged Councilman that I'll never get to see you. You'll be too busy traveling. Is it true?" His voice cracked.

His father rested his hand softly on Makai's shoulder. "I will have lots of work, yes, and I will have to travel to Union often, but I'll always have time for your mother and you."

"But not as much as now." His wings dipped along with his head.

"It's a difficult job, but I want you to know you're just as important to me, more important."

Makai looked up. "Then why do you want to do it anyway? The traits are unified, we don't need the Council. There's nothing so important they need you!"

"You're right, son, the traits were unified by the First Council, and again by the Second after the Lirin wars. However, traitism is still rampant in Illirin, and the Council takes measures to further unity and integration, fair trade and good will. It's a never ending job."

"There's no traitism anymore, Father, there's tons of Legged at my school and we get along great."

He shook his head. "The Winged and Legged have always been close allies. Besides, the kids at your school are friendlier than some others. I'm glad you don't experience it, but it's a big problem in many places."

Young Makai frowned. "That's awful..."

"And that is why I want to be the Winged Councilman. I want to prove that we can unify and make a better Illirin. I'd like to have the chance to try." He squeezed his son's shoulder and stood back up.

Makai opened his wings, now excited by the idea. "Then I want you to win. You're the best, and everyone else should know it."

Gabe came to, still holding the picture in his hands. When did that happen? The memory came in so clear, but he must have been young.

He wiped a streak of dust off the surface of the desk. Everything in the room felt more *his*. More memory seeped in, not always in the dramatic flashbacks, but kind of like the tide coming in one wave at a time, slowly filling the hole in his mind.

He bent over to open the bottom drawer. He pushed some papers to the side, and underneath he found a wooden box. Setting it carefully on the desk, he rubbed his finger over the hinges. It was important. No, meaningful.

Inside he found some more photographs, a few medals—trinkets. It was supposed to be more. Stuck in the corner, he found a folded piece of paper. He opened the note.

> *I want you to know I love you both. I don't mean to upset you, but I have to follow my heart. I've been breaking the Schism to visit a girl named Heather. You'd love her, I know you would. I'm going to stay with her on Earth. I know you probably think I haven't thought this through, and you're wrong. I know it's illegal, but it can't be all bad, not when people like Heather live there. I can't come home often, but I will visit. I'll miss you both.*
> *Makai*

Heather…his memories seemed to always go back to her. He didn't deliver this note, did he? He picked out another photo, his mother posing in the kitchen with a culinary masterpiece. Pain crept in around his skull again, forcing him to lean over. His body fought back to repress the flood of memories, but the gate was already open. The throbbing grew, and he passed out, but not to unconsciousness. His mind spun around in jumbled recollection.

"How long have you been doing this, Makai!" Father yelled, apparently unafraid to wake the neighbors. His short white hair now had wisps of gray, and frown lines riddled his brow, evidence of the aging his office inflicted.

He wasn't going to back down. "Few months. So? I really don't see the big deal, I'm not hurting anyone."

"You're interfering with humans, you're breaking the Schism, and you're meddling in things that have been off-limits since our worlds divided. It *was* for a reason, Makai! I didn't raise you to think you're above the law."

"I don't think that—"

"Then *why* are you doing this? Of all things, breaking the Schism, my son. Don't you see how wrong this is?" *Father huffed, out of breath.*

He didn't mean to put his father in this position. Wasn't love more important? "But, but…we're in love. I couldn't help it, I had to talk to her and now I can't stop. I want to marry her."

The silence separated them like a wall. He waited for words, angry and loud. They didn't come.

"I know it's crazy. I know it is, but it's the truth. It's what's happened. I can't un-love her now. What do you want me to do?"

Father closed his mouth and recomposed himself. He stiffened his jaw. "You did this to yourself, Makai. You've caused not only your own heartbreak, but this poor human girl's as well. You cannot go back, and you know that."

"But Father!"

"But nothing. The Schism happened because of our interfering on Earth. It is forbidden, even for young love. I'm sorry, but this is how it is."

He clenched his fists, anger welling up. He wanted to lash out at his father, blame him. So what if it was his own fault. It didn't matter, he was still angry.

"Son," Father's tone was softer. "I know what it's like to feel a love so strong. I'll supervise one last visit, so you can say goodbye. But that's all I can do."

He nodded to agree, but would he come back through after taking that trip?

Everything blurred again, and flashbacks bombarded Gabe's mind. He remembered sneaking out to go see Heather and returning late at night. The memory was so real, the cold wind dimpled his arms with bumps. He smelled the violet kalettes of spring blossoming in the flower pots.

The calm night broke into dread as Makai heard the front door of his home slam open. Hidden by the columns on a neighbor's porch, he turned his head around the corner, and two seemingly traitless figures ran headlong from his house. Should he follow? He stopped. His mother was just inside. He abandoned stealth and ran through the front door.

"Mother?" he called. She was probably just asleep and would be startled to find out he hadn't been home.

No answer. He walked through the living area and then called again, louder, "Mother?" The silence made him nervous, and he moved faster. "Mother!"

He stopped walking; his heart stopped beating. There, on the floor of the kitchen lay his mother. So still, he saw only movement in the pool of blood expanding by her head. Her vibrant lavender skin faded to an ashen gray.

Makai scrambled to the floor and cradled her face. "Mother? Please...please..." She was gone. He put his forehead against her sweaty skin, still warm. Everything in him drained out, leaving him hollow. His chest shuddered with dry sobs, over and over, taking all his breath. It hurt, he'd suffocate like this.

His forehead still touched his mother's, but the warm spot disappeared. Cold. Dead. It wasn't real. Time inched forward.

He lifted his head and caught the empty gaze of her glazed eyes. Real. They murdered his mother, those men who fled his home. They killed her. She would never smile again, never hug him, never ask about his day.

The clock ticked once again. He tensed everywhere—jaw, fists, and tendons down to his wrists. He stood, wings spread. They couldn't get away with taking her life!

Makai hurried to the study. He took Father's old tri-blade that hung above the desk. He didn't bother fastening the hit to his belt; he shoved the sheath in his waistband and ran out the door.

The instant he cleared the threshold, he leapt into the sky. Who were they? He didn't notice a trait, so they must be Seers. He squeezed the hilt of the blade. No matter how fast they were, he was faster. A Seer could never outrun a Winged in the air.

It wasn't long before he caught sight of them heading for the edge of the forest, still in Winged territory. The two Seers made it just inside the tree line when Makai reached the murderers. Flying past the first few trees, he rose above them.

He drew the tri-blade, clicked the release to open the prongs, and folded his wings to dive blade-first on top of one man. He drove the blade into the back of his neck, and found his footing on the ground before the other could cry out. The murderer tried to flee. Makai leaped into the air and descended on the second man, slicing his neck in an effortless swing.

He stood up, his adrenaline-filled body still shaking from anger. He breathed hard, in and out. *Remember to breathe.*

On the ground, two bodies lay spread out, blood splattered across the tree roots. Wind blew leaves over the corpses as if they belonged on the forest floor.

He gripped the wet hilt and sheathed the blade. The blood looked purple against the palm of his hand. What had he done? If he had waited for the authorities, they would have gotten away.

They deserved it! They murdered his mother. It was retribution! His stomach lurched anyway. Leftover dinner rose in his throat, and he threw up. He steadied himself against the tree, waiting in vain for the sick feeling to leave.

The damage was already done. He walked back out of the forest edge to contact his father and to face his grief.

His unconscious body broke into a sweat. He breathed rapidly, and tears streamed down his face from his closed eyes. The memories kept flowing, and soon he relived the encounter that next happened with his father.

Makai cleaned himself up before leaving the house. He tried not to disturb anything so the guardians couldn't tell he had returned. As his father instructed, he made his way quietly outside the city. The clearing by the woods wasn't far, but remote enough to be out of prying eyes. He had been there many times to watch the thinning that came by.

A shadow approached against the dawning sun. He wanted to hide, to cry, to fly away, anything but face him.

"Makai," said Father's hoarse voice. "This is hard for you, too. I know why you...I understand."

He waited for his father to continue. "But?"

"No 'but,'" He sighed. "I shouldn't admit it, but I'm glad you got them. They..." He swallowed. No words breached the next minute, a silent moment of understanding.

Makai spoke first. "What am I going to do? So you're mildly okay with vigilante revenge, but I don't think the guardians are."

"No, they aren't. That's why we're here." His father gestured to the edge of the woods. "The thinning you use to see Heather, it's near here, right?"

The darkening sky kept Makai from seeing his expression. Where in the world could he be going with this?

Father abruptly wrapped his arm around him and pulled him close, cradled by a wing. "You'll go to her, marry, and have that life, son. But to everyone here, you were captured and killed by a third murderer. The other two, you killed in self-defense. This story is the only way you'll be safe. I'll miss you more than you can know. Maybe one day, when you have children of your own..."

He leaned back to look his father in the eyes. "But what about the Seers? Who sent them? This wasn't random. It was a message or threat to you. Something is going on, what's happening?"

"It doesn't concern you anymore. Even if you're needed to pass on the riddle, the magic will take care of it if you don't return. Leaving is the only way to protect you. If you stayed, you'd have to face justice for your crimes, and I can't lose you, too." His father squeezed his eyes shut.

"But Father..."

He gripped Makai's shoulders. "Didn't you say you wanted a life with that girl? You have your chance. Start over and be happy."

Makai pulled his father back into a hug. "I'll miss you. Please be okay. Protect yourself. Send for me if you need me, I'll come."

He looked into his son's eyes and fought back the tears. He put forth a smile to send him off. "You cannot return, but remember that I love you, Makai."

"I love you, too, Father."

The remainder of his memories filled the recesses of his brain. He remembered everything from childhood to climbing in the car with Heather, the tree in the road, and the blackness that followed. His life flashed before his eyes, but he wasn't dying…or was he? That part of him he remembered, and the new part he had become, would never be the same.

Thirteen

"Hey."

A hand rested on Gabe's shoulder. He blinked his eyes open, trying to focus. His face squished against the papers and photographs on his desk. Sitting up, he peeled the pictures from his cheek.

A human girl looked at him. "You okay?"

He wobbled on his chair. "Who're you? What's…?" The girl looked confused. Wait, that was Lea. She came with him, and they were trying to jog his memory. He'd forgotten. All the missing pieces locked into place, the old and new. "Right, Lea. Yeah, I'm okay."

She helped him out of the chair, and he stumbled on shaky legs. "You've been out of it for over an hour. I was starting to get worried." She glanced sideways. "Okay, so not *starting* to. I was worried."

"I'm okay, really." He could still feel the way the blood had slid over his hand, the weight of the blade. He wiped his palms down his jeans. It's only a memory.

Lea rubbed her arm and glanced at the door. "We've been here a long time. Tank's getting low too."

He sighed, gazing at nothing in particular. He got what he wanted, but in place of relief, his stomach churned sour. Why couldn't he let it go? The black wall left his mind. At least he was grateful for that.

Lea rested her hand on his forearm and leaned in. "You remember anything?"

He nodded, but not with the enthusiasm she likely expected.

"That's good." She added, "Right?"

Gabe gave her a half-smile. "FYI, if your subconscious suppresses memories, it probably has a good reason." She waited, so he felt he needed to explain more. "I'm not liking myself very much right now."

"You remember everything then, not just bits?"

"Yeah."

She brushed his wing with her fingertips. "I'll be right there to listen. We can talk through everything, whatever you want. When we get back." She bit her lip. "We are going back, right? Together?"

"Yes, yes, and we should leave right now," he said, turning toward the door.

"O...*kay.*" Lea raised an eyebrow. "I'm not sure where we can—"

"I know where the thinning that crosses campus at night is right about now. It's not to campus yet, but it'll drop us off close enough."

"Right, you would know that, huh." She sounded uneasy.

Gabe started to head out when a door shut downstairs.

"I know someone's here!" a deep voice yelled. "I'm armed! The guardians are on the way."

Lea and Gabe looked at each other. He held up his finger. "Shhh. Stay here." She nodded once and backed out of the way.

Turning the corner on the landing, Gabe saw his father, Jeken Ilat. He crouched at the bottom of the stairwell holding his tri-blade drawn and opened. When he caught sight of Gabe, his jaw slackened and the tri-blade clattered on the floor.

"Makai." Jeken breathed.

Gabe took a step down. "I'm sorry. I know I shouldn't be here. It's difficult to explain, but I—"

Jeken ran to his son and wrapped his arms around him harder than a child clutching a lovey. "Makai, you're alive." He pulled back to see his son's face. The worry lines in his brow had deepened into creases. "I'm so happy to see you safe."

So much time had passed, but Gabe remembered leaving only minutes ago. Father's warnings were fresh. "But, you told me never to return."

Jeken led him down the rest of the stairs. "I know I did. I had Ceru try to find you through the thinnings to check up on you, but he lost track over a year ago. I received a cryptic message recently, and then nothing. I thought…" He paused. "I'm glad I was wrong."

"You're not mad?" The knot tightened inside. Facing his father now renewed his shame, and as much as he wanted to stay, he didn't want to face him.

He smiled more than Gabe recalled. "No, I'm not. Yes, you shouldn't have come back, but I'd be lying if I said I wasn't happy to see you." Jeken's features hardened and returned a dark frown that seemed like it had taken residence on his face often. "Although, things are complicated right now."

Gabe replied, "I wouldn't have returned, but I got into an accident and lost my memory."

"That's probably why Ceru lost track of you, your patterns changed."

"And I'll be going right away, now that I remember I can't stay."

Jeken gripped Gabe's upper arm. "You need to know what's going on. For the first time in two-hundred years, the Council is close to disbanding. I'm sure there's a conspiracy unraveling things from inside, but I don't have proof."

"What can I do?"

"Stay safe. If the next Councilman needs you to pass on the riddle—"

"There won't be a next anytime soon."

Jeken said, "I'm trying to—" A *clang* echoed from upstairs. He spun toward the stairwell. "Come down here now!"

Lea sheepishly turned the corner and met them in the living area. Gabe exchanged a glance. *Don't worry, Lea, it's safe.* His father would understand. At least, he hoped he would.

Jeken observed her for a minute. "Heather?"

"No. Heather died in the accident. This is Lea. She helped me recover my memory."

"Uh, hi." She waved with the tips of her fingers while biting her lips together.

"Oh," Jeken said. An awkward pause followed. "I didn't know humans could survive here."

Lea proudly pointed to the tube in her nose. "Oxygen tank."

Gabe stood closer to Lea, hoping to ease her nerves. What could his father be thinking? After a year, he randomly appeared here with a human decked out for dive. At least he seemed all right with it. "Right, so…yes. Um, Lea, this is my father, Jeken Ilat."

She held out her hand. "It's a pleasure to meet you…uh, Mister Ilat?"

Jeken chuckled and gripped her hand in a firm shake. "Councilman Ilat to most, but yes, we say 'Mister' here."

"Yeah, about that. I was wondering why Illirins speak English?" Lea asked.

Gabe smirked. That was so like her, always searching for answers.

"During the time of the First Council, our ancestors met with the people of Earth. They first crossed over on the British Isles, and they cooperated with the wizards there to instill a common language, both amongst the traits and with the people on Earth." Jeken paused. "Does that answer your question?"

"Yes, fascinating!"

"The awkward history lesson over now?" Gabe twitched his wings. Was this really happening? His father and Lea brought his two lives colliding together. Too much to deal with. "Besides, we really do need to get going."

"Of course." Jeken pulled Gabe to the side and whispered, "I have more I need to discuss with you, and it must be *alone*. Everything we stand for is in danger."

"Yes, Father."

He let his son go, and turned around to pick up the tri-blade. He put it in the worn sheath, and pointed the hilt toward Gabe. "Take this with you."

"I don't need a weapon."

"I want you to protect yourself." He forced it into Gabe's palm and closed his fingers. "You know how to fight. Take it and stay safe."

"But I—" Gabe tried to reply, but caught the gaze of authority in his eyes. "Yes sir."

Jeken bowed his head to Lea. "It was lovely meeting you. I only wish it were under better circumstances. Look after him, will you."

"Of course, Councilman." Lea hefted her backpack.

He gave his father a quick hug. "Thank you."

"Love you, son. Now go, before the guardians arrive."

Gabe gave one last look to his father and took Lea's hand. "Let's go."

He led her out the back door. They went a different direction and left the residential area for a clearing behind the city. Gabe checked for anyone around them and slit the thinning.

The cabbie kept the radio turned up, so Gabe had an excuse to stay quiet. Lea made a few comments about the music, but thankfully didn't ask him anything. What would he tell her? What *could* he tell her? What would someone as gentle as Lea say to someone with blood on his hands?

She'd never understand. Hell, he didn't even understand. He wasn't a traitist, was he? Everything he knew conflicted with what he felt. He wanted to shut down, ignore everything. Maybe it would be better in the morning.

Somehow he avoided talking the whole trip back. Unfortunately, Lea still followed him when he came up the stairs to his room. Couldn't she take a hint?

"I'm exhausted. I think I'm just gonna veg out and turn in early." Gabe avoided eye contact as he put his key in the lock.

"It's six o'clock."

He walked in and tossed his keys on the bunk. "I'm not in the mood to talk right now."

Lea ignored his attempt to close the door and invited herself in. "I think I've done an excellent job not asking you questions, letting you obsess, or whatever it is you're doing. But I'm not going to let you sulk alone all night and have an identity crisis by yourself. So, you're going to let me be your friend and talk to me. *Capiche?*" She folded her arms, dropped onto the bed, and crossed her legs. Nothing would move her. Good God, she was stubborn.

He gave in and sighed. "Friend." He also sat, leaving space between them. "That's the problem. I've been trying to think of a way to tell you my past and have you still like me." He unclipped the sheath from his belt and held it flat. "I've got nothing."

"Boy, someone's being über dramatic." She poked him, but he didn't respond. "Listen, you're not gonna scare me away. You're stuck with me, and whatever you remembered won't change that."

He traced the cracks in the leather with his finger. "You're too nice. You can't possibly understand. Self-admitted, you couldn't fight someone to save your parents, let alone stab somebody who took one from you." The bed squeaked as she moved, probably away from him.

"What happened?" Her usual tone was gone.

Gabe tossed the blade on the rug, juxtaposed with the coffee stain…two lives. He took a breath. "I came home late. I found my mother murdered—"

"Oh no!" she gasped.

He let the momentum keep him going. "The two Seer men fled the house. I followed, and I killed them. I avenged her." He closed his eyes, trying to slow his heart. "I wasn't thinking. It was stupid. I was so angry."

Lea's fingers graced his shoulder, but he shrugged away. She said softly, "I'm so sorry…losing your mom like that."

He looked at her. She was concerned—for *him*, not his victims. He shook his head. "And what about them? I killed two men. I'm just as guilty as they are, even more. Someone else sent them, but for me, it's on my head."

She shrunk back under the bunk. "What do you want me to say? You're a monster? You're justified? I wasn't there, I don't know everything." She sat up and looked him in the eye. "But I do know you, and you're a good person."

He scoffed. "Yeah? How can you be so sure? I'm not. I don't even know who the hell I am anymore, if I ever knew. I wanted to remember my past so badly. I wanted to know who I was, and now that I know, I don't like it." He leaned his head against the metal pole of the bunk bed. "I always believed what I was taught about people, about unity, but every time I see those eyes, that anger takes over. Maybe I am a traitist. Add that to the list of my 'good' qualities."

Lea got up and pulled out a sketchpad from his opened portfolio. She flipped to a pencil drawing of Heather and held it in front of Gabe's face. "I know *you*. You're kind, funny, and a better artist than me." She dropped the pad enough so he could see her. "You don't have to be who you were, be who you *are*."

"It's not that easy anymore!" Gabe stood and banged his hand against the rail. "I still feel these things. I can try to push it back, but it keeps welling up. All I've experienced and everything I know is there, conflicting with new things I've learned. It's impossible to ignore who I was."

She got up in his face. "I didn't say it was easy to be who you want. I said you *could*. Who's more the real you, the one influenced by his society and experiences, or the one who made decisions based on nothing but his heart?"

He moved past her to pick up the tri-blade. He unsheathed it to see the steel, pristine and sharp. No trace of the blood from when he last held it. Was it really just as easy to clean up, to start over?

No, it wasn't. Gabe was his blank slate, and he couldn't get that back. But, he wasn't Makai anymore either. He didn't see things the same way. He was lost. How could he choose?

Lea's image reflected in the blade—two lives. He put it away and gripped the leather in his hand. It wasn't about choosing a side; he was both. He could move forward however he wanted, but he couldn't change his past.

He turned around and replied, "Neither…and both." Somehow, he smiled. "You're right, I'm not Makai Ilat anymore, but I'm also not Gabriel Jones."

"I kinda like Gabe." Lea tapped her fingers against the binding of the sketchpad. "He helped me, saved my parents, and I enjoy his company."

He snapped the sheath onto the belt loop of his jeans. "I'll be Gabe then, but Gabe Ilat. I'll take my family name and all the baggage that goes with it."

"Good, because I was gonna have a hard time calling you Makai."

She seemed completely unaware of what she had done. She was his guide, his star. What would he do without her?

Lea still clutched that pad filled with drawings of Heather. A new guilt twisted in his chest. Maybe it was gratitude. That's all it was. She made him something new, something better. Who wouldn't be grateful for that?

He wanted to say more but all he could think of was, "Thank you."

"Didn't do nuthin.'" Lea smiled like always. "You looked through some pictures and passed out. I just rifled through your things to entertain myself."

He blinked. "What? You..."

She wrinkled her nose.

"Ha, ha. No, I'm saying thank you for annoying me into dealing with my crap, instead of wallowing in it." Gabe found himself resting his hand on the hilt at his waist.

"Oh, that? Then you're welcome."

He tried to ignore the tug on his heart. "I think you're the dork, Lea."

"Takes one to know one."

And she'd be the one to know him. She'd pulled him from a dark past into someone he could be proud of. If only he could say it. Gripped between Lea's powerful hands, that sketch of Heather formed a wall he wouldn't break.

Fourteen

Even Heten Nor's private chambers were not immune to the touch of the desert. Heten gritted his teeth and brushed some sand out of the carvings in the corner of the table. It was disgusting to have to eat and worry about it getting in the food.

He heard a commotion outside his doors. A crash followed the guard's protest. The double doors flew open, slammed against the walls, and his ally the wizard stormed in, the wind from the doors billowing his cape.

"Nor!" the wizard yelled as he closed the distance to the table. He pounded his fists, rattling the plate. Fire ignited around his hands. "Your *precious* daughter failed, and failed big time. What happened to 'Family, I can trust with the most important tasks?'" he said dripping in sarcasm.

The fire disappeared, and he lowered his voice. "She not only lost Makai's interest, but he's well on his way to getting his memory back, if he hasn't already. What do you plan to do about this?"

Heten listened, his expression giving up nothing. He took another bite of his sandwich and placed it on the plate. He then lifted his eyes to look into the infuriated face of his business associate. "Please, take a seat, Wizard. I've been expecting you."

The wizard threw the leather chair backward, the patterned rug lessening the crash. "Don't play this with me. I want answers now! If you're not any closer to obtaining the Stand of Unity, then our deal is on tenuous terms." He took a breath. "My family has been waiting centuries for this opportunity, and you will not ruin it for me."

Heten rolled his eyes. What an idiot. The human didn't have a clue. "Are you just aching for a flare of the dramatic? Think before you presume to know more than me. I'm aware of the changes, and I've taken care of it. Now sit. I refuse to discuss business with a *hothead*."

The wizard stiffened his jaw and bent to pick up the chair. He banged it against the floor and took a seat. "Better?" he sneered.

"Much." Heten laced his fingers together atop the table. "Vermillia failed her mission, yes. She was even tardy in returning here out of fear of punishment. She protested quite vocally, and out of the kindness of my heart, I have given her a second chance. She is in the process of obtaining the final riddle for the unlocking spell and location of the Stand. If she cannot get the information, she will seal the leak. She knows what happens if she fails this time." He added, "She will not fail."

The wizard blinked, cocking his head. "*Final* riddle?"

"Oh yes, you were too busy irrationally screaming for me to tell you. I've gotten the remaining three councilmen to give up their pieces of the puzzle." His thin lips grew into a sly grin. "My methods have caused some brilliant dissent within the Council that has spread to the most traditional cities of the other traits. The resulting discord will aid us greatly when we begin the assault."

His demeanor took a radical change. "Nor, I've underestimated you. I heartily apologize."

"Accepted. After all, we are close allies in this endeavor." Heten's eyes narrowed. "Allies deserve more respect that you've shown today. Remember that." That impudent thug better learn to show deference. So what if this human could tap the aether, or if his power was superior to any Illirin, Heten had an army.

The wizard leaned back in his chair, crossing his legs. "Mutual respect, I agree."

Heten kept his eyes locked. The wizard was hiding something, but at least he was holding true to his word. The moment of tension passed, and an air of agreement returned to the room. Heten ate another bite and dabbed his mouth with a satin napkin.

Heten said, "I do have another matter to discuss with you. If you hadn't dropped by, I was about to summon you."

"And that is?"

"It's about the deal I brokered with your mother. I've been able to ensure you are unopposed in the upcoming battle, but recently there's been a hitch in the plan. Merlin's descendant may have the opportunity to learn of her ability to tap aether. I can take measures to prevent this, but it may involve killing a human, and even my men are hesitant to take that leap."

He pondered this information for a few minutes. "Don't do anything. You've done your part. If she learns of her power now, it's already too late since we're making our move soon. I have an idea, leave her to me."

"As you wish." Heten nodded. He better not screw this up.

"Is there anything I should take care of before we get the Stand?"

"Make sure you're prepared to hold our defenses and bolster our offense. You must be in top form."

The wizard smiled. "I'm always practicing, but if we're close I can work on a larger scale. Don't worry, I'm ready."

The buzzing grew louder. Gabe pushed his ear into the pillow to mute the noise. It didn't help. He flopped over, hitting the alarm with his arm and knocking it to the floor. The muffled buzz continued from below. Wait, the alarm. He was going to be late for class! He tossed off his covers and barely took the time to dress, before grabbing a protein shake and running out the door.

The day passed just like any other day, but not for Gabe. He was a new person. Clearer skies, stronger smells from the blossoming flowers, and even the way the sun lit the world seemed crisper, like a high-definition view of everything. Before now, he'd been drifting through a dream. He knew who he was. His feet hit solid ground with each step, firm and real.

Gabe sat in class listening to another boring lecture on politics. Why did any of this matter? The election didn't affect him; he wasn't voting. The other students in class diligently took notes, and he tapped his pencil against the desk. He didn't belong anymore. He started attending the university to get close to Heather. After the accident, school became a tool to help regain his memory. Now that he didn't have either of those pieces, why was he there at all? But, if he wasn't a college student, where would he go? What would he do?

Yesterday, when he had gone home, Father sounded urgent. What could cause the Council to disband? It was unthinkable. He should find out, and Father had asked him to come back to talk about it.

He glanced up at the professor. Right after classes, he'd go home and find out what Father wanted to say. Aside from that, he missed him. It's easy to be defiant and say you'll leave forever until you actually do. As it turns out, leaving your life behind is hard.

After classes finished, Gabe returned to the dorm and grabbed a quick bite for lunch from the stash of snacks in the corner. Thank goodness Matt didn't take all the food. He checked the clock, just after twelve-thirty. If he hurried back to the auditorium building, he could catch the thinning close to home. He headed out and locked the door behind him.

As he made his way across campus, he watched the students travel from one building to another. He looked for her brown braid amongst the flowing crowd. Lea wouldn't randomly pass by, of course. That didn't take away the unsettled feeling that wrapped around him. To return to Illirin without her sent a pang of guilt into his chest. He should've told her, but Father insisted he go alone. No way would Lea take no for an answer, that was for sure. So he'd meet up with his father and return as quickly as possible. She wouldn't even know he was gone.

Someone had left the front door to the house ajar. Gabe held his breath. No, not again. He drew the tri-blade and walked inside. In the living area, shiny green wings blocked the view of a man kneeling by the desk.

Gabe crouched to defend. "Who are you?"

The green Winged man stood, turning to face him. He looked about his father's age, and his brown hair was disheveled from rummaging about the floor. He did a double-take. "Makai?"

"Ceru Klair?" Gabe let his arm relax by his side. Right, Father mentioned Ceru knew about the ruse surrounding his own "death."

Gabe said, "Yeah, it's me."

Ceru hurried over and gave him a one-arm hug with a pat on the back. "I thought you might have died for real. Lost track of you some time ago."

"Yeah, long story." He surveyed the room. The lamp was broken on the floor, papers scattered everywhere, and an end table flipped over. He nudged Ceru to the side to see that he had been looking at a small bloodstain on the rug. He whipped his head around. "Where is my father?"

"I don't know. Only just got here myself. I was trying to figure that out."

Gabe's heart raced, but he tried to keep cool. "Who's after him? Do you have any ideas?"

"Things with the Council have deteriorated since you left. One of the councilmen is behind some scheme. He's gotten everyone paranoid and working against each other." Ceru continued to look through the wreckage for any clues. "Jeken's told me some things, and I've seen the evidence of the paranoia when I've traveled."

"I don't understand. Why would a councilman be trying to break up the Council?"

"Your father believes he's after the Stand of Unity."

Why would someone want the Stand? It was reserved for a worldwide emergency, something that would involve halting Illirin's rotation and binding with Earth. What could someone personally gain from such a thing?

Gabe asked, "Why?"

Ceru shook his head. "We're still not sure what the plan is. There are rumors of a human wizard in all this mess."

"It's the Seer Councilman, isn't it. Heten Nor, right?"

"Yes," he replied, turning his attention behind Gabe. He found a scrap of fabric under the table, a silky material swirling in coral flowers. "What's this?"

Gabe took the swatch from him. Heather wore that on their date. "The Seer girl who tried to kill me, she wore that blouse."

"Then we know who has him." Ceru added, "And the good news is, if they really are after the Stand of Unity, then your father is still alive. He won't tell them anything."

"Bad news is we better find him fast." He thought out loud. "There's no way she had time to get him out of Winged territory unseen. She had to take him somewhere close but hidden."

"The Eastern Mountains have hundreds of caves throughout the base. They're not far from here."

Gabe was already halfway to the door. "Let's go. I hope we have enough time to search them."

Gabe and Ceru took to the air only a few steps outside. They had to get there in time, they had to. That Seer girl would be traveling by foot with an uncooperative hostage, so they could easily make up the difference. Hopefully, she wouldn't have a lot of time to interrogate his father.

They landed in a clearing at the base of the rising mountain. Anyone could climb the gentle incline, and there were at least thirty caverns within sight.

Gabe started to lose his calm. "How are we going to narrow this down? He could be anywhere!"

"Ssshhhhh, I thought I heard something."

They stood still as a faint voice echoed from deep within the caves. Gabe looked at Ceru and pointed to the right side.

Ceru nodded and took off in the opposite direction.

Gabe hurried to the first opening and listened for the sound— nothing. He waited a few moments and moved on to the next cave. Periodically, he heard the distant noise and adjusted his route. He tried to keep his mind on the task, but each entry he visited without finding him wasted more time. He had to save his father. He couldn't lose him, too.

Picking up his pace, he tripped over a rock and tumbled onto the flat landing several feet below. His scraped elbow hurt. He hurried back to his feet and heard it in detail—a scream.

"Ceru!" he yelled. "Over here! We have to hurry."

Ceru joined him and they sped into the cave. Gabe cursed the uneven floor coated in gravel. The rock walls echoed his every movement, destroying any chance they had of surprising the kidnapper.

A few hundred feet into the tunnel, Gabe heard another agonizing scream. His eyes popped. *Father!* He tried to run, but his feet slipped on the gravel. He fell hard, catching himself with his hands. The heels of his hands stung.

"Careful." Ceru picked him up.

"No time," he replied, and once on his feet, he sprinted forward. He twisted his ankle on the slick rock, but he kept going. His thundering heart kept him from feeling the pain in his foot. All that mattered was getting there.

At last he got close enough that he could hear the woman's voice.

"Has your tongue loosened yet?" she said.

Labored breathing answered as the only reply. A burst of red-orange light flared against the wall, and his father screamed.

"Stop!" Gabe cried. He ran as fast as he could handle through the last of the narrow cavern.

"Too bad, you're out of time, old man," she growled.

His father released a stifled cry, and Gabe rounded the corner. He caught sight of her orange hair as she fled through the back passageway out of the inner chamber. His body nearly tore in half, to both follow her and go to his father. He chose his father, and rushed to his side.

Heavy manacles chained Jeken to the cavern wall. He slumped against the floor, his wings covered in severe burns. Smaller scorch marks riddled his arms and legs.

Gabe lifted his father's face with his hands. "Father. Father…"

He inhaled sharply and then took a few shallow breaths. He opened his eyes. "Ma…kai …"

Ceru caught up and jammed his pocket knife into the locks on Jeken's restraints. "Hold on, we'll get you a medic. Just hold on."

"You'll be okay, I'm here. You'll be okay…okay." Gabe then noticed the cause of the last cry—a tri-blade embedded to the hilt, deep in his father's side. All three blades pierced in different places, and he was bleeding heavily, just as the weapon was designed.

He repeated his mantra. "You'll be okay…okay."

Jeken coughed trying to catch his breath. "Makai, please…you must…"

"Save your strength," he said and looked to Ceru. "Do you know how to heal? Help him, please."

Ceru frowned. "I don't know how. I can barely tap aether, let alone…" He turned his eyes back to the cuffs. He finished releasing the restraints, and Jeken fell into Gabe's arms, his wings dangled limp and spread loose from his back.

Gabe lifted him. His father felt heavy, like he wasn't using his own muscles.

"Wait." Jeken coughed. "Makai, your sister. You have a sister." He lifted his head to look at his son. "Before I met your mother—"

"Father, please, let me move you. We'll get you to a medic."

"Listen." He lifted his arm to reach for Gabe, and his hand fell like a weight on his knee. "Promise you'll protect her. Look out for her. Please."

"Father."

"Promise." He squeezed his eyes shut, gritting his teeth against the surge of pain.

Gabe gripped his hand. "I swear. But I won't need to, come on."

Ceru crouched and laid his hand on his friend's shoulder. He glanced at Gabe and then gave Jeken a closed-lip smile. "I'm here, old man. I'll look after him."

Jeken nodded in return.

"No!" Gabe shouted. "No. Come on now, let's go!" He tried to lift him, but his hands slipped. It was a bad grip, that's all. He wouldn't look, but he saw the flood of red anyway. Slick blood blanketed his father's side, pooling on the cavern floor like a sheet of silk.

Jeken forced his eyes open. "Ma…kai. Son. I love you." His eyes began to close against his will.

"Father. Come on, please. Get up."

The last resistance in his body left, and he went limp against Gabe's lap. This wasn't happening. He was going to be okay. They had to save him, they had to.

Gabe tried to stand with his father's arm over his shoulder, but he was nothing but dead weight. He fell back to his knees, and the arm slipped. His father's body slumped next to him with a sick thud.

Bending over, he grabbed his head and buried his face against the icy ground. He curled tight, every sinew stretched hard against a pain that surged from within. He punched the ground over and over, but he couldn't get it out. *No. No. No.*

Tears fell freely to the cavern floor, enough to form little puddles in the dimpled stone. His father was dead. They tortured and killed him. First his mother, now his father, and for what? Councilman Nor's Seers and some conspiracy? Was that worth killing his family!

The anger from before boiled hot. He shook. Leaning back, he stretched his wings and screamed. He stared back at the passage the Seer murderer fled through. His body tensed, ready to follow after. But no, he couldn't. Not now; he had more important things to do.

Ceru knelt beside Gabe and touched the arm of his wing, folding the slats closed. Ceru also had wet cheeks, red splotches across the whites of his eyes. "He's my oldest and dearest friend. I understand, I do." He stopped to take a breath and wipe his face. "I'll help you carry him."

Gabe could only nod. He had no more left to say. All the words he wanted to share were for his father's ears, and he could no longer hear them.

Fifteen

Gabe hadn't said a word since his father died. He followed Ceru, letting his body go through motions to do what needed to be done. But his mind was blank. He tried to retreat to that place he knew when he lost his memory. Maybe then he wouldn't feel.

After they finished the logistics with the morgue, they made their way back to Ceru's home. No way would Gabe go back to his own house, not now, maybe not ever.

He sat at the kitchen table, hands around a hot mug of tea, and stared past the green-tinged water. Specks of leaves in the ripples gave way to his father's face cringed in agony, blood caked in his graying hair. Even his mother flashed by, faded as a violet with the color drained. He squeezed the mug hard, wanting to hurl the damn thing against that peaceful sage wall. He didn't. Even without the pool of tea, the images lingered behind his eyelids. Nothing could get it out of his head.

"Makai?" Ceru's calm voice interrupted his horrible montage.

He looked up at the haggard face of the old family friend, and gulped some tea to open up his throat. "Why the hell did I take so long coming back?" he asked himself. "Why go to class? If I had only gotten back sooner. Damn it!" He pounded the table, which rattled the mugs.

"Probably wouldn't have changed anything. We don't know how long she had him."

"I could have done something!" He gritted his teeth. "Did you know he gave me his blade? He couldn't even defend himself because of me. I—"

The wooden chair scraped as Ceru stood up. "This is not your fault, and I won't listen to you blame yourself for this. The blame rests on Nor and his assassin, not you."

"You're right." Gabe's chest ached, muscles tender from either crying or trying not to. Everything had happened so fast, and now that he had a moment to pause, he yearned for distraction. But there was nothing left to keep him from reliving that scene over again, feeling the weight of his father in his arms, and seeing his last words crease his face with worry more than pain. *"Makai, your sister. You have a sister."* Why didn't he tell him before?

He held the mug again, the warmth pressed against his fingers. "Why did he wait until he was dying to tell me I have a sister? He said it was before he met my mother, so it's not like it'd be a scandal."

Ceru turned to the counter to heat more water. He lit the burner and filled the kettle with unsteady hands. The kettle dropped onto the stove with a clang. "You'll understand when you meet her. Her name is Aime Nee, and she lives in Union with her nurse."

"You know her?"

"I know about her. I've never met her, but I've known your father since we were in school. We're like brothers. He doesn't…didn't…have any secrets from me."

"But he did from me." Gabe rubbed his fingers on the smooth table, his cobalt hands the same as his father's.

"Makai, he—"

"Don't call me that, please," he said. "Call me Gabe."

"Your human name?"

"Yes."

"I don't understand. That name is an alias. You want to discard your given name because Jeken kept your sister a secret?" Ceru poured the steaming water into his mug.

"That's not why. It's just that I identify more with it now, that's all." He didn't want to hear his old name. He had decided to be who he wanted—to be Gabe. Makai made all the mistakes. He wanted to move on without the shame holding him back.

No, the name Makai didn't fill him with guilt, it hurt to hear. All that name made him think of was his family, and they were dead.

Ceru sat back down and shrugged. "If that's what you want. Gabe it is."

"Thanks. Do you know why he couldn't tell me about my sister?" he asked.

"Yes." Ceru lifted his mug, obscuring his face. "But it isn't my place to share. Please, you'll have to learn from her."

"Fine." Gabe swirled the tea and didn't drink any.

Silence returned to the dimming kitchen, the sun creeping below the windowsill. Talking to Ceru sucked, because all they could discuss were things Gabe didn't want to talk about. The silence was worse, making him drift into his own thoughts.

Nor had his father killed, probably his mother too. Why his family? What did they do to deserve this? So, his father was a councilman and held the riddle. Nor wanted the Stand, but why? It was always *why*.

Ceru busied himself with putting things away and cleaning an already spotless room. When there was nothing else to pretend to do, he said, "Mak...Gabe. You must be thinking about why Councilman Nor wants the Stand of Unity."

Gabe nodded. "I can't figure it out."

He sat and pulled the chair in. "I've been going over theories with your father, and if a human wizard really is involved, it isn't good." He rested his forearms on the table. "I don't know if you remember the history of the time before the Schism, but when human wizards siphon magic from our aether it's more powerful. Something about the differences on Earth and living without magic enhances the effects for them."

"So you're thinking Nor wants to use this guy to bring Illirin to war and take over?"

"Yes. Or something like that."

"I don't understand. What would be in it for a human to help Nor?" Gabe asked.

Ceru tapped a spoon on the table. "Earth is probably in danger from this individual as well."

Nor wanted to bring war to Illirin, but going after Earth, too? That was insane! He wouldn't let that happen, not if he could help it. "We can't let them get the Stand."

"That is up to you. You're Jeken's riddle keeper." Ceru paused. "Which brings me to something I wanted to talk to you about."

Gabe raised his eyebrow.

"We need to leave for Union tomorrow morning. We need to tell the other council members what has happened and swear you in."

"What?" His eyes popped.

Ceru scratched his head through tangled brown hair. "You know what. The riddle keeper becomes interim Councilman until an election can be organized. Besides, you need to be there to pass the riddle on to the next Winged Councilman."

"How long will that take?" He didn't expect this. He had to go back in the morning. Lea would freak if he wasn't at drawing class.

Ceru lifted his wings as he straightened his back. "It varies, but I want to hurry and get the election set up as fast as possible…two weeks, maybe three." He looked at Gabe. "I want you to run."

"Again, what?" Gabe shook his head. "Have you lost your mind? I'm barely of age. I don't know what the hell I'm doing."

"Everyone knows you. They know you share your father's views, and they know your character. You understand what Illirin needs, what the Winged need. I see so much of your father in you, and I won't be the only one. You'll have the advisers, so it's not like you'd be doing it alone."

"Oh no, no, no. Temporary figurehead, okay, but I am not cut out for Councilman. That's a life term thing. You gotta find someone else."

Ceru reached across the table and covered Gabe's hand with his. "The idea is overwhelming, I get it. But the fact is, there isn't time to find someone else. Jeken's death is completely unexpected, so no one has prepared for a new election. Those that would run on short notice are in it for selfish reasons. Jeken said the Council is in serious trouble, and I think you're the only one who has a chance to save it." He sat back. "Listen, you already know what's happening, so you're prepared. You will have an instant following, and the existing councilmen already know you. I think you have enough trust to repair whatever Nor's done. No one else has that."

"I don't have time!" He pulled his hand away and stood up fast enough to slide the chair clear away. "You're wrong. I'm really not that great. I can't stay anyway, you know, the whole revenge thing, pretend death and all that."

Ceru sighed. "With what's happened, it's clear someone is after your family. Your claim of self-defense will stand, but we'll say you escaped and were in hiding, which is mostly true."

Was Ceru crazy? He couldn't lead his trait and more importantly, he had to get back to Earth. Being in Illirin was painful, and he wanted to get away. He noticed he'd splayed his wings some, and closed them again.

The corners of Ceru's eyes turned down. "You do understand, don't you?"

"What, that you're insane? Yeah, got that."

"No. You know you can't return to Earth, right?"

Like something punched Gabe straight in the gut, he dropped back onto the chair, which was now two feet from the table. "What?" He was getting tired of saying that.

"Every time you go through it weakens the Schism, and any weakness makes it easier for this wizard to tap Illirin's magic. You're risking the safety of Illirin *and* Earth. You're the one who has what Nor wants. If you return, you'll risk the life of anyone you call a friend."

His stomach lurched, the gulp of tea threatening to make a reappearance. Ceru was right, he couldn't go back. He'd get Lea killed. His heart squeezed. All the feelings he suppressed for Heather's memory weren't going away. He was only waiting for a better time, and now it wouldn't come. He did love Lea, and now he would lose it before it began.

No, it wasn't the same. She would live, and he could protect her. He could still love her by keeping her safe. That made it okay, but why couldn't he breathe? His chest had locked up, sore and gripped in a vice.

"I'm sorry." Ceru frowned.

It took him several minutes, but he admitted, "You're right. Of course, you're right." He looked up. "We need to go to Union anyway so I can see Aime."

"And what about running?"

Gabe scooted the chair back under and rested his arms against the table. "I still think you're crazy, but you have a point. If the Council is as unstable as you say, we need to get someone in there fast to repair the damage, or the Winged will be filling a soon-to-be empty seat."

He sighed, giving in. "I can try."

"You'll be amazing, I know you, and I know you can do it." The subtle dip of Ceru's shoulders showed relief.

"You're biased."

Ceru smirked. "Maybe, but I really believe in you. Not just because you're an Ilat, but because you have the strength and heart."

Gabe actually found it in him to smile. "Thanks, Ceru. I need that confidence." A little pain pricked at him. The confidence belonged to Lea.

"You've got it."

Gabe and Ceru discussed plans, politics, and conspiracies for a while, and by the time they finished, they had only a few hours to sleep. Gabe planned to make one last visit to Earth, but it was too late. He'd have to wait for the following night, which was okay, because he needed that time to build his resolve. Really, he wasn't in a rush to end his life on Earth.

Sixteen

At dawn, Gabe and Ceru ate a quick breakfast and took off for the capital city of Union, close to the center of the continent. The First Council created Union, the first and largest of the integrated cities, to bring the traits together. Not only were the Council chambers there, but it was home to a myriad of businesses. Over the years it became the center of trade for all of Illirin.

The flight took several hours, since they had to stop and rest a couple of times. Gabe knew Ceru wanted to get to work right away, but he had to visit his sister first. Ceru headed for the Council Hall so Gabe could visit Amie alone. By that evening, everyone would know about his father's assassination. She had the right to hear it from family before it became news.

Gabe walked through the hallways of the apartment building and stopped in front of Room 115, a ground-level unit. He rolled his sore shoulder and tucked his tired wings. The long flight did a number on his back. Thank goodness he didn't have to climb the stairs. He took a deep breath and knocked, and after a minute the door opened a crack.

An older Tailed woman with canary skin smiled through the opening. She must be the nurse Ceru mentioned.

"Hello," she said.

"Hi, um, I'm here to see Aime Nee. Is she in?"

The nurse eyed him for a minute. "May I ask who you are?"

"Oh sorry, yes. I'm Gab...Makai Ilat, her brother. I really need to speak with her."

She looked surprised by his announcement, and then held up her finger. "One minute. Let me see if she's up for having visitors." She ducked into the apartment, leaving the door open a crack. Gabe couldn't help himself and peeked inside.

He saw a nicely sized unit painted in pastel shades. An oversized painting hung above the sofa, and a vase of fresh flowers sat on the glass coffee table. Even the flower print coasters were meticulously arranged. Martha Stewart would be proud.

In the back hallway, almost out of sight, the Tailed nurse talked with someone. "He says he's your brother. What do you want me to say?"

"Really? Wow. What kind of idiot con artist is this? Get rid of him, I'm feeling 'unwell' today," she replied.

Gabe stuck in his head. "No, Aime, it's really me. I need to speak with you."

The nurse spun around and came toward him. "Oh no, no. You do not come in here without permission. How rude!" She tried to shoo him away.

"Wait," his sister said. "Let him in."

The nurse sighed and opened the door just wide enough. His sister waited in the dimly lit hallway. He could only make out her salmon skin and chin-length hair, stark white like the Ilats tend to have. The shadow of her wings showed they were petite, half the usual wingspan. Maybe she couldn't fly. Is that why she needed a nurse?

"Thank you." He nodded.

Aime watched him for a few minutes, keeping her distance. "You look like him, but how is it possible? Makai was killed. Who're you?"

Gabe took a step toward her, but she moved back. "It's me, I promise. I've been in hiding." He kept to the story. "After my mother was killed, we thought I'd be targeted again. Things have changed, and that's why I'm here."

"You sound like him too. Can it really be?"

"Yes."

She stepped forward under the chandelier in the living area. Light revealed her delicate features that surrounded Seer eyes.

Gabe inhaled sharply, and his wings flared with the rush of anger, which he tried to suppress. Unintentional, but his shock did not go unnoticed.

Her curiosity vanished, and her eyelids narrowed over cross-shaped pupils. "I thought you would be different, but no. You, too." She turned, giving him a view of the small wings tensed over her shoulders. "You can go."

"No, wait Aime, please. I didn't mean—"

She whipped her head around, holding her wings tight against her back. "Didn't mean *what* exactly? Hrm? To be a bigot? A traitist? Or maybe you're just curious how someone like me can exist. That's *impossible,* right?"

He shrugged off the nurse's hand when she tried to lead him out. "Aime, no. I'm sorry. This is a little hard for me. I know only a few are responsible, but it's hard to see those eyes and not think of what they've taken from me." He took a breath. "I apologize. I'm working on it, but you must give me some leniency."

She crossed her arms. "Out with it. Why are you here? I thought Father didn't tell a soul about me."

"He didn't. I only learned about you yesterday—"

"What changed?"

She was forcing him to say it quickly. He wanted to soften the blow, but she made it impossible. "Yesterday…Father was killed," he choked out.

Her hands covered her mouth, and the anger left her face. Weakened knees forced her into the plush ivory chair behind her. *"No, no, no, no."* She started to cry. "No. He was going have dinner with me next week."

That was probably the worst way to blurt it out. Now that she wasn't attacking him, he felt even worse. He could have at least warned her to sit down or something.

He knelt in front of her. "I'm sorry. I didn't want to tell you this way, but I didn't want you to hear it on the news."

She caught her breath. "What happened?"

Father's body, scorched and bloody, appeared in his mind. He clenched his jaw, forcing the image away. What could he say? She didn't need the details; they only made it worse. He kept eyes on the knickknacks lining the bookshelf. "It was a murder. You don't want to know more than that."

She moved her face into his line of sight, tears running down her cheeks. "Who did this? I want to know who." For the first time, he saw something new in Seer eyes. Instead of the cold hate he imagined, he saw a grief that can only come from love.

He sighed. "I don't know her name."

"Right," she said with an edge.

"I'm sorry…" He wanted to make things better. He had to try. "I'm sorry I reacted the way I did. You didn't deserve that."

"Damn right," she shot back. She looked at him and frowned. "That was out of line too, sorry. I know to expect it. I just thought you would be different."

He tried looking in her eyes…those eyes. "I am, or I will be. I think I've gotten the kick I needed to pull my head out of my ass."

"Hope so." Her furrowed brow softened some before more tears rushed in. She shook her head. "He was all I had. He can't be gone."

She leaned back into the soft chenille.

Gabe reached out and hesitated. She might not want his compassion. Hearing her sobs renewed his own pain, so he went ahead and put his hand on hers. "I'm here for you, too. Father's wish was that I look after you."

Aime raised her eyebrow and wiped her face. "Really? I'm not an invalid, I only play one. I don't need babysitting." The dichotomy between the tears and the sarcasm was almost funny.

"I'm sure he knew that. I think this is more about what's coming than your ability to protect yourself from idiots like me."

Her lip curled up for only a moment. "What's coming?"

"These murders, the conspiracy, it's probably leading to a war. That's what I'm to protect you from, and not just you, *everyone*."

"Oh, yes?"

Gabe inhaled and stood up. "You'll see this evening. Speaking of which, I need to go. I just had to meet you first." He squeezed her hand. "I'm sorry to be the messenger." He raised his eyebrows with a smirk. "Next time, please don't shoot the messenger."

She half-laughed. "Right. I hope to see you again soon, Makai. I want to give you a second chance for a first impression."

He nodded. "Call me Gabe, new name and new start. I'll contact you soon."

The nurse moved to lead him out the door.

"Oh, and watch the news tonight," he said.

"If you say so."

Gabe left feeling a mix of things. She surprised him, and it wasn't just her parentage. There was something remarkable about her. He couldn't nail it, but he knew one thing. He definitely had to talk with her again. A sister, he had a sister.

The columns in front of the Council Hall loomed overhead, supporting the massive balcony. Gabe touched the smooth marble, soft but firm under his fingers. As enormous as the entry felt now, it seemed smaller than his last visit. Without his father holding his hand, the whole world shrank. He couldn't be a child anymore. What would his father say? Responsibility. He had responsibilities now. He had to grow up and attempt to fulfill his role. He could play the part, though it belonged to a better man. Even an understudy would do if he could learn the lines.

When Gabe entered the Council Hall, the receptionist guided him to a conference room on the top floor.

Ceru answered the door. "Come in, hurry!" Pulling him inside, he said, "You're cutting it close. I told you we had to get the inauguration ready for this evening, and it's almost time."

"Sorry." Gabe rubbed his wrist.

The three advisers had been working on preparations with Ceru. Piles of papers littered the huge conference table in the center of the room.

"So," a portly gray Winged said as his handshake nearly ripped off Gabe's arm. "You're Makai Ilat, eh! I think last time I saw you, you were just a boy, oh my!"

"Yeah, um…"

The tall adviser came from his other side and repeated the arm-breaking shake. "It's a pleasure. My name is Gorli."

Gabe smiled through closed teeth. "Nice to meet you, too." Were they trying to kill him?

The last adviser sat on the far side of the table. He took his time and approached in a normal manner. Bowing his head, he said, "I'm so sorry for your loss."

Gabe replied, "Thanks."

Finally, someone with any kind of sense.

Ceru introduced him and the portly gentleman. "This is Senni and you met Obram. Your father worked with them for quite a few years. They were recently re-elected, so you can lean on their experience."

At that, all three gentlemen gave the appropriate condolences and seemed to get over the excitement of meeting Gabe. What did Ceru tell them about him? The way they acted, they probably thought he could piss rainbows. This was going to be harder than he imagined. He didn't know how to act or what to say. Why did he agree to this?

Gabe sank deep into the wide leather seat at the end of the table. He mostly listened as they began discussing the particulars of the broadcast and inauguration. Only the Winged representation needed to be present, and they wouldn't have to wait for the other councilmen to arrive.

After they worked through the details, Senni took the time to ask. "So Makai, have you prepared for a speech following the ceremony?"

Gabe shook his head. "I haven't had time to think of anything."

"In this situation, I don't think anyone will expect too much, not to worry," Gorli said.

"Nonsense." Obram waved his hand. "I'm sure those Ilat genes can wow the crowd. Aren't I right?" He winked at Gabe.

Gabe tried to keep a neutral face. If he couldn't survive his own advisers, how could he make it through a speech?

"For your address," Senni said, bringing the conversation back. "There's some standard verbiage about the success of unity and betterment of Illirin. You can use most of that. I was more concerned with whether you had anything specific you want to say?"

Gabe closed his eyes to think. He imagined the stares from the others focused on him. The pressure made him uncomfortable. Guess he'd have to get used to that.

What would his father do in this situation? What would he say? He sighed heavily. His father wouldn't *be* in this situation. They only needed him because his father wasn't there.

Gabe looked up across the table. "Yes. I do."

He explained his idea. The advisers hesitantly agreed to allow it, thanks to Ceru keeping them in their place. He fell into this political ocean without a clue, but Ceru kept him afloat. He needed him by his side. After it was over, he'd let him know.

The time for the inauguration approached. They dressed Gabe in a fine suit, and a makeup woman slathered his face in anti-shine goo. They turned him into a doll all dressed up and ready for tea. He'd lose his mind if he had to put up with that all the time. They assured him it was just for the cameras, and afterward he could go without the goo.

Ten minutes later he stood on the balcony in front of a crowd of at least a thousand. All different traits made up the viewers in the courtyard, a full spectrum of Illirin faces waiting to hear the news.

An official journalist took the podium to report Jeken Ilat's passing and announce the forthcoming inauguration of his riddle keeper. Murmurs of surprise echoed throughout the crowd. Councilmen usually retire allowing for a drawn-out election process, so riddle keepers were rarely needed. The identity of a riddle keeper was a secret, but since most councilmen choose a family member or close friend, it surprised no one to see Gabe standing there. Well, they were surprised he lived at all, not that he was his father's formal confidant.

Next came Ceru to introduce Gabe. He told the story about Gabe's "death" and how he went into hiding, sharing as little real information as possible. He spun the words in a way that made you think you understood everything, when he actually told you nothing. Absolutely perfect.

The lights shifted to Gabe, and he swallowed a ball of gunk down his parched throat. Slow steps took him to the podium, adrenaline pumping hard. Was this fight or flight? He wanted to run, but his father would want him to be strong. He'd disappointed him too many times. Now, he had to do more than play the role—time to fight.

The first part was easy. He simply repeated what the judge said, raised his hand, and followed the ritual outlined in the book. The judge finished when he pinned the token of the office to Gabe's lapel, the Winged icon. The little silver pin pulled like a sudden weight holding him to the marble floor.

The applause faded, and he started to hyperventilate. Calm down…he had to calm down. He traced his fingers over the pin, its smooth surface and barely rounded corners. The tiny wing represented his trait, just like he did. It was time to say what he needed to say and what Illirin needed to hear.

He pulled the microphone in and spoke to both the crowd and cameras. "When someone begins a speech he says, 'it's a pleasure to be here today,' but I won't. It's *not* a pleasure to be here today, to stand before you.

"I'm here because my father, Councilman Jeken Ilat, is *not* here. He's the councilman the Winged deserve. He's the councilman Illirin deserves. He worked his entire life to make things better for everyone, and he was great at it. I'm only here because some people don't think that way. They don't want what's best for everyone, they work only for themselves, and their work is tearing Illirin apart."

Wide eyes and gaping mouths covered most of the faces in the crowd, shocked by Gabe's revelation. After all, those living their day to day lives had no idea what pressures were building. Time to change that.

He continued, "I can't make accusations without proof, but I promise I will not allow those responsible to continue to endanger Illirin and our peace. I promise to live up to Jeken Ilat's ideals, and to bring people together, not apart. And most importantly, I swear to fight for Illirin, our unity, and our future. I will not give in to traitist pressures. I will drive for the unity the Council represents."

He paused a few seconds and then issued a direct challenge to Heten Nor. "The Council is the symbol of unity. I will return it to unity, no matter what it takes."

The crowd applauded, unaware of the hidden threat. Only Nor could know his challenge. Gabe would stop him. He had to.

He waited for the applause to end. "I would also like to announce my intention to run in the upcoming election for Winged Councilman. Thank you." He stepped down from the podium amongst the wild cheers. He should smile at the praise, but his gut bunched up. Could he really deliver on his promises? He only said what he thought his father would. He hoped he wouldn't regret being so bold.

Seventeen

When Gabe's phone went to voice mail the day after they returned from Illirin, Lea didn't think much of it. He went through an ordeal and probably wanted to chill. So, she went to class, microwaved some pot stickers, and had a quiet evening in front of the television.

While lying on the sofa watching *Law and Order*, a nagging flickered in the back of her mind. She didn't want to bother Gabe for no reason, especially if he was trying to unwind, but something felt wrong.

She pulled out her phone and let her finger hover over the send button. If she bothered him, what would he think? It's not like she was his girlfriend and could just check up on him. She sighed. Would he ever think of her that way? After all, his head must still be full of Heather. She didn't want to push him.

No…that little twist of envy turned into fear. She didn't want to compete, to be compared to his first love. It was better to just step back.

She put the phone away. He'd be at drawing class tomorrow morning, portfolios were due, so stop worrying. The television became the optimal distraction device, yet again. Thank you rerun marathon.

The next morning, Lea awoke with that uneasy feeling still itching in her head. She headed to class and bounded into the room as usual. She glanced over to Gabe's empty stool. A few minutes into class, everyone else had arrived ready for the final critique, but still no Gabe. Maybe he overslept? Nawh, he probably wanted to skip class. He got his memory back, so why bother coming.

Lea put her drawing on the easel to wait for her turn, and she looked back at Gabe's empty place. That odd feeling itched around her again; she couldn't shake it. Without warning, she sprinted from the classroom. Her instincts were almost always right. She needed to see him to know he was okay. If she saw him in his dorm, she would feel better.

She ran all the way across campus, only stopping to catch her breath once she stood outside his room.

"Gabe?" She tapped on the door. No answer. He must be asleep. She knocked louder. "Gabe." No answer. She pounded on the door three times, and silence followed. She pulled out her phone and called his cell—straight to voice mail.

Her cell fell from her hand and bounced across the carpet till it hit the wall. That jerk. He returned to Illirin without her. He didn't even *tell* her. That was the nagging feeling. He left her and went back, the only conclusion that made sense. How could he go without saying anything?

She picked up her phone and took a few deep breaths before heading back to her apartment. If he went to Illirin, she would follow him. Once she found that oversized smurf, she was gonna give him a piece of her mind.

Classes ended and the halls filled with people, but minutes later they emptied as fast as a street drains after a flash flood. Disappointment struck every time she checked the clock, one minute passed, or two. Was he okay? He went alone. What if something happened?

He didn't have to go alone. She banged her fist on the bench. That ass, he didn't even tell her! She wavered between worry and fury, never sure which was stronger.

At long last, the clock read almost one. She readied the oxy backpack and stood in the middle of the hall where the thinning appeared.

As Gabe had done before, she reached into the cooler air and clawed at the thinning. Her hand kept going forward. Nothing happened. She used both hands and waved her arms around like a poorly trained mime.

"No!" she yelped. "Aaahhhhhh!" She grabbed an empty soda can and chucked it down the hall, the clatter drowned out by the organ. She couldn't go without him. He was always the one to open the doorway. Now she was stuck, able to do *nothing*. She hit her leg with her fist, but that didn't ease the horrible feeling of being so useless. She stopped, took a few breaths, and tried to resign herself to waiting. It's all she could do.

Lea spent the rest of the day delving into different activities to stay occupied. She could have slept since the next nearby thinning arrived so late at night, but sleep was out of the question. So she studied, watched television, and baked three dozen cookies. Yeah, they were the kind you scoop out of a tub, but it still counted as baking. If Gabe's apology was good enough, maybe she'd even let him have some. He'd have to grovel, yes, some nice groveling would do.

The day eased into evening and then night. After midnight, Lea returned to campus. She triple-checked her calculations, and the thinning would appear between the RTVF building and the University Union. Deserted and quiet. Last time she searched for a thinning near the Union in the middle of the night, Gabe showed up. Maybe she'd be as lucky.

The lampposts along the walkway cast away the night, creating a lighted refuge. Only the digits on Lea's watch and the black speckled sky revealed the time. She found a wooden bench and waited, waited, waited.

A few minutes before three, Lea got up to stand near the thinning.

Please come. Please be safe.

In the muggy night, each heartbeat echoed in her ears. Her digestive system warbled in overdrive. Was it worry? Was it upset? All she knew was that she hated it.

At last, the light appeared in an uneven line opening from the other side. Gabe's blue, Winged form stepped through the portal, and as it closed, his wings vanished and his coloring faded to normal. He looked straight at her. Somehow, he expected her to be waiting for him.

Lea took in air again, sighing in relief. "You're okay."

Then she pursed her lips, biting them on the inside of her mouth. She stomped over and hit him on the chest with her palms. "Now that I know you're not maimed or dead, I'm so mad at you!" She clenched her fists. "I've been waiting here, thinking of synonyms for 'mad,' and all I could think of was 'mad,' *that's* how mad I am!"

Gabe didn't reply so she kept going. "You left me! You went back without me or...or even *telling* me you were going! Don't I deserve that much? I've been sick worrying, and I just can't. I...I." She huffed. "Why?"

"I didn't know how long it would take, and I thought it might be dangerous."

"You thought it might be dangerous, so you went *alone*?"

"Yes."

He answered too fast. Lea faltered back a step, blinking at him. She wanted to stay mad at him. He drove her crazy, and he deserved an ass-kicking for it. But, something seemed off. She studied his face, dark circles beneath his eyes and pale skin. He was more than just physically exhausted.

"What's wrong?" She relaxed her hands by her sides. "What happened?"

He inhaled deeply. "My father was assassinated."

"No! I'm so sorry. Is there anything..." She touched his forearm.

He shook his head. "No. But there's a lot going on at home. The Council is in trouble. Someone is plotting to start a war, and Earth is in danger too. You could be in danger. I've got to—"

"Tell me everything." She slid her hand down to grab his. "Let's go back to the dorm. We'll figure out what we can do. I'll help you."

He closed his hand over hers and stopped her. "I don't have a lot of time."

"What do you mean?" She turned. Why was he looking at her like that? The back of her neck prickled again.

His voice struggled to lift the weighty silence. "Every time I cross over, it weakens the barrier between our worlds. It gives power to those who want to wage war." He paused like he was waiting for her to reply, pressing his mouth in a tight line. She nodded, so he continued, "Lea, this is the only way I can protect you. I cannot break the Schism again." He glanced away. "I can't come back anymore."

It took a minute for it to click in her brain. He wasn't coming back. He was going to leave, forever? Her ribcage squeezed in. She couldn't breathe.

"No, no. *No!*" She gripped his arm like she'd never let go. "You can't leave. I need you, I lov—"

Gabe pressed his finger to her lips. He all but whispered, "Stop. This is hard enough as it is. Please…don't make it worse." His finger trembled as it lifted away.

That fingertip stole Lea's power of speech. She wanted to reply, to say anything. But only the voice in her head could speak, and even it had fled.

Next thing she knew, Gabe pulled her close, wrapping his arms tight around her. Shocks ran through her, both excited and afraid. He slid his head next to hers, lips by her ear. "I couldn't just disappear without seeing you. You…you've done more for me than you understand. You made me who I am. I can't ever repay you. All I can do is protect you, and I will, the best that I can."

He squeezed her again, holding her for an eternity and only a moment, and she breathed in his rain-kissed scent. Lea had only dreamed of him holding her like that, but this wasn't a dream. This was turning into a nightmare.

He released the embrace but kept his hands gripped on her shoulders. He looked into her eyes as she fought back tears she didn't want him to see.

"Thank you. For everything and more, thank you." He let go and then brushed her cheek with his hand. Her skin tingled where he touched her. "I will never, ever forget you." He waited until the last possible second. "Goodbye."

The word crashed into her like a truck, knocking her back a step. So final.

Stop! Wait, please. You can stay, and if you can't, take me with you. Please. I'll go with you. I need you. She pleaded only in her mind. She was mute. *I need you.* She had to tell him, but nothing would come out.

He turned around and steeled himself before tearing the thinning.

She stretched her arm toward him and squeaked, "Gabe."

He paused at hearing his name, but it was too late. He walked through the portal and it sealed behind him.

The last week of school crept along even though end-of-semester activities kept Lea constantly on the move, taking finals and turning in projects. She even had to slap some projects together last minute. It was important to pass so she could graduate, but she didn't care about it like she should. She didn't have her heart in it. Her heart felt very far away.

After her last final, Lea returned to her lonely apartment and dropped the keys in the metal dish by the door. She took in the landscape of her plain living room, which had nothing to see except the few trinkets on the mantel of the unused fireplace. She picked up the framed picture of her, Gabe, and Matt—the three amigos. There she was grinning like an idiot, so happy. She wanted to slam it upside down and never look at it again. After all, those days were over.

She moved to flip the picture but stopped. It was her only memento, her only picture of him. She sighed and placed it back in its rightful place, next to the heirloom journal. She missed him, but she didn't want to forget him. Not that she could forget if she tried. Every time she talked to her parents, she'd remember what he did for them. Would she ever think of him so infrequently? For now, he kept creeping back into her mind unbidden, but not entirely unwanted.

She checked her watch, still had an hour or so before she had to leave for the airport. She glanced at the picture again, Matt. She hadn't spoken with him for ages. He probably thought she and Gabe both fell off the face of the earth. How ironic, it was true for one of them. She reached in her pocket for her cell and gave him a call.

"Hey," Matt answered, his voice surprised. "Lea. Sup?"

"Hi Matt, just callin' to see how you're doing." Why did she feel so weird? "How's your mom?"

"Oh yeah, um, good, doing better." He paused. "But yeah, I'll have more free time coming up."

"That's good."

"So, um, I'm not too far from campus. Just 'bout a forty-minute drive. We could all meet at the theatre by the highway for a movie soon. Heard from Gabe?"

Lea chewed her lip. "Um no, haven't heard from him in a while."

Matt chuckled. "Bet he and Heather eloped on us. Told him I wanted to be invited."

"I'm sure he would have invited us if that were the case." Man, that felt weird to say. Poor Matt was so in the dark, but how could she tell him? How could she explain? At some point, he'd have to find out Gabe was gone for good, but she just couldn't do it now. That'd finalize it for good and make it more real.

"You okay?" His voice changed tone.

Oh crap, she must've given something away. She turned on her happy mode. "Oh yeah, great, super actually. I'm about to fly out to help my parents settle into a new place for a few weeks."

"Oh."

"Though I'll be back before summer is over, so we can all try to catch a movie then. Even continue the *Street Fighter* tourney." Maybe the promises of fun times would cover her flub.

"Sounds great," he replied.

"Well, gotta go. Traffic by the airport sucks."

"Indeed." He added, "Have a great trip, Lea."

"Yeah, later."

"Later."

She hung up, and relief rushed over her now that the conversation had ended. She loved hanging out with him and Gabe, but she something odd came from Matt. Would things be okay with just the two of them? They had done it before, but not without more of that strange feeling hanging around. Besides, she needed a little alone time. Well, not alone, but her parents were certainly a welcome change. She finished zipping up the tiny toiletries in her quart-sized baggie and got ready to leave.

Eighteen

When Gabe left the field near Wren, he never turned back. Muffled crying had come through the thinning, and he couldn't even think about seeing Lea like that. She was the strong one, and he managed to break her. Why did she have to say anything? Damn it. He must be the biggest jerk on either plane. Worse than that, now he knew for certain she felt every bit as bad as he did.

The last remnants of the sherbet dawn began to fade into morning when he returned to the Council Hall. Flying all night allowed him to empty his mind. Unfortunately since he had landed, the thoughts weaseled their way back in.

Distraction, that's what he needed. After he got some rest, Ceru was sure to have plenty for him to do.

Gabe walked, more like stumbled, through the hallway until he found the office Ceru was using. He opened the door to find him already shuffling through papers at this early hour. Gabe nodded to him and hobbled to the small sofa against the wall.

"Did you sleep?" Ceru asked, placing a packet of papers on the desk.

Gabe shook his head and put his feet up on the tufted leather.

Ceru examined the new arrival. "You look terrible." He jabbed his finger toward Gabe. "You went back, didn't you?"

Prying his head off the armrest, Gabe said, "Yes, I did. I couldn't leave and not say goodbye. But it's done now. I cut ties. I'm all yours."

"That was a stupid risk you took."

He dropped back to the armrest. "I've broken the Schism dozens of times. Once more wasn't going to do anything meaningful."

"Not that." Ceru tightened his wings and put his elbows on the desk. "No one knew where you were. What if something happened to you? You don't have a riddle keeper."

Gabe said, "So what. The First Council thought of everything, right? Besides, if there wasn't a way to resurrect the Winged riddle, then the Stand would be safe from Nor regardless."

"You can't be so cavalier! You're responsible for more than yourself now, even if it's only temporary. I told you that you couldn't go back to Earth, and I didn't think I had to list every reason why."

Gabe forced himself to sit up so he could see Ceru properly. "You asked me to sever a limb. The least you could do is stop bitching about me tying a tourniquet."

Ceru closed his eyes, the tired creases on his face drawing his frown. "I am sorry. I'm only trying to look out for you."

"I know." He sighed and leaned all the way back. He zoned out at the ceiling for a few minutes and then asked, "Is there someplace I can stay?"

"Well, there are the houses set aside for councilmen, but…" He paused. "I'm not sure it's a good idea for you to go there, now that I think about it."

Gabe said, "Can you get someone, a third party, to make a reservation at some non-luxury inn under 'Gabe Jones?'"

"Sure. I can get you a guardian escort, too."

He shook his head. "No. That'd draw his attention."

Ceru leaned back, the chair tilted against the wall. "You're probably right. In that case, you should also lie low and try not to go out. Now everyone knows your face, and Nor can have eyes anywhere."

"I know, I know." He tried to think, but his mind fogged over. "Big target, got it. Don't get killed, check." He lifted his heavy head off the sofa to look at Ceru again. "Which reminds me, *if* you're not absolutely nuts and I somehow get elected, I..." He cleared his throat. "I know it'd be more dangerous for you, but you're the only one I can trust. You're the closest to family I've got, aside from my new sister."

The chair squeaked as Ceru sat up straight. "You want me to be riddle keeper?"

"Yes."

A gentle smile appeared on his face. "I'm touched. I accept, dangers included."

"Thanks, Ceru," Gabe yawned, turned over, and passed out.

It took many days of resting at the inn for Gabe to recover from the tornado of events, including his all-nighter and the funeral. Rest was great and all, but he was getting bored. He couldn't even turn on the television without seeing a repeat of his speech. If he never saw that thing again, it'd be too soon, and he still had more than a week left to bask in campaign ads and posters. Gratefully, he was in Union, because back in Winged territory where it mattered, he'd see himself everywhere. He'd have to return to Wren for the event, but till then he could stay out of the public eye.

Ceru couldn't expect him to keep himself cooped up in that tiny room the entire time, so he called Aime to set up their dinner. He got dressed and ready to meet her at the restaurant, a small semiformal place in a less-traveled area of the city.

By the time Gabe arrived that evening, the lighting inside the restaurant had dimmed for the romantic crowd. His mouth watered, the smell of gourmet food wafting into the foyer. What an unusual restaurant. Instead of an open dining room, a narrow hallway branched into cozy private nooks. Candlelit sconces lined the walls, and indigo curtains hung partway down the entry of each room. Aime sure knew how to pick, this was ideal.

The hostess led him down the hall and to a private two-seater on the left. Inside, Aime waved at him to join her. He noticed her eyes appeared "normal," but once the hostess left, she blinked a few times and the Seer pupils returned.

He smiled, holding out his hand. "Gabe Ilat, it's a pleasure to meet you."

"Taking that new first impression literally, I see." She shook and allowed him to sit. "Aime Nee, pleasure is all mine."

"I'd like to completely ignore my being an insensitive idiot and start off the right way."

"Me, too." She smiled and put the napkin on her lap. "Just so you're aware, the waiter knows me. I don't have to keep up my magic while we're here."

"The magic that hides your eyes?"

"Yes. It's very draining, and while I don't actually need Leena as a nurse, it's nice she's there to help with dinner sometimes."

He frowned. "I'm sorry you have to go through so much trouble to go out."

She shrugged and opened her menu. "I'm used to it. No point in getting worked up over something I can't change. I haven't known anything else, so it's not as bad as you think."

He took a sip of water. She seemed okay with it, but it had to bother her. Otherwise she wouldn't have been so irate before.

The design of the restaurant dampened the usual noises from the kitchen, leaving them to fill the quiet with their own conversation. The candle on the table flickered, and he blinked the spots away. They had to talk about something else. Taking up some time, the waiter came by and listened to their orders. Though when he left, Gabe felt even more lost for words.

Aime folded her hands in her lap and took the dive. "I must say, you've surprised me."

"How so?"

"I expected you were father's riddle keeper, but to run for permanent office? He never led me to believe you wanted to follow in his footsteps."

Gabe chuckled. "Okay, so the career choice is sort of a within-the-last-week decision." He then asked, "Father talked about me? What did he say?"

"Nothing terrible, I promise. He mentioned how you've always been strong willed and a free spirit. Once, he said you took after him more than he thought. A rebellious streak?"

He looked at his half sister's face and smirked, "Oh yeah, I can see that now. I never pictured *him* a rebel. He was always so straightlaced."

Aime smiled and then her mouth turned down. "I miss him already."

"Me too." He sighed.

His father had fallen in love with a Seer. *Young love,* huh? It must be why he acted so understanding about Heather. Apparently they shared that in common, but how else was he like his father? He glimpsed a new dimension to this man he thought he knew, and it ached that he couldn't talk to him again to learn more. Aime summed it up right.

The waiter returned with their entrees and distracted them from gloomy thoughts. Aime took a bite of her fish. "So...Gabe? Doesn't sound very common. The name change thing have something to do with why you're a rebel?"

Gabe pierced a few pieces of pasta, stirring them on the plate. "It's a long story, boring."

"I've got time." She tilted her head a fraction.

"In that case then, it's not that long. I used to watch the thinnings. Yeah, I know, one of those losers. Anyway, I met this human girl and we hit it off." He munched a bite of pasta.

She almost choked on her food and coughed a few times, before she said in hushed tones, "You broke the Schism?"

His cheeks flushed. "Yeah, um, maybe like a zillion times."

Her mouth hung open. "Okay, so I see it, a rebellious streak. Definitely not what I had imagined. Mak...Gabe, how could you?"

"I was brash and thought I knew better. Long story short, that's where I was in hiding all this time, and Gabe is my human name." Maybe she'd let it go with that. He didn't want to talk about it. That part of his life was over. "Mmmmm, this cream sauce is exceptional."

"I thought you said it was a long story?" She continued to look at him, and he avoided her gaze. "Gabe?"

"I'm still a bit raw from the whole thing. My law-breaking days are over, maybe even for good, especially since I'm councilman now. Can't I leave it at that?"

"Fine, you don't have to tell me anything. I just thought I could be here to listen. I hoped to grow our relationship, not be superficial acquaintances that share some genetic material." She lifted her glass and took a sip, barely obscuring her disappointment.

"You guilt-trip like a pro."

"Thank you," she chirped.

"I can sum everything up in a series of clichés if you want. 'Ignorance is bliss,' 'you don't know what you've got till it's gone,' and 'if you love someone, let them go.'" He could weasel his way out of talking with a joke. She gave him a half-lidded "yeah right" look. Damn, it didn't work.

He sighed and recounted his time on Earth, from Heather to the accident, and losing his memory. He talked about how he felt without his past, and how he met Lea and learned to focus on being who he wanted. He gave Lea credit for helping him recover his memory, but overall, he tried to keep his story brief and loose on the details. He couldn't hide in his voice how things had affected him. Every time he mentioned Lea's name, he paused a second, giving away his regret.

When he finished, Aime quietly drank from her glass and gazed at the breadbasket. She reached across the table to touch his wrist. "I apologize for how I reacted to you yesterday. You've had a rough time too, even without our recent loss."

"You were right to be angry. I was an ass. Honestly, I've probably acted a little traitist since my mother's murder. I'm thankful for you, Aime. You've put me back on track. I can't think that way. I need to put blame where it belongs."

"So you meant it then? What you said in your speech, you really believe that way?"

"Of course I did, er, do. I'm not perfect. But, I know what's right and what I need to work for. But before any of that, I need to save the Council."

Her white hair curved under her chin as she cocked her head. "What do you mean by that?"

Uh oh, said too much. "Nothing, just political babble. Heh, still new to all of this."

She put down her fork. "I'll give you some leeway because we just met, but don't insult my intelligence. What's going on?"

"I've said too much already. It's just some ego clashing within the Council, and I want to help smooth things over. Small stuff, I can handle it."

"Father never told me what was really going on either. What is it with you Ilat men? Afraid I'll wither like some cut flowers? I can handle more than you give me credit for, I promise you that."

"No." Gabe sighed. "It's not that. I can't talk about it, and really, the less you know the safer you'll be. Which reminds me, after the election I'm going to have to keep a low profile for a while. It wouldn't be safe for you to be seen with me."

"That doesn't sound good."

He put his fork down, half of his meal untouched. "It isn't. Hopefully, we'll find a way to resolve this issue soon."

"Maybe you're the one who needs looking after." She smirked.

"You're probably right." He returned a smile.

Aime was certainly more than she seemed. She appeared delicate but sounded anything but. Heck, she could see him the same way, the councilman who broke the Schism and took a human name. Who was stranger out of the pair?

For a minute, he studied her face. Before, he'd have thought she was pretty despite her Seer eyes, but now she was more impressive because of them.

He said, "I wish I had gotten to know you a long time ago. I regret that Father felt you were a secret he needed to keep from me."

She combed her hair behind her ear with her fingertips. "That's very sweet. I wish things were different too, but I understand why he handled it this way. Let's not focus on regrets. We should look forward to getting to know each other better."

"I'd like that very much." He added, "I'll find the time right after I figure out a way to make myself safer to be around."

"I hope you exaggerate."

Resigned, he replied, "If only."

The wind blowing past Gabe's ears became the kind of white noise you use to relax or help you sleep. The rushing sound, combined with the rhythmic beating of his wings, lulled him into a meditative state, a feeling he could only find in the air. To his left, Ceru's green wings pumped in a similar rhythm to his. They'd left early enough to travel at a nice, relaxing pace. Sadly, the pastry Ceru brought him for breakfast was long gone, and he could feel the sugar rush ebbing away.

They couldn't have asked for better weather for their long-distance flight, which put him in a good mood despite the uncertainty of the Election Day. Yes, Gabe was the first to put his hat in the ring, and he had all the advantages, but after a few days, two well-respected businessmen put their names on the ballot. The individuals running were known for charity work and helping with Winged issues. They worked with inter-trait trades and had various credits of experience to advertise.

Being so much older than him, they knew more about everything. One of them could easily win the election. That should bother him, worry him, but it didn't. He wasn't cut out for this. Why did he agree to run in the first place? Ceru had caught him off guard when his father died. It wasn't fair. His peaceful focus vanished, and his worry manifested in unsteady flight.

He concentrated to straighten himself out before shouting over the wind, "It's too late, isn't it?"

Ceru turned his head. "We've got plenty of time."

"No, to take my name out."

A chuckle stuck out amongst the rushing wind. "The polls opened this morning. Yes, it's too late." Ceru surveyed the ground below. "We should stop to rest anyway. I'll warm up your cold feet while we're on the ground."

Gabe followed, and they landed in a field near a small cluster of trees they could use for shade. He took off his pack and grabbed the water bottle to quench his thirst. The cold liquid hit his stomach, awakening his sense of hunger.

"Here." Ceru held up another death-by-sugar pastry.

Gabe's stomach turned. "Uh, no thanks, jittery enough without the rush." He looked through his pack for something else. An old protein shake hid inside the bottom from when Lea packed the bag for their excursion. The roaring hunger left to make room for the other kind of emptiness. He sighed. It wasn't worth it to keep a memento of a past life, might as well just drink it. He downed the shake and tossed the can away. He didn't mind littering, just this once.

He looked back at Ceru sitting against the tree next to his. Ceru finished off another pastry, seeming just as in control as always.

"This is a mistake," Gabe blurted out. "I shouldn't be on the ballot today. Why did I let you talk me into this?"

Ceru combed his unruly hair with his fingers. "Why do you think that?"

"I'm not qualified. When these people vote, they're voting for my father's name. They don't know me. I don't know what I'm doing. I'm too young to have any life experience to be a councilman, to represent the Winged to the other traits. What if I screw up?"

The lighthearted chuckle in response made Gabe balk. "What's the joke?"

"That you can't see what everyone else can, or at least I can." The corners of Ceru's eyes lifted like a smile. "You have more life experience than anyone else in Illirin. Think about it. You've dealt with your share of tragedy. You've been thrown into the midst of a conspiracy, and *you* chose to work out the details, to fight back. Even the fact you lived on Earth gives you a perspective that no one else has. You experienced other cultures, and you can think of unique questions and solutions. What other kinds of 'life experience' do you think you need?"

"I don't know..." He rested his hand on the pack at his side. "But, I think I'm in this for the wrong reasons. I didn't want to put the target on someone else's back. I didn't want to pass the riddle and give Nor more opportunities to get what he wants, but I wasn't thinking long term. What am I supposed to do?"

"You know the first goal would be to calm the suspicions Nor has spread to the other councilmen. Tell me, what would you do first?"

Gabe pushed the stray strands of hair out of his face. He had actually spent a lot of time thinking about it. "Well, I'd probably find time to talk to one of the others alone, possibly Brennan, the Legged councilman, he'd be the most likely to trust me. I'd ask him to catch me up on what's been going on, because I'm new and everything, and work my way to finding out what Nor told him. Once I had an idea of the rumor, I think I'd try to gather more information from the others, but I wouldn't refute Nor until I searched for some evidence of his lies. To get them on my side, I know I'd need proof."

When he was finished thinking out loud, his eyes refocused, and he saw Ceru grin. "What? What is it?"

"You already have a plan. I couldn't even think of how to proceed, and you've got it all worked out. Don't you see? You're a natural leader."

"There's your insanity peeking through again." Gabe let his wings hang loose to relax their sore arms.

Ceru ate a bite of his pastry and pointed at him. "I remember back when you were just a kid, and your friend went missing on that trip. Your father said you didn't wait for the teacher to come back. You organized those kids and sent them out searching."

Gabe threw up his hands. "And I got in serious trouble for that, too. I disappointed him all the time, especially when I broke the Schism. Leader? Ha. I'm just shy of a criminal."

Ceru relaxed back against his tree and pulled his pack into his lap to tie it up. Pulling the string tight, Ceru said, "That's the problem sometimes. Leaders are terrible at following. Jeken saw it, and it was hard on him. He wanted to be a good parent and guide you to obey like you should. We'd get together, and he'd laugh at something you did, so proud of your instincts, but he couldn't encourage you. He got into enough trouble himself, and some of those stories I know he'd kill me if I shared."

Who was that man Ceru described? Not his father. The more he learned, the less he recognized the man who raised him. "Did I know him at all?"

"You did. The parts of him he didn't show you were the things already in you. You didn't only get his coloring." Ceru smiled but his eyes drooped. "I feel like I didn't lose all of my friend."

Were they really so alike? He always wanted to make his father proud, but every time he screwed up, the idea slipped away. Now Ceru looked at him like he could've done something right, if only he'd known his father better. The warmth faded to a cold pain. He'd never know for sure now that his father was dead. Though Ceru knew his father better than anyone. What if he was right?

Gabe said, "Okay, *if* I believe you, and assume I've got some gift, that's great and everything, but I still feel lost. I mean, fixing Nor's damage is one thing, but what about after? Other than talking with the other councilmen, I have no idea what my father actually did day to day. What about bringing proposals to the Winged Minister?"

"You've got Senni, Obram, and Gorli. They've been through all that a few times. You're worried about on-the-job training. No one knows the details when they start something new. The important thing is to find a leader, and that's you."

"You seem so certain..."

Ceru looked to the side for a moment and picked a small flower from the grass. "I don't have any children of my own, never married. Jeken kind of let me live vicariously, and it's almost like you're family to me. I watched a lot of you growing up, which I know makes me sound more biased, but I think I'm just more aware of your abilities." He handed Gabe the blossom. "The only thing you need is confidence."

He shied away from Ceru's gaze, and Lea's voice popped into his head. *"Self-fulfilling prophecy is a real thing. Suck it up."* Even now she was guiding him. Turning back to Ceru, he saw they were both right. "Yeah, I'm terrible at it, but I'll try to have more faith."

"Good." Ceru's shoulders relaxed.

Gabe gulped some more water and zipped the bottle up in his pack. "We should get going."

Ceru stood, stretching his arms and wings. "We're getting close. Shouldn't be too much longer."

"One thing though, now that I kinda-sorta want to win the election." Gabe paused. "What if I don't?"

Ceru heaved. "We'll have a harder time trying to save the Council, and the new councilman and riddle keeper, from Nor."

"But, you'd still help me try?"

He chuckled. "I knew you wouldn't drop it either. I'm in this with you."

Gabe only nodded in return. He felt it too, that Ceru was kind of like an uncle or something. He should be happy, full of warm fuzzies for the family-like bond. But, he didn't have a good record with his parental figures.

Decorations adorned with the Winged icon filled the press conference area. The enormous campaign banner that hung on the back wall drew Gabe into the past, only the first name was wrong. As a child, he spent a lot of time helping at Father's headquarters. His father ran a drawn-out campaign, a marathon against many candidates compared to his own miniscule sprint. In a few hours, the election would end the same as every other in history. The Winged would select a new representative, a new beginning. Earlier, Gabe wanted nothing to do with that new start, but now…now he was hoping to be given the chance.

Gabe found a spot to stand away from the podium where he had a good view of the huge screen on the wall, accessible but also not front and center. By the time the press arrived, the screen showed a journalist reporting the votes as they came in. A crowd of supporters flocked into the small room, and most of them had known Jeken personally. He saw a few familiar faces from his school-aged days, Hawlk, Kyla, and even Rusty Roran. Rusty must have used some of his leave to come. Touched, Gabe would have to find time to talk to them between the announcements and the obligatory hand shaking.

The energy in the room rose and fell with each message. As they tallied the votes for a city, the totals on the screen for each candidate changed. Gabe had a good lead at first, but the votes from the candidates' cities narrowed the gap. The enthusiastic murmurs seemed to shift to anxious small talk amongst Jeken's older supporters. What did it matter if they weren't voting for him, but his father?

Gabe stepped back a little closer to the wall and a little further from the stage. He removed the Winged pin and put it in his pocket. What if he no longer had the right to wear it? He flipped it around in his fingers, warm and flat to the touch.

A young Winged woman only a few years older than him approached. He stopped flipping the pin.

"Good evening, Councilman." She offered, and he shook her hand. "Sorra Volan."

Gabe replied, "Thank you, Sorra, that's what we're hoping for, right? Heh."

She giggled. "Technically you're councilman until we hear otherwise, but I know you've already won. You must."

"Do you know something I don't?"

She shook her head. "You're different than the others. It's subtle, but you have something more. I believe you when you speak, and that's rare in this world."

He stood a little straighter. She meant that, every word. "I thought I was riding my father's legacy."

She gripped her white clutch with both hands. "Well, that's a faulty strategy. Our trait is too cautious to elect someone without substance. I vote for a person, not a name."

"There hasn't been enough time. No one knows any of the candidates, not really."

Sorra's wings remained still, showing her ease. "The others maybe, but we've all seen and heard you throughout the years. You've probably forgotten, but about five years ago I saw you with your father when they opened the bridge to the Finned's Island. He gave you credit for the idea, and you barely accepted the praise. That's only one example, but I could tell you were both intelligent and humble. The rest of the Winged have had plenty of opportunities to see you, too."

"Thank you." His ears burned, probably a deep purple.

She took his hand to shake again. "I hope you win, Councilman."

Gabe smiled. "Me too."

Sorra walked back into the crowd to mingle with the others, the pressure of her handshake still on his palm. When he began, he signed on to play a role, but these people saw him as more than an idle figurehead. They weren't voting for *Ilat*, they were voting for *him*. Whatever strength Ceru and Lea saw within him, others could see it, too. *Suck it up and have some faith.* Lea's voice haunted him again. Okay, she was right. He finally got it.

It was almost like everything had led to this moment. Losing his mother, running away with Heather, his father's assassination, meeting Matt, and especially Lea; it all changed him and guided him to this place. A crappy way to get there, but maybe it was meant to be. If he had a real purpose, then he could diminish the pain, even if only a little.

From the speakers towering in each corner of the room, the pitch of the journalist's voice changed. The final counts came in, a curtain of silence fell, and the crowd hung on every word. Gabe could only read the lips that announced his victory through the deafening applause.

Cameras flashed, and Ceru pushed him to the podium. He read his acceptance speech to the press that Senni had drawn up. After that, the mass of congratulations and questions came at him, but he answered without nerves getting in his way. He was clearheaded for the first time. At long last, he knew who he was. He was Councilman Gabe Ilat, representative of the Winged.

Nineteen

Lea parked her car in the space in front of her apartment. Outside, the air burned at forty million degrees compared to the "summer" in western New York. She had just returned after spending a month settling her parents into their new place. Grandma had transferred some money to an anonymous bank account for them early on, and then they both found jobs that paid, well, *enough*. Not like Dad could get an engineering gig with that fake ID, so retail would have to suffice for now. With luck they had found a dirt-cheap house rental in Buffalo, probably the only people glad the economy was in the toilet.

Her parents didn't unpack their things from storage for obvious reasons, so Lea spent most of the time assembling furniture shipped in flat boxes, each an entertaining puzzle of particleboard pieces. Dad would open the wordless instruction book and pretend to read in Swedish. She'd double over in laughter, while Mom smiled quietly. Evidently, her father's genes won the sense of humor contest.

Time spent with them happened in an alternate reality where everything worked out right, and she'd been able to ignore the loss present in the back of her mind. The happy weeks in New York ended way too soon. Lea had to return to her life. She needed to register for classes, and maybe find a job now that she no longer consumed her life with research.

She opened the door to her dark apartment, stagnant and empty. Like a physical force, the solitude crushed her. No laughing, no distractions, only herself in a blank slate of a living room. What she had avoided came flying back, and that tiny speck of pain inundated the front of her thoughts. She immediately honed in on the picture leaning against the journal and the kind blue eyes she missed.

Sighing, she dropped her suitcase next to the door, flicked on the light, and went to the mantel to punish herself. She traced her finger over the edges of the plastic frame. She missed him, but that wasn't all. What was this feeling? Her hands quivered while she held the frame. Even her stomach began to sink like she was frightened. What was there to be anxious about? Was it her sixth sense again? It felt similar but different, like someone added a secret spice to her favorite chili.

She set the picture down and urged the thoughts away. After all, she couldn't do a dammed thing, and if she focused on that she'd break something. She already had one fist-sized dent in the wall coming out of her security deposit, she didn't need another.

Lea spent the remainder of the evening doing laundry and filling out job applications online. When she worked, she could keep her attention on typing or folding shirts. But as soon as she finished, that strange worry crawled back in. Sometimes it was mild, sometimes it was strong, but it was always mixed with a tinge of longing.

Over the next few days, Lea settled in with some grocery shopping and other errands. She had a hard time slipping back into her solitary life. She wanted to confide in someone, talk about everything that had happened. Maybe she could talk to Matt. They could go back in time and have a video game night, or watch movies in the dorm.

But no, that was a bad idea. What if he got up the courage to speak the unsaid words that always hung around him? She still didn't know exactly what to tell him anyway.

After another week, she couldn't take it anymore. She had to talk to someone, and at this point it could be anyone. Matt was her best bet after all, so she selected his name and hit send before she had a chance to think it over.

He picked up. "Lea, hey!"

"Hi Matt, I'm back in town. I know you wanted to get together soon so..." She forced her confidence.

"Oh yeah, hey, um...when were you thinking?"

"Today, tonight, whenever. Job hunt fail, so I'm pretty free."

After a short pause he replied, "I'm sorry...I've got D&D tonight so I can't."

"That's okay, some other time then."

"I'll give you a call, promise."

She shouldn't have asked for tonight. That was weird. What the heck was she thinking?

"No problem, I'll see ya later." She hung up and shoved the phone deep in her pocket.

How mortifying. Why did she assume he had feelings for her that she wanted to avoid? If that were true, he wouldn't have chosen playing nerd make-believe over a chance to hang out. She pegged him wrong. What else was she missing? She was great at deducing things from scientific data, but that's where it ended. People were different, people were changing and evolving, and she had it all wrong.

But wait...Matt didn't have feelings for her. Great! She could hang out with him again without worry. Sure, Gabe would be absent, but if she could recapture a little of that happiness, maybe she could make it through without him...without him.

An ache pulled from deep in her core, but she tried to push it away. It sucked. Every time she thought she'd gotten over it, she'd remember his goofy smile, his warm arms, and without him there, she may as well be in the vacuum of space. Nothing touched her, not even the air.

Before meeting him, she bottled her feelings so easily, tucking them behind a wall where they couldn't hurt her. Gabe ruined that. He stole her mask, and her heart. It wasn't fair.

What was that noise? Lea got up from the sofa. The rattling grew louder. The wind banging the window sounded like a storm building, but the sky had been clear only moments beforehand. The weather report even predicted unrelenting sun and cloudless skies for the whole week, lows only dipping into the eighties.

She lifted the mini blinds to see what looked like a tornado rising from the field northwest of the university stadium. Clear skies surrounded the funnel until the top began spreading outward to envelop the sky in a thick blanket of grey thunderheads. The tornado started on the ground? Without a storm?

Lea pinched her arm, ouch. Oh crap, this was real. The classic freight train noise blared louder as the funnel widened. Lightning struck from the fresh clouds and hit a telephone pole, raining sparks over the apartment complex under construction nearby.

Should she take shelter or keep watching? Reason lost the battle, and she continued to stare at the anomaly. Oh, that was weird. The tornado remained stationary like a column to support the whirling sky. Then without warning, the mysterious funnel vanished as suddenly as it arrived. In only seconds, she could see the stars, and calm breezes tickled the leaves of the tree by her building.

She stumbled back onto the sofa. What the heck was that? She spent more than half her life researching all the weirdness surrounding the fourth dimension, and that was by far the strangest thing she had ever seen. It was impossible.

The hairs on her neck tingled. Trembling, she gazed through the window into the quiet night. Her eyes followed the windowsill over to the mantel and the picture. The journal, her family heirloom. Didn't the inscription say something about strange events?

Lea retrieved the journal and blew dust off of the leather cover. The locking mechanism on the side had no keyhole, so as far as she knew, it had never been opened. Her family had passed the curious journal through the generations. It looked so worthless, but all the women who received the tiny book treasured it, and she was no exception. She cradled the journal in her hands, instinctively resting her thumb on the smooth metal plate. She adjusted her glasses and read the inscription aloud.

> *"When something strange can't be explained, the time will come to be. This book you have, hold in your hand, you are the only key."*

What did it mean? Whatever it was, it must be significant.

The metal lock warmed under her thumb. It glowed momentarily and then clicked. She slid her thumb, and the lock opened. She gasped.

She rubbed the pad of her finger along the edge. She was the first to open the book, an honor but also an unknown. The binding crackled as she bent back the cover and flipped to the first page. Thick and splendid old-book smell hit her nose. Legible handwriting, but the author used a quill tip, and the uneven ink made it harder to read.

> *Prophecy is an infuriatingly imprecise art, and I therefore apologize in advance for anything I have missed or am unable to share with you. What I understand is that you will need my knowledge in the future, so I'm recording it here for you. If you're reading this, the magic energy I've imbued has successfully kept it passing through the generations to reach you. Now Lea—*

Lea hurled the book across the room. How the hell did it know her name? That was impossible, it was just, not, possible! Prophecy? Magic? She studied science, not fiction. She must have imagined it. The weird tornado and now this? She hadn't been sleeping well, but she didn't think it had gotten this bad.

She glanced at the book lying cockeyed in the hallway, and curiosity struck her again. She might have imagined it, but she could never ignore a question staring her in the face. She cautiously opened the book and continued to read.

> *Now Lea, do not stop reading! I know this may alarm you, but hear me out. I don't know what year you will be born, but I clearly saw you in my vision. The world is in danger. Well, more accurately, the world will be in danger. I wish to help you and the people of your time.*

  I cannot assume you know much, so I'll start at the beginning. My name is Merlin, your grandfather of however many generations. Illirin, the plane that borders ours, possesses aether unlike anything on Earth. As a Wizard, I can siphon and use magic from Illirin, and you've inherited this gift. Learning to channel the energy of magic is more of an art, but I'll do my best to guide you. It will be more difficult for you to tap aether, but I can explain why.

  In my time, the Illirins who live here are peaceful, and we've learned a lot from each other about both science and magic. I've helped to further our exciting partnership, and I wish it could continue indefinitely. Unfortunately, mankind is tarnished with greed. Some have used Illirin's gifts for war, to attack Camelot and other neighboring kingdoms. My counter efforts cause just as much damage, and the loss of life and property is staggering.

  Magic on Earth is powerful, and its potential for devastation is too great. The Illirins we have worked with over the years can no longer permit their world to cause such suffering, and I completely agree. Shortly, we will divide our worlds which will sever our connection to Illirin's aether. The Illirin leaders ensure me that the rotation of their world will make it so hard to tap aether, that it will be impossible to cause any meaningful harm. Only the most talented will be able to use magic at all, and the energy would be very weak.

  This brings me to today. In my vision, someone used magic on a wider scale, though the division remained intact. One such event guided you to open this journal. Someone in your era can use magic despite the divide. Worse than that, something may heal the divide, giving this person unimaginable power. He or she is a descendant of my rival, Morgana.

  With this power, Morgana's descendant is a threat to both Earth and our neighbors in Illirin. You are the only hope to stand against them, because whether or not the divide endures, you can oppose them and protect the world from tyranny. You will face Morgana's heir, and I shall help you prepare.

Not to be boastful, but my abilities to harness magic are superb. I've seen it, and you have my strength. You are, will be, a powerful sorceress. Some aspects of magic you must learn on your own, but I can teach you the rest.

"Hold on here," Lea asked out loud. "You expect me to *fight* someone? This is crazy, you're crazy." She was talking to an inanimate object. "No, *I'm* crazy."

Overwhelmed by what she learned, she closed the journal. Merlin, like *Sword in the Stone* Merlin? The Arthurian legends were simply myths, not history. Weren't they?

She looked at the tattered book. Merlin wrote that he put magic in it. She could feel it, now that she understood what it was, the same tingling of her sixth sense. Was that magic working on her? Maybe this was real.

She skimmed back through the few pages she had read. He wrote of Illirin and even knew the dimension's name. Her jaw hung open. That was proof it was all true. After the divide, no one knew about Illirin until she and Gabe crossed over. Merlin was right. She had to keep reading.

Morgana's descendant has an advantage over you. He or she can already tap aether, and you'll be starting at the beginning. Their family likely passed down the knowledge of Illirin. We did not, because magic here is just too dangerous, and not everyone can be trusted with the key to such power. I'll do my best to prepare you—.

Hit by an intangible feeling, Lea looked up from the yellowed pages. Morgana's descendant was here, and he or she created that huge tornado through the Schism, or the divide as Merlin called it. A faint voice echoed in her mind. *Every time I cross over it weakens the barrier between our worlds. It gives power to those who want to wage war.* The danger Gabe wanted to save her from was already here…Morgana's heir! He left to protect her from something hiding in her backyard. He didn't even know. And she was supposedly destined to face this person?

She yelled, "You dumb ass! You didn't know what the hell was really happening, and you left anyway. Damn it!" She dug her fingers into the binding to keep herself from chucking the journal into the wall, again. She flipped through the pages, mostly detailed instructions she didn't have time to read. She returned the book to the mantel, her eyes catching Gabe's in the photo. She needed to tell him what she learned. She had to help him.

So what if she'd use warning him as an excuse. She needed to talk to him, to see him. She just needed him. How could she contact Gabe? She couldn't open a thinning without him and had no idea where he'd be.

The thinnings, that's right. You could see Earth through them from the other side. That's how Gabe got to know Heather in the first place. It'd be a long, long shot, but maybe he still had a habit of peeking in on Earth. A little flicker tickled her inside, like a butterfly coming back to life. Maybe he cared enough to look for her.

Twenty

The first flight, the first day of school, the first time breaking the Schism—during his life Gabe went through a lot of "firsts," but they meant nothing compared to walking through the Council chamber doors. He didn't have the usual jitters that accompany the new, because the job seemed like an afterthought. No nerves, no worries about performance; instead he focused all his energy into putting on a smile like Lea used to do. A mask to hide the hate.

On the other side of the table, Nor had already taken his seat. The others rose to introduce themselves, but not him…not the murderer. Gabe played his part, all handshakes and nods, Nor remaining always in his line of sight. The anger grew, rising up into his throat like a wave of nausea, and with the same will not to throw up, he shoved it back down. Down, down, with a smile.

Nor slowly stood and extended his hand across the table. "You must be the new Councilman Ilat. Pleasure to meet you."

Gabe reached over and gripped his hand. He squeezed Nor's fingers so he could feel the bones cracking into each other. "Hi."

"I'm looking forward to working with you." Nor extracted his hand from Gabe's. He slithered back down into his chair.

"Here's your seat." The Finned Councilman patted the top of the wide, leather chair as he sat in his own.

The oval table had five seats, and Gabe took his place, his spot on the Council. Through some miracle, he made it through that first meeting, and the next, and then the next. Over the weeks, it got easier to ignore Nor's smug grin and the darkness lurking just behind his fake geniality. He never made it easy though.

Nor would act polite, but everything he said undermined Gabe's efforts to find common ground. They'd be working well on a resolution, break for lunch, and then someone would strike the deal down. Nor had to be getting to the others in private. The whole mess drained him, mind and body. He almost wished he was back with Obram and Gorli learning about the formal request procedures—almost.

On the upside, the Council was still working together. Nor hadn't succeeded in driving their paranoia to that level, not yet. And only one week remained in the session, thank the stars. He didn't know how much more he could take without losing his diplomatic calm.

At the end of the day, Gabe stepped through the tall doors of the Council Hall and stretched his wings as wide as they went. He had gotten through to Councilman Brennan of the Legged. A small victory in the scheme of things, but he let it lift his spirits. He'd take his wins where he could get them. It helped that Nor hadn't been at the last few meetings. He felt confident in Nor's absence, and the negotiations produced more results because of it. For once, he left the chambers in a good mood.

It didn't take long for Gabe to get to the other side of the city, where he'd been staying in a modest apartment. He put his key in the door and paused. Something shuffled inside.

He let go of the knob as the door pulled open. Someone grabbed his arm and yanked him down. Gabe swung his other arm out to the side at a second pair of legs and pulled a knee forward, causing the attacker to fall.

The first man wrenched Gabe's arm behind his back, crushing his wings against him. The assailant tried to force him to his knees. He wouldn't go down, even though it meant his arm was near breaking. Biting his cheek against the pain, he threw his head backward. He heard the crack of the man's nose against his skull. Gabe's arm dropped free.

He turned away from the door, but the other man got to his feet to block him. The Seer's eyes focused in a distant look. Crap, he was gonna use magic. Gabe bent over and rammed into his chest, plowing him into the wall. Gabe stumbled to the side, and the Seer reached to grab him, missing his wing by an inch.

Gabe sprinted to the end of the hall, both men in pursuit. He crossed his arms in front of his face and crashed through the window, sending glittering shards raining down. The broken glass kept him curled too long, and he almost hit the ground. His wings opened to catch the wind softening the blow, but he landed hard enough to pound a sting up his shins. He rebounded with sore knees back into the air.

Dipping his wing to turn, he raced into the fading twilight. Damn suit was too tight, and he couldn't go as fast with his shoulders bunched up. The would-be kidnappers couldn't keep up, but the more distance he put between them, the better chance he had of losing them for good. He'd get some new clothes when he landed, something less noticeable.

Why had he stayed in one place so long? He wasn't thinking. He got sloppy, but at least it didn't cost him anything this time.

The Council would have to do without him for the final week. Union wasn't safe. He'd find shelter in Wren. And now that Nor made a move, all his previous plans were useless. Ceru would know what to do. He'd contact Ceru from Wren and make a new plan.

Stopping to rest would waste time. He kept flying in a consistent rhythm to save energy, though it was a fast one. The further he got, the slower his rhythm became. Each pull on his wings hurt the muscles the Seers had injured. He could scarcely glide by the time the outskirts of the city inched into sight. So close, but too far. He landed in the clearing by the forest edge so he wouldn't fall out of the sky from exhaustion.

Gabe sat and breathed deep to slow his heart rate. There, that's better. To the side, he noticed something a few feet away, a thinning. He knew that thinning well—too well. Maybe he landed here on purpose hoping it was close. He wanted to be strong, to believe he could move forward. But he wasn't strong. He wanted to see her, wanted to know she was okay.

He crawled over to peer through. The thinning hadn't arrived at the campus yet, but he could see some landmarks close to Lea's apartment. He sighed. It wasn't anywhere useful. Besides, it was summer, so she wouldn't be on campus anyway. He continued to watch through the thinning for a few minutes to reminisce. A poster on a light post caught his eye, hung slanted at a weird angle which didn't face either the street or sidewalk. There, on the lost cat poster, was a picture of Lea. *What?*

He read, *"Please help, she's in danger and lost. If you find her, contact me by Saturday night if possible."* She didn't own a cat and the wording was strange.

"She's in danger…" he whispered. It couldn't be true, not after he left her to keep her safe. He looked at the sign closer for any clues. Saturday night…and that wasn't her phone number, it ended in 0300. She'd be at that thinning, the one overnight.

Did *she* put up these signs for him, or did someone else? If she was in danger it could be some kind of trap. If it was a trap, it was a good one, because he was going to walk right into it.

The following night, Gabe arrived at the spot well before the thinning arrived. He watched it travel, fading in and out before it rested where he stood. Through the foggy window, lamps lit the walkway near the Union, and Lea waited by the bench checking her watch. He released a breath and his shoulders relaxed. She must have planted the signs.

He looked around once before he ripped the Schism and jumped a foot down to the sidewalk in front of her. The portal closed, and it took a moment for his eyes to adjust. There she stood, but not pissed off like the last time. She wore an odd expression, closed mouth and unblinking eyes. What was she thinking?

"You came…" Lea whispered.

"You're lucky I even saw the sign. I wasn't supposed to be anywhere near there." She was okay, thank God she was okay.

"Ya know, I'm glad you're still kind of a stalker."

Gabe chuckled. "I thought you wanted my help."

"I do." She paused, looking into his eyes. "I need you."

"I'll do anything." He didn't care about his responsibilities. He had to help her. He'd do anything for her.

Lea closed the distance between them. "You didn't know when you disappeared on me, the danger you—"

"Wait." He held up his hand. Before she explained, he needed to say it.

She grabbed his wrist and yanked his hand down. "You will not *shush* me again! This is importa—"

Gabe pulled her into his arms. She inhaled sharply, stopping her tirade.

"I was so worried. I thought something had…" He took a breath. "I won't let anything happen to you. I can't." He brushed the hair off her forehead and traced his finger by her jaw. "I love you."

Her mouth opened just a little, with wide doe eyes and no more words. Lea, speechless?

Gabe smirked. "Thought I couldn't shut you up?"

Her lips curled into a smile. "No fair."

Lea tilted her chin, and Gabe responded in kind, closing his eyes for a kiss.

He expected soft lips, but was greeted with cool air. The weight in his arms increased, and his eyes popped open. Lea's unconscious head dangled back over his arm. She went loose and heavy, taking him to the ground. He leaned her upper body against him as he knelt on the concrete.

"Lea!" he yelled shaking her, "Lea! Lea!" No response. His heart thumped loud in his ears. "Help!" he shouted into the night, *"Help!"* The Union had a twenty-four-hour computer lab. He yelled again, "Somebody…*help!*"

She felt so heavy, another limp body lying in his lap. No. No. He held shuddering fingers under her nose; she was breathing.

Footsteps approached in front of them. He looked up to see Matt wearing his D&D cape and boots, coming from a game. "I don't know what happened, she just passed out!" He was frantic, but Matt was calm.

Matt put his hands out. "Here, let me. I'll take her."

Gabe nodded and helped guide Lea into his arms.

Matt put one arm under her knees, the other behind her back, and lifted her. He looked down at Gabe, and his expression shifted from the concerned roommate to a scornful glare. He plucked a dart from Lea's neck and tossed it to the ground.

"Oh, grow up, it's just a tranq." He rolled his eyes. "You are such an idiot, Makai." He laughed and hefted Lea in his arms before he turned.

Gabe stared at the back of his friend's head. This wasn't happening. Matt was his roommate. He didn't know his name. He didn't know anything about…and then Gabe's eyes widened. "It's you." All this time his friend had been lying to him. "It's you? The wizard—"

"Too little, too late." Matt turned around halfway and said, "Oh, and some parting advice, just tell Nor what he wants. He might let you live." He started to walk away. "Adios *amigo*. Ha ha."

Gabe didn't have the opportunity to let it all sink in. The bushes by the Union rustled and two figures appeared. He reached for the blade at his waist, but a sharp pain bit into his neck. His vision went black.

Gabe awoke little by little, drowsiness hanging over him like a shroud. It took a few minutes from the beginning of consciousness to open his eyes. He sat on the floor against the wall of a barren metal room, no benches, no bucket, nothing. The only door on the opposite wall had a small window of thick glass, not that he could see anything from the floor.

He tried to lift his arms, but was stopped short by the chains fastened to the wall. The cuffs pressed snug against his wrists, no leeway to slip them off. His movement in the room must have alerted someone that he had awakened, because a short time later the door opened, and Heten Nor walked in.

"I trust you slept well, Councilman Ilat?" Nor smirked.

"Councilman Ilat was my father." Gabe glared into Nor's Seer eyes. Behind the odd pupils of his trait lived his darkness. The trait looked the same, but Nor's eyes were nothing like his sister's.

"Well, you've done an excellent job impersonating him these past weeks."

Gabe crossed his arms as best as he could with the restraint of the chains. "Do whatever it is you're planning. You won't get anything from me."

He wasn't scared like he should be. Maybe he had gotten used to the idea, or maybe he wanted to prove he was as brave as his father. Whatever it was, he was ready to face death. Illirin and Earth depended on him. Lea depended on him.

Nor replied, "What if I asked 'pretty please?' You wouldn't be the first to give me his riddle, so you can take comfort in that."

"Never. You'll have to kill me, just like my father."

Nor exaggerated a sigh. "I thought you might say as much. You Winged have to be so *noble*." He paused. "Well, since we both know that torture is a waste of time, we should move on to more fruitful negotiations, don't you agree?" Nor regarded him with a relaxed posture, unconcerned and hiding something.

Gabe's skin crawled.

"I can tell you want to do the right thing and protect your people. It's easy to be noble when you must only forfeit your own life." Nor glared intently at Gabe's terrified mouth, opening wide and trembling. "Is it still called *noble* when you sacrifice someone else? Hrm?"

Nor snapped his fingers, and the door opened.

Gabe breathed, "No…"

Another Seer brought in Lea, arms bound behind her and gagged with a rag. She looked terrified, and rightfully so. She struggled as the Seer handed her to Nor.

Nor yanked her bindings, pressing her back against him. He drew a blade, clicked open the prongs, and held it to her neck. She winced. Her eyes darted around, scared and shaken. "Unlike in chambers this is a simple question, so you don't have long to answer. *Yes* or *no*?"

"Don't hurt her, don't hurt her. Let her go. Don't hurt her." Gabe's voice shook.

"Or?" He pushed the blade into contact with her throat. A bead of blood formed at the edge and ran down her neck. She went rigid, her chest still without breathing.

All of Gabe's strength left him. Nor won. He wouldn't let her die, even to protect everyone else from a war. His head dropped. "You win. I'll tell you. Just let her go."

Nor grinned and sheathed the blade. "Now. I am not a patient man."

Gabe took a deep breath and closed his eyes. The riddle wasn't a simple piece of memorized prose. The First Council embedded magic in the words to ensure they remained unchanged and passing through time. The only other time he touched the flow of aether was when he acquired the riddle. Now, he had to remember how to find the magic again to recount the words.

A vibration of energy began in his chest and flowed up through his back. His eyes glazed over with a faint glow.

He stared forward as he recited, "All about blows the wind, blue horizon sea's no end. Wings fly swiftly to the granite peak, but the others need to take the week. All together, first in place, recite the words that open this space. Unity comes not from one, and once again we call our friends."

The glimmer in Gabe's eyes vanished, and he faltered on his feet as the energy left him. He looked back at Nor still gripping Lea's arms in a tight hold. "You have it. Let her go."

Nor nodded. "That goes perfectly with the rest. Thank you very much, Councilman Ilat. It was a pleasure doing business with you."

"Let her go!" Gabe yanked his chains.

"Yes, well, there's a small problem with that." Nor's expression darkened further. "I'm about to become an emperor, and I must have respect from all my future subjects. You Winged are so proud of your strength. You've spent centuries looking down on us as weaklings. I can't have anyone thinking I'm weak, now can I?" He drew the blade quickly and took it to Lea's neck. She tried to scream but the gag muffled all but a soft squeal.

"No!" Gabe shouted. The cuffs bit into his wrists.

An evil smile spread over Nor's lips as he slid the blade across her throat. He released the bindings, and she collapsed to the floor, her body tangled like a pile of blood-soaked rags.

"No!" Gabe raged against the chains. *"Noooo!"*

Nor yawned and snapped his fingers again. The servant from before came in and dragged Lea's body into the hallway. Nor followed, leaving only a thin trail of blood behind the closed door.

Gabe kept screaming, his rage the only thing in control. He writhed against the chains digging deeper into his wrists, though he felt no pain. A rabid beast fighting captivity replaced his mind with wild fury. His vision went white. No thought, no feeling at all, and within the madness, time refused to pass. Or was it speeding by?

His anger welled from deep within an ancient space. The flow of aether connected, and magic coursed through his body. Electricity crackled around his arms as sharp white sparks. A charge as powerful as lightning exploded, and he broke the chains with a strength that was not his own.

Running entirely on survival instinct, Gabe punched through the small glass window and unlatched the door. The startled guard spun around and reached for his blade. Gabe swung his arms up and slammed the guard's head against the wall. He ran down the hall letting his gut guide him. He turned a corner and found a stairwell. He glanced through the window on the next floor and saw daylight. He had to shove a couple people out of his way, but he made it outside and into the air.

He didn't think, couldn't think, just kept going and going. He flew long past reason until his wings gave out. In his weakened state he would have crashed, but he was able to tuck his head to roll, slamming into the base of a large tree where he was greeted by welcomed darkness.

Twenty-One

The screams bounced off the metal walls, overlapping and echoing into a kind of victory music. The melody filled Heten Nor with unadulterated joy. He paused to listen and released the flow of magic disguising the prisoner.

Her skin faded back to its normal aqua tint, and her features regained their Illirin appearance. The one thing that did not change was the dead look on her face. Heten motioned for the servant to take the body away, and he continued to move through the compound to meet back with the wizard.

Even climbing the stairs, he could still hear the screams from that Winged whelp. The boy had been born with everything, all the privileges the world had to offer. Not only the Winged trait, but he had a councilman for a father with money and power that even the rest of his kind would envy. Heten hated him for it, for his luck, for his arrogance, and for his innate belief he was better than everyone else. Now it was his turn to suffer on the bottom. Heten couldn't take his trait, but he would take away his power once he had the Stand, and for now, he wiped the arrogance off his face.

Heten relished the screams until he was too far to hear them. Without knocking, he opened the door to the wizard's room.

Matt stood next to the desk in the center. "You could announce yourself, you know."

"I did not want to waste the time." Heten straightened the cuffs of his sleeves. He noticed a red smear on the edge. He would have to change later.

"So?"

He walked in and took a seat behind Matt's desk. "We leave tonight to collect the Stand. It won't be long now."

Matt said, "Great. I'll be ready. Did Makai react like we planned?"

"Yes, and we'll help him to escape if he can't on his own. He will surely feel the need to 'stop us' no matter what. He'll validate our war, and the other traits may welcome a benevolent despot."

"Whatever you say." Matt shrugged. "I'll get ready to leave later. I need to talk to Lea first. She'll be up soon."

"I still don't know why you wanted me to use a prisoner. She is your opponent. It took a lot of effort to keep her from learning anything useful, and now you bring her here."

"She's more use to me alive, I promise."

Heten scoffed. "If you say so. Your decision better not backfire, Wizard."

"Don't worry. We'll have the Stand soon, and then nothing can stop us." Matt gave a cursory bow and left.

That human was getting a little too full of himself. Heten couldn't risk offending him before the war. Afterward, he would have to watch that boy every moment. The wizard would gain incredible power over magic, but Heten had the power that mattered.

Something soft and warm tucked around Lea where she lay. Not the arms she last remembered, but a bed with a fluffy comforter. The crisp air smelled clean and light. Dishes rattled to her side, and she slowly blinked to dislodge the sleep crusties.

A magenta-skinned girl set down a tray with a pitcher and glass. The girl caught Lea's eye and hurried out of the room.

Lea sat up surrounded by pink pillows. The walls, floor, and even ceiling were the same gray metal, making the ornate bed frame and flowery comforter seem terribly out of place. No more out of place than she was in Illirin though.

How did she get here? What happened? She grabbed her glasses off the nightstand and put them on. Her hair hung around her shoulders, freed from its usual braid. That's weird.

What was the last thing she remembered? She waited for Gabe, and he showed up. Then, she blushed. He loved her. The warm static tickled her arms and back where he had held her. She had closed her eyes to kiss him, and then…nothing. Then she woke up here.

A shudder ran through her, and the back of her neck prickled—her warning. She felt it many times before, but never this intense. This scared her.

The door opened, and Lea flopped back onto the pillow to feign sleeping. The door squeaked closed, and footsteps approached the bed. Something scraped over the floor, and she felt someone lean near her. She tried to even her breathing, but she had no idea how well she succeeded.

"Lea?" The voice sounded familiar. "I thought you were awake."

She bolted upright to see Matt sitting in the folding chair next to the bed. "Matt?" She blinked. "What are you doing here? Wait…where is *here*? Where's Gabe?"

"Don't worry, you're safe. Everything is okay." He smiled, but it didn't put her at ease.

"What's going on!"

Matt rested his hand on top of the bed. "This place is called Illirin."

"Yeah, the girl with the pink skin tipped me off. I mean more specific, and more of the *why* am I here." She spoke as fast as her heart raced. She hated not knowing anything. It shortened her already millimeter-long fuse.

He sighed. "Will you give me a chance to explain?"

Lea found a corner of the velvet blanket and twirled it between her fingers. "Yes, sorry. Just a little freaked right now."

Matt nodded. "I brought you here to keep you safe."

Her mouth gaped. "What?" She hit the bed with balled fists. First Gabe and now Matt, was she that incompetent? "I am so frackin' sick of people protecting me. From what this time?"

He cocked his head with a goofy grin. "'Frackin,' *Battlestar* reference...nice."

"Safe from *what*, Matt?"

He took a breath, tapping his fingers against the comforter. "From Gabe," he replied.

Lea covered her face with her hands. Nothing could sound crazier. "Don't you get a warning before you enter the *Twilight Zone?*"

"I'm serious. I wish I wasn't but—"

She whipped her head around and looked him in the eyes. "That's ludicrous. Gabe would never hurt me."

"Maybe before, but..." He shook his head. "He's had a psychotic break. He thinks someone assassinated his father, but he died of a heart attack. Something snapped, and now he's come up with these conspiracy theories. He's going to start a war with the Seers. After all the suffering they've endured at the hands of the Winged, one spark from him will ignite a revolution."

"None of that makes any sense. I just talked to him, and he was fine." It couldn't be true. Gabe was more than normal. He said he loved her; that had to be real.

"How much have you talked to Makai since he regained his memory?"

She bit her lip and grabbed at the blanket again. "A few times." She hadn't talked to him a lot because he left. That was weird by itself. She wouldn't believe it, she couldn't.

The chair scraped the floor as he leaned back. "I'm sorry, but it's true. He's lost his mind, and he's dangerous. You'll be safer here where I can look after you."

Was Matt right about Gabe? She turned to see him relaxed in a folding chair, but that chair was in another plane. What were they doing in Illirin? Matt never knew about the ED Project, so how did he even learn about this place? Something wasn't right.

She sat up a little straighter, her back against the ornate headboard. "How do you know about Illirin?"

"I've always known. My family has connections here going back centuries. They've waited a very long time for someone to be born with the gift again, and that someone is me. I'm a wizard."

Her eyes widened. It was him. The tornado near campus, that's why he couldn't hang out. She was looking into the face of Morgana's heir. It was too late to hide her shock, but she could recover.

She heaved an exasperated sigh. "I realize you enjoy role-playing games, but I never thought you were one of those dorks who believed that stuff was real." It was Matt after all. She just had to treat him the same as always, and not someone a mysterious little book said she'd have to fight.

He laughed and raked his fingers through his hair. "No, not like that kind of wizard. I have a gene variance or enzyme, something like that, but I was born with the ability to interact with four-dimensional features like the magic of Illirin's aether. It's why I can breathe here too." He pointed to a vent near the ceiling of the bedroom. "This room is oxygenated, but I can go anywhere I want."

"You really expect me to believe this?" Lea crossed her arms.

"I do." Matt reached across the comforter and took hold of her fingertips. She reluctantly released her hand and let him hold it between his.

He said, "And we are kindred spirits, you and I. You also have the gene…you're a sorceress. Well, not yet. You'll have to tap the aether for the first time to make the changes in your body that allow you to breathe. That's really why I brought you here. I want to help you learn your gift."

She pulled her hand under his into a fist, and he let go. "I'm a scientist, not a sorceress. The only magic I know how to do is break relativity." She squinted. "Okay, *bend*, bending relativity."

"You just have to bend it a little further." He chuckled. "Doesn't Clarke's Law say that any truly advanced science is indistinguishable from magic? Most people would think the existence of this fourth dimension is impossible, but here we are. They coined terms like *magic* and *wizard* in feudal times. They didn't understand what this really is."

"So what is it then?" She leaned in.

"The aether consists of an energy of infinite possibilities, 'magic.' The gifted can transform that energy into whatever they want. The four-dimensional properties allow you to use your mind to bend the energy into a new form. It's like how the genes in your body tell your cells what to become, except this energy can become anything. You could send it out as an element like fire, or carry your will into an object, or transform something else. Like I said, the possibilities are infinite. The ability to bend magic varies from person to person, but you get the idea."

"You somehow seem smarter than I thought," she said.

"Well, um…thanks for the backhanded compliment. I do more than just play games, you know."

Lea winced. "Sorry. I…this is all new to me." At least he'd think it was, she hoped. Keep acting, show the smile.

Matt took her hand between his again, and an excited grin spread wide. "And I'll teach you everything I know. We can do amazing things together. You'll see."

He squeezed her knuckles, and her body tensed. Why was he looking at her like that? She didn't want to read into things again, but she couldn't help it. Now she felt awkward on top of being a captive. What was Matt thinking?

She glanced to the side. Change the subject. "So, you said this room has oxygen. Is it the only one?"

He let her hand go to point at the door. "There are a few others I've had prepared for you in this hallway, and the guard outside will help to make sure you make it there. I know it's confining, but it's only until you learn your gift."

"Right."

Matt raised his eyebrow.

Crap, what did he see? Could he tell she didn't trust him? She stiffened to keep herself still. Her pulse pounded. He had to be able to hear how stupid loud it was.

"What is it?" He stood, resting his hand on her shoulder.

"I'm okay. Just tired, and it's a lot to process."

"Of course." He bent over her and paused before planting a gentle kiss on her forehead. The spot cooled when he lifted away. "I'll come get you for lunch in a little. Feel better."

"Thanks."

He left the room, and Lea allowed herself to shake. Her nerves were so close to betraying her, and her mind ricocheted like a hyperactive kid in a bounce house.

She got out of the bed to grab the glass of water from the tray. With an unsteady hand, she took a sip and let the water pool in her cheeks, giving back lost moisture. Matt brought her here, but what was the real reason? He was her friend. He helped her study, they hung out together, but she knew nothing about who he really was. He said he wanted to protect her, and he claimed Gabe…no, Makai, he claimed *Makai* was dangerous.

Matt knew Gabe's identity, and with his connection to Illirin, he must have always known. He never told Gabe who he was or helped him remember. Her body went cold. The glass clanked against the tray as she dropped her hand.

He lied from the beginning…always lying.

She caught a sob in her throat and struggled to hold it in. She didn't want to cry, this was dumb. It only felt like she was losing a friend, but he was still there, wasn't he? He had always been a wizard or whatever, even if she didn't know it then. But the lies were more than that, and a prophecy said he was an enemy. She didn't want him to be an enemy. Maybe he wouldn't have to be.

She inhaled through her nose and calmed herself. What she needed was to find a way out of there. Dammit, if only she finished reading the journal. She was trapped without guidance, without this supposed magic, and in a single room that had enough oxygen for her to not pass out and die.

Worst of all, she was without Gabe again. Matt could have just taken her and left him alone. Yeah right. Acid rose up her throat. She called him out of hiding, and now who knows what's happened to him. If he was hurt, it was her fault.

She closed her eyes to remember the moments before she blacked out—Gabe's strong arms and that little worried bump in his eyebrows. He said he loved her.

Upon opening her eyes, her daydream smile faded. The lifeless metal room had a few decorations, a vase of fake flowers, and a couple of pink pillows. It was a lame attempt to turn a barrack into a bedroom for a girl. She might not be a prisoner in name, but she felt every bit like one.

The squeak of the door woke Lea from her nap. She must have passed out again, though probably not for long. With only the soft tap of her shoes to announce her, the magenta girl from earlier slipped into the room. She looked the most human of any Illirin that Lea had seen. The shiny colorful skin and pointed ears seemed like the only defining characteristics.

The girl approached Lea and held out a folded bundle of fabric. It was then Lea noticed the girl's eyes and her strangely shaped pupils. She must be a Seer.

"This dress is for you, if you'd like," the girl said, her voice timid. She handed Lea the bundle.

Lea held the top and let the dress fall open. The simple red gown had a silver-beaded trim around the neckline and waist. Long, flowing sleeves opened at the shoulder with trimmed slits throughout, almost lacey. It was sort of like the costumes in those period films like *Robin Hood*, but at the same time it had touches from later fashions.

"Thank you," Lea said after admiring the dress. The girl turned to leave, and Lea held out her hand. "It's beautiful, so I don't mean any offense. But what's wrong with my own clothes? I've seen people here wear lots of more modern-looking things."

The girl turned and kept her eyes down. "It's the style of our trait. You may have seen others mimic the humans seen through the thinnings, but Seers are more traditional."

"Ahh...thanks."

She bowed her head. "If you'd like something else I can—"

"No, no. This is more than fine. I love it. Thank you."

She bowed again and left as quiet as a whisper.

Lea took another quick look at the dress. It's probably a good idea to blend in, as much as possible anyway. She took off her worn cargo pants and T-shirt, and pulled the gown over her head. The silky lining slid soft against her skin, nice but weird. She tended to choose practical clothing, and opportunities to dress up didn't come often.

She straightened the sleeves and stepped in front of the dresser mirror. Was that really her? She pulled at her loose hair, twirling it in her fingers. The color red grabbed attention, and though her eccentricity got noticed, this was attention of a different kind. It made her uncomfortable.

A loud buzz interrupted her thoughts. The intercom on the wall blinked and Matt's voice came through. "Lea? Hey, you ready? Press the button to talk."

She did as he asked. "Yeah…um …yes. Ready for what?"

"I'll come get you for lunch."

The light blinked off and the intercom clicked. Only a minute or so later she heard a knock, and Matt opened the door. "The dining room is right down the hall." He held out his hand for her.

She took it and followed him into the hall only after taking a deep breath. The hallway looked like the same metal as her room, all uniform and all very dull. Nothing about the building seemed ordinary. Like, who could picture someone working or having tea in a tin can? The florescent lighting and grated ceiling only added to the martial atmosphere. It had to be some sort of military building. That didn't make her feel any better.

A couple of guards stood in the hallway, backs straight against the walls. They wore uniforms and had blades similar to the one Gabe's father had given him. How odd that they had such advanced technology like Earth, but still used glorified knives. Where were the rifles?

When they entered the dining room, Lea exhaled and filled her lungs. The air felt cold and sharp, likely from the added oxygen. The dining room contained one long wooden table surrounded by chairs. Pretty red lanterns hung on the walls with a few paintings around the room. It had the same semi-decorative feeling as her "bedroom," like someone quickly added a few details to cover up the purpose of the building. Behind the façade she could imagine the real function for the small dining room, a meeting hall for strategy sessions or briefings. But the new decor and place settings established it as a place for her to eat. Someone went through a lot of work to set up these rooms just for her.

Matt acted the gentleman and pulled out a chair. She took a seat, and of course he sat next to her.

"So…" He smiled. "Seems we're out of pizza, but I hear the soup is awesome."

"I'm sure it's fine." Lea couldn't look at him. She inspected the room, failing miserably at hiding her unease.

"I'm still me, ya know." Matt twirled the spoon on the table. It hit his fingers and slid into the plate with a clink.

She bit her lip. "I know..."

"No you don't," he said. "You're acting like I'm a stranger or something. It doesn't matter where we are. I'm still Matt, I still like gaming, I still like sci-fi, and I still..." He blushed and continued twirling the spoon. Someone came in and delivered the soup and sandwiches, reprieving Lea from Matt's weird soliloquy.

She felt his eyes on her, but she focused on tasting her soup. The warm tomato-ish cream slid over her tongue. It wasn't half bad. Beside her, Matt heaved a sigh, and she turned to see him sulking over his food. She set her spoon down hard, her white-tinged fingers gripping the handle.

"What do you expect from me? Nothing is normal, *nothing*. First you bring me to another dimension and then tell me Gabe's insane and going to start a war. We're in some kind of bunker, and you want me to pretend we're eating lunch in the dorm cafeteria?"

"No, I just want you to stop acting like, I dunno." He stopped. "Never mind."

Now he was the one who wouldn't meet her eyes. Did she hurt his feelings? His mouth took on a downturned tilt, and then the guilt hit her hard. No matter what she learned, he was still the Matt she knew in there somewhere.

She sighed. "I'm sorry. I don't mean to lash out, I'm just...scared."

Matt spun his head. "You don't need to be. You're safe here. I'll make sure of it."

"Can you really promise that? You mention war, and we're in a base, which seems like the opposite of going to a safe place." She had to know what she was dealing with, even if he'd figure out she knew more than she let on. She dared to ask, "They seem prepared for a war already, and really, what's your part in this? You're not Illirin. It has nothing to do with you."

He said, "It does have to do with me. My parents made sure to tell me how important it was that I learn everything about this place. People like us are rarer than red diamonds. Being gifted means you have a stake in Illirin—it just does." He twisted the signet ring engraved with an *M* around his finger. "More importantly, we have friends here, and I want to help them. You don't understand what the Seers have endured. They've been persecuted forever, subjugated by not one, but four other traits, and I'm going to help them even the playing field."

"You want to be some kind of hero to these people?" Lea slurped another spoonful.

"No, it's not like that."

"Then what's in it for you?"

Matt stopped twisting the ring, resting his fingertip over the top. "Honestly, I do want to help these people, but more importantly I must keep the promises that have been made."

He seemed distant, keeping his thoughts to himself. What did those promises entail? Judging from his lies, it couldn't be anything good.

She leaned her head over the table so he would look at her. "You don't have to keep them, you know."

"I do." He smiled, though not quite naturally. "And, I want to. You asked what I'd gain, and it's simple. It never hurts to have friends in power. In my business classes they encourage it, call it 'networking,' and I'm networking inter-dimensionally. I'm sure my professors would be proud."

Perking back up, he ate a bite of his sandwich. "Besides, I can help make a change here, real change. Things will be more equal for everyone, and the persecution will stop. If you think about it, 'equality' is an empty word at home too. We could benefit from some of the ideas the Seers have."

Lea didn't know what to say. As Matt spoke, he became more confident, like he understood how to be himself in Illirin more than on Earth. He was so certain he'd make a difference here. But how? What could he do? She remembered the guards in the hall. Maybe he was trading Earth's secrets?

"Sounds great, but what exactly can you do to make this change? Give these guys some guns?" She nodded her head toward the guard standing by the door. "They've got TVs and intercoms, but carry swords? Doesn't that seem bizarre?"

Matt laughed and had to cover his mouth to keep from spitting out his food. "Sorry, I'm sorry. I forget you don't know," he said. "Explosive-based weapons like guns don't work, because combustive fuels can't ignite in four-dimensional space. The elements found in gunpowder, oil, gasoline don't exist here. Everything is powered by the aether. The energy becomes electricity. It's perfect, clean unlimited power."

A spark seemed to flash in his eyes. "Doesn't that sound incredible? Just imagine."

"It is incredible." It was. If Earth had the same resource, it would change everything. She would have thought more about it, but she noticed his smile. He seemed genuine, or at least what she thought was genuine.

He inhaled deeply. "The aether is magnificent. When you touch it, you feel an immense connection, and for the first time in your life you feel…whole." The awe in his face was nothing she'd ever seen before. "Haven't you always felt like you were alone? Like you saw the world on a different wavelength, that no one else quite 'got' you?"

Lea caught herself staring at him without answering. Of course people 'got' her, at least Gabe did.

Matt said, "I knew the instant I met you that you were like me. You knew what it was to be unique. You were the only other one who could understand." He paused. "I want to help you feel it, to know what I do. We aren't outcasts. We're extraordinary."

How do you respond to that? She had always been alone, but that was her choice, wasn't it? Now she wasn't so sure. No one saw through her mask until Gabe, but he was Illirin. He didn't fit in with the normal mold either, which matched with Matt's theory. Where was the proof? The answer was simple; the proof was in the aether—magic.

"I do want to learn," she admitted.

"And you will."

With the enthusiasm from Matt fading into the background, a quiet settled between them again. Lea took purposeful bites of her sandwich. Could he hear how loud she chewed? That tension exaggerated everything, every tick, each nervous flinch broadcasted to the world.

Matt cleared his throat. "So…um…that dress looks pretty on you." Pink graced his cheeks, and he turned back to his lunch.

Heat rushed into her own face, though more from embarrassment than anything. "Thanks, but it's not really my style. I'm more of a denim and earth tones kinda girl. Ya know, understated and boring, etcetera."

He replied while still looking into his soup. "It suits you more. You're the polar opposite of boring."

The wooden chair squeaked under her. "That the magnetic pole or true North?"

"Magnetic," he said, his shoulders relaxing. "Definitely magnetic."

"Business classes, really? You're too nerdy to be a business major." She felt herself ease against the chair back.

"Yeah? What makes me so nerdy I can't get an MBA?"

"I'm not aware many CEOs have video game speed records."

He chuckled and crossed his arms behind his head dramatically. "I think having the world speed record for *Street Fighter* is a claim to Internet notoriety *and* an excellent resume bullet point."

They ate their lunch and shifted their conversation to discussing their old video game tournaments. Matt tried to explain how button mashing would never overcome strategy. Lea counter argued, and actually made Matt spit-take with her "logic."

She was able to relax enough to enjoy her old friend, even if it wouldn't last. Those days were long gone, filed away in the past. A little pain nudged at her heart. Matt seemed like the guy she remembered, but there was something new in him. Maybe she was catching glimpses under his mask. She didn't like what she saw.

When lunch ended, Matt escorted her back to her room. He pointed out the different functions on the intercom. "So if you need anything at all, ask for help. Someone will come right away."

"You won't be around?" Lea asked.

He shook his head. "Not for tonight, but I'll probably be back tomorrow night or the following day. I'll come here as soon as I can, and help teach you to tap the aether. It's an instinctual thing, so it might be hard to explain."

"Where are you going?"

"I can't tell you."

"Why?" She moved to try and look him in the eyes.

He rolled his shoulders back. "I have something I need to do. I'll be back soon, I promise."

"I don't under—"

"You'll be taken care of, don't worry. I'll be back." He softly touched her shoulder and kissed her on her forehead.

She froze.

He gave her a weak smile as he left.

A damp imprint remained on her forehead where he kissed her. It felt wrong. She looked at the closed door and sighed. It didn't even need a lock. How long could she breathe that thin air, five, ten minutes? She wanted to follow him, find out what was happening. The tingle on her neck intensified. He was up to something, and it wasn't good. Her gut agreed—it couldn't be good.

Twenty-Two

The pounding headache felt like a relaxing scalp massage compared to the hurt in the rest of Gabe's body. He untangled his surprisingly unbroken limbs and sat up against the rough bark of the tree. Must be evening, the sunlight dipped behind the branches allowing only thin slivers of yellow to peek between the shadows. But, where was he?

A pain sharper than the rest drew him to his wrists. The shackles were still there smeared with some blood from digging into his skin. No, it really happened…he got her killed.

He bent over his knees and began to shake, not fast, but in slow waves as realization of his loss sharpened into focus. He wept hot tears into his hands and wrapped his wings tight around his shoulders, as if they could protect him from the pain. He got her killed. Lea was dead. He got her killed.

His chest ached, and once again he felt the physical manifestation of a broken heart. Lea was dead, her eyes forever stuck open in that terrified gaze. Both his parents had been murdered. Each lifeless face flashed into his mind, their bodies limp and bloody. One gruesome death was enough to scar someone, and he carried three. When he closed his eyes, he saw nothing but blood, and open, horrifying reality greeted him. What had he done to cause this?

The Winged riddle, it was always about the riddle. He gave Nor what he wanted, and he killed Lea anyway. Whatever moisture left in his throat disappeared. He gave Nor the riddle, and now he would find the Stand. Gabe doomed Illirin to a war they'd lose to Nor. He traded his trait's safety for what, a broken promise? His mistake would screw over a world, maybe even two.

The enormity of Gabe's errors crushed him, squeezing from outside and within his ribs so he couldn't breathe. If his own despair killed him, it would be a fitting end. He made too many mistakes, and now it was too late to do anything about it. How could he fix what he had done?

He couldn't bring back Lea, his father, or his mother. He couldn't undo his relationship with Heather and losing her too. Breaking the Schism to meet her was his first mistake. If he hadn't created a life on Earth, Heather wouldn't have died in that car, he wouldn't have met Lea, and she'd be safe. He could've been there for his father, maybe protected him.

It stung as he wiped the tears from his bloodshot eyes. Wishing he led a different life wasn't going to change anything. Dwelling on it only drove him further down his spiral of self-blame. So, he couldn't atone for giving the riddle to Nor, but he could do his best to stop him. Maybe if the Winged attacked first, before the Stand was in place, they'd have a chance.

Gabe stood and stretched some of the ache from his wings. The energy that brought him there returned to him. He could blame himself all he wanted, but the truth was none of it would have happened without Nor. Nor was behind his parents deaths. Nor murdered Lea in cold blood. His own blood boiled again.

Nor won't get away with it! He deserved to die for his existing crimes, let alone what he planned to do.

With his renewed fury, Gabe took to the air and found enough landmarks to spot his location. Not far from Concord, an integrated city in Tailed territory, so he made his way there and found a small clothing store.

He balled up the short chains on the shackles into his fists and ducked inside. Heading to the back, he glanced around. Coast clear. He needed something to cover the cuffs for now, so he could wait until he returned to Union to bother getting them off. Good, they had Winged jackets in XXL. It would have to do.

He finished putting it on, and then turned the corner. It didn't look like the clerk had noticed him come in, perfect. Act casual. Nor's spies could be anywhere.

"Do you have a phone I can use?" He walked up to the register.

"Sure, it's back here." The clerk led Gabe to a doorway behind the counter. A phone hung on the wall of the break room.

Gabe nodded. "Thanks." He waited for the clerk to leave and then dialed Ceru's private number.

"Hello?" Ceru answered.

"Ceru," Gabe whispered, "It's me."

"Are you all right? Where are you? Where have you been? What happened?" He fired questions off one after another.

"Sssshhhh. No time. Is the Winged Minister in Union or still back home?"

Ceru gasped. "Union…why? What's happened?"

"I'll be there by morning." Gabe hung up. He couldn't explain since he wasn't somewhere private enough to speak. More than that, he needed to hold on to this anger to keep him going. He couldn't afford to delve back into the pit until he completed his mission. The only good he could do was at least try to save Illirin from a madman. He had to try.

Gabe arrived in Union before dawn. He found a scrap of metal to pick the shackles in an alley before snatching a couple hours of sleep—about all his mind would allow him anyway. He got up and headed for the Winged centre, where he'd find the Winged Minister.

Dirt coated his jeans, and his cut-up wrists left trails of blood down his forearms. Some of his white hair got loose from the ponytail and hung in his face. He marched through the doors of the official building, and while he certainly didn't look like the Winged Councilman from the posters, he carried himself with purpose.

Guards blocked the staircase leading to the Minister's meeting room. With stiff steps, Gabe approached the men. They remained at attention, eyes locked forward like statues who never needed to blink.

"Exc—" The receptionist coughed with a squeak in her voice. "Sorry, excuse me."

Gabe turned his head.

She startled and held her hands close to her chest, though they seemed to shake even then. He must look frightening. "Do you have an appointment? We have to do—" Another squeaky cough. "Um, background checks and there's a wait—"

"This is an emergency." Gabe pointed to the Winged pin, making sure she saw the bloody gouges in his wrist.

"Councilman," she gasped. "I didn't recognize…" The receptionist fixed the kink in her skirt and nodded to the guards. "Of course you've been vetted. I'm sorry. Yes, the Minister's first appointment isn't for an hour so you should have time to discuss—" She stared at his wrist and his bloodstained jeans. "Yes. Okay, I'll let him know you're here." She hurried back to the front desk.

One of the guards pivoted and walked up the stairs. Gabe followed. The guard stood by the side of the door, knocked a couple times, and opened it inward.

The anger that had pulled Gabe forward this far focused into an energy he could use to bolster his argument. He must convince the Minister to fight Nor's men first, before they brought the war to the rest of Illirin. His father had said the Minister was honorable and always willing to listen to his thoughts, and in this case, Gabe prayed he'd give Jeken's son as much trust.

Inside the receiving office, the Minister sat behind a wide desk, leaning over his elbows. The glow of a screen reflected off his face. He lifted off the desk and sat up, his wings folded neat and tucked formally behind him like someone lying one hand atop another.

"Come on in, Councilman." The Minister's white teeth stood out against his indigo coloring, though his smile vanished as Gabe walked through the doors. "What happened? I left a message with your office yesterday. I was hoping to meet with you."

The Minister stood and extended his hand. He almost pulled away, like he wasn't quite sure what the procedures dictated when the Councilman showed up looking like a tattered refugee.

Gabe reached to complete the handshake. "I'm sorry to barge in on you like this, Minister, but it's an emergency. I wish we had different circumstances for our first meeting."

"And what circumstances are those?" He gestured to the chair in front of the desk.

Gabe didn't sit. His body wouldn't let him even pretend to relax. "Heten Nor held me captive. He's planning to start a war, and with the Stand of Unity, he can have his human wizard tear Illirin apart."

"Wait. What?" The Minister's neat wings splayed wide.

"Very soon he'll have the Stand. We need to stop him before he gets it working, or it'll be too late." The words tumbled out fast and unfiltered. "I escaped from the compound, and I know where it is. I can mark it on a map. It's not too far into the desert. If you call the generals now, they can get the army there by tonight. Probably really late, but we don't have a lot of time."

The Minister's chest heaved in one slow motion. "Back up, Councilman. How do you know all of this? You're asking me to declare war on the Seers, on your word alone?"

Whatever miracle that kept Gabe calm stopped working, and he smacked his hands flat on the edge of the desk. The two guards inside the room jumped forward, blades pointed at Gabe.

"He has *all* the riddles!" Gabe let that sink in while the weight of his shame pulled him down again. A confession without absolution.

The Minister waved the guards back. He looked Gabe over, closed-mouth and motionless but for the flicker in his eyes. Whatever chance Gabe had to earn the Minister's respect was gone. His father died to protect the riddle, and here Gabe came, begging for a war to fix his inadequacies. It didn't matter what the Minister thought of him as long as they stopped Nor.

"I swear…we have to act fast, please." Gabe kept from making eye contact.

A long pause followed, filled with the sound of a single finger tapping the tune of the Minister's thoughts. "Tell me everything you know, then I will call General Betil."

A quick flight landed Gabe atop the balcony of the Council Hall. He hurried through the doors and down the wide staircase into the main lobby.

Ceru had been waiting near the entrance. Gabe passed by him heading toward his office.

"What's happened? Are you all right?" Ceru ran after.

The door swung open and banged into the chair rail. "The Minister's declared war with the Seers. The army leaves soon, and I've got to deliver some information."

When Ceru closed the office door behind them, Gabe braced himself for the barrage of questions.

"War? I thought things were going well. What happened?" Ceru forced his wings closed.

He silently approached the desk, leaving his back turned to Ceru. "Not long from now, Nor will have the Stand of Unity. He does have a wizard working with him. Our only chance is to strike first and hopefully weaken his forces before they can activate the Stand."

"That's impossible. Even if Nor could figure out its location, he couldn't retrieve it without the final riddle."

Gabe winced as he imagined the eyes of his uncle piercing the back of his head. He let him down, he let his father down, and he failed his office. He failed them all, everyone, especially Lea.

"What happened?" Ceru asked again.

He couldn't bear to look at him. He exhaled slowly. "You can only take so much before you shatter. Despite how I look, the only thing holding me together is how much I need redemption…and vengeance."

"I don't understand. Tell me."

He turned his head to see the confusion and worry written on Ceru's face. "I gave it to him, and he killed her anyway. An innocent human girl, whose only crime was knowing me." He choked, the tears filling his eyes without permission. "Nor murdered her. I got her killed."

His last memory of Lea came to his mind, a lifeless heap on the floor. He leaned on his hand against the desk to keep from falling. "Everyone I touch is killed. You probably need to watch yourself. I'm a hazard to your well-being."

Ceru reached out to him, but he pulled away. "You didn't cause their deaths. You're a victim, too. It's not your fault."

He shook his head. "Maybe not, but this war is, and the least I can do is try to win it. I must try to clean up the mess I made."

"You can't blame yourself. There were three others who gave Nor their secrets."

Gabe replied, "They didn't know the stakes like I did. My father died protecting the riddle, and I gave it up for *nothing*. I failed. You put your money on the wrong guy."

"I don't think I did." Ceru walked in front of Gabe, forcing him to see his face.

Gabe expected disappointment, but the downturned eyes and furrowed brow looked more like concern. Why couldn't Ceru just be upset with him? As much as he wanted compassion, he needed to keep the fire hot. The only thing he had left was to kill Nor, and for that he needed his rage.

He inhaled to compose himself once again. "Either way, we need to stop Nor before he uses the Stand. I'm going into the fight with the soldiers, and when I find him, I will kill him myself."

Ceru shook his head. "No, you can't go into the battle. He's most protected at his base, and with the wizard there, heading straight for Nor is suicide!"

Gabe proceeded to go around the desk to find the papers he needed. He opened drawers and pulled stacks out on the desk.

Ceru yelled, "You don't even deny it!"

"What do you want me to say?"

"That you'll stay here and act like a leader, not a lunatic."

"Sorry, no can do. I kill Nor. It's all I have." Gabe shoved a folded paper in his pocket.

"That's not true!" Ceru said, "Me, Aime, your whole damn trait!"

He stopped looking through the papers for a second and glanced up at Ceru. "I'm sorry I can't keep my promise, but maybe you can. If we can't stop it and the war comes to Union, please get Aime to safety for me."

"You can do it yourself."

Gabe kicked the side of the desk. "Damn it Ceru! I *will* fight in this battle. It is my only chance to fix it. Once everyone knows Nor has the Stand, they'll know what I've done. I have to be there, don't you understand?"

Ceru sighed. "I don't agree with it, but I get your reasons." He frowned. "This isn't like you."

"It isn't me."

"I hope you come around soon."

Gabe rolled up the maps and headed for the door. "Wouldn't put money on it." He firmly grasped Ceru's forearm and shook. "Thank you for everything. You were as much a friend to me as you were to my father, and I appreciate it more than you know."

"Always." He put his hand over Gabe's. "Come home."

He replied with a weak smile and left the office. He had to get the maps to General Betil and set off with the army. If they left soon, they could make it to the desert by that night, and even that seemed too slow. Time, never enough time.

The Stand of Unity—an artifact, a relic that conjured images of something both powerful and valuable. No one alive knew what it looked like, but most imagined the Stand to be a golden staff encrusted with jewels, an ornate representation of the power it possessed. Some thought the Stand must be enormous in order to hold two worlds together.

How wrong they were. Heten Nor grinned at the disconnect, seeing the reality he held in his hands. The Stand was a simple metal staff about shoulder height. The head flared out with five flat sides that came to a point, like the shape of a carved jewel. Each side engraved with a trait symbol and some words in the ancient languages belonging to them. No jewels, no gold, and so unassuming that it could have rested against the wall in someone's home without drawing notice.

The extensive measures the First Council went through to protect the Stand seemed almost unnecessary. No one would think to steal such a boring and worthless hunk of metal. Well, not for its monetary value anyway.

Heten gripped the staff, and the power embedded within flowed freely into his palm like a charge. Worth more than any riches, this power could give him everything. At long last, he'd have the respect he deserved from the other traits.

Even as a Councilman, he could see the disdain in the eyes of the others, especially the damned Winged. Did the gift of flight and superior strength make them better? No, but that didn't stop them from walking, or would it be *flying*, over the Seers. They spouted principles of equality, but all the while enjoyed the benefits of their ancient victories. The best lands and most profitable businesses were always wasted on the arrogant Winged.

He ran his fingers over the simple carvings, and his eyes lit with a promise. The lucky would soon become the unfortunate. The Winged would never accept him, never accept losing all they won with their *blessed* strength. With the wizard doing the dirty work, he could reap the rewards. The rest of the traits would welcome him for delivering them from such an unbalanced world. More than an emperor, he'd be the savior of Illirin.

"Are you done admiring it now?" Matt wiped the dirt from his face. "It took a lot longer to get here and find this thing, even with my help to speed the journey."

Heten smirked. "Blame the overprotective councilmen who decided to hide it deep within the mountain on a remote island. We have the Stand now, time is ours. Don't worry so much."

"If your little show for Makai pissed him off enough, the Winged army could already be there. We have to install the Stand and ready the forces to defend the compound."

"Our army is waiting for us outside of Union. First, we strike the heart. The riddles clearly indicated the Stand can only work at the center of Illirin." Heten continued to spin the staff between his fingers while they walked out of the cave.

"What?" Matt stopped. "The army is gone? But Lea…the Winged will attack the compound!"

Heten flicked his wrist. "And they won't be defending Union. Don't worry about your little girlfriend. I left her floor and the ones above guarded enough. What's the worst that happens? They capture her and try to hold the compound, thus dividing their forces. Win. Win."

"You're using her—"

He turned his head to Matt. "Angry you didn't get to first? You'll still get your chance. We'll re-capture the compound, and you'll rescue your princess and become a hero. You should be thanking me, I'll be a good…what do the humans say… 'wing man?'" He laughed. "Oh, the irony."

"If they hurt her Nor…" Matt gritted his teeth.

"They won't. She's an innocent and a *human*. Stop worrying your spiky little head, and prepare yourself. We need to get to Union, set the Stand, and join the army for our first of many great victories." Heten held the staff for Matt to put his hand on as well. "Are you ready, Wizard?"

Matt glared a moment before looking back to the Stand. He grasped it below the top, his eyes widening as the power flowed into his skin. "Yes." He smiled at Heten. "I am."

Twenty-Three

Crisp white stars cut through the inky night of the desert sky. Without the lights of the city, true black blanketed the world with a darkness that you could almost bundle up in, safe and warm. Gabe spent what he assumed was hours staring at the pinpricks of light above. A good way to empty his mind and meditate, and after his restless nightmare-filled "sleep," he definitely needed a different way to recover. It didn't recuperate like sleep did, but it was better than nothing. How many hours had he slept since he awoke from the tranquilizer? Not sure, but he could count them on one hand.

The shade of black seemed to lighten, and the stars faded off in the distance. Dawn hadn't broken yet, but he could hear the others waking and moving around. It was time. Today he would pay back Nor for all he stole from him. His fury had an outlet at last.

Gabe moved slowly to allow his muscles to stretch. He spent a few minutes loosening his stiff shoulders and knees, and he did the same exercises he saw the others doing. Gazing out over the makeshift camp, hundreds of Winged soldiers geared up for battle, and a good number looked to be about his age. Just like him, they'd never been in a real assault before. They shared more in common than they had differences.

In some ways, he felt more prepared than the others. Gabe possessed a drive they couldn't possibly match, and real motivation had the power to overcome any shortcoming. Lea's near-obsessive determination taught him that. Even then, when they met that night outside the Union, she had a fierce energy bottled inside, a contagious spirit.

The vice in his chest tightened, and he banished the memory. Lea's lesson would help avenge her. Very soon.

He opened the pack and pulled out the arm guards he brought with him. One by one, he strapped the curved metal guards to his shoulders, upper arms, and forearms. They were the only shields the soldiers used. The silvery cloth of the uniforms could deflect glancing blows, but it was hardly armor. Winged fighters used speed and agility as a defense without relying on sheets of metal to cover their bodies. Gabe tested his arm guard with his fist, perfectly fitted. It would do nicely.

Just over the crest of a dune, General Betil finished discussing plans with the other generals. Gabe rolled his shoulders one more time and straightened his uniform before catching up to him. He tapped the general's arm. "Where do you want me to go?"

"Remain here with the reinforcements, of course." His eyes traced Gabe's uniform and noticed the arm guards strapped and ready. "You thought—"

"Yes, I'm fighting with the army. I've been here before and I can recognize the layout, maybe get to where we need faster."

"You're no trained soldier, and I don't believe our Councilman should risk his life in battle."

Gabe clenched his fists at his sides. "I was the second in my class when I came of age. I can fight. Just because I didn't join the army doesn't mean I don't know what I'm doing." He took a breath. "Nor had my mother murdered and had my father tortured and assassinated. This battle involves me more than anyone else."

"Which is exactly why you should stay out of it. You can't objectively follow orders."

"I will, I swear! You must allow me to fight. This is my fault. It's the only way I can make up for the mess I've made. Give me this chance, I beg you." Gabe stood at attention, to show the general he was disciplined; he couldn't stop his hands from shaking.

Betil exhaled. "I'm sorry, but the answer is no. I respect your passion, and you've done your part by bringing this to the Minister's attention. You've done what you can in your position. We'll capture the Stand and keep things from getting out of control."

"But—"

"No. You must remain here to meet with Councilman Brennan and his forces when they arrive. *That* is your duty. Leave the combat to the trained soldiers."

Gabe sighed and dipped his head to Betil. "Fine. Do as you must."

Betil bowed deeper in return and continued on to his group of soldiers, while Gabe walked away in the opposite direction.

Stay back at base and wait…yeah, right. Brennan could figure things out for himself. Gabe had to take responsibility for causing this war, but that was only part of it. He needed to kill Nor himself. His parents deserved justice…Lea deserved justice. No one else knew how much Nor hated him, or what he had taken away. This was personal.

Gabe shuffled in with a group of soldiers assigned to the first wave in General Jural's unit. They wore the same uniform, so as long as he kept his head down he could blend in well enough.

The ranks of soldiers assembled on the uneven sands. Straight rows crested in waves of silver stretching over the dunes. Gabe lowered his head. Would someone recognize him? He was just another speck in the gray ocean waiting to crash into Nor's base, but every glance sent a wad of dry spit into his throat to keep him from breathing.

General Betil addressed the collected soldiers. "Remember your training, work swiftly and precisely, and we will succeed. Though many will defend in close quarters with tri-blades, Seers are notoriously gifted with magic. Fortunately, tapping aether takes concentration, and in fast-paced battles they should only have enough time to use a natural element. Expect fire, electricity, or forceful blasts of wind, but watch out for anything more. We should be able to defend ourselves with arm guards and speed. The few soldiers who can tap aether will lead and protect the rear of each unit." He put his fist on his heart. "May the wind be to your back. Good luck!"

The men around Gabe saluted, and he followed suit just a second behind the rest. Gabe felt eerily at peace. He wanted this chance to face Nor more than anything. Going through a bunch of others to get to him was a technicality.

The time for the battle quickly approached. Gabe double-checked the clasp on his sheath and elbowed the solder to his left.

"Sorry," he muttered.

The solder turned, and instead of the obligatory 'okay,' he stammered, "Councilman?"

Crap! Gabe turned his head the other way, but it was too late.

The soldier saluted. "Councilman...what..."

Other faces twisted their direction. Gabe shook his head. No, this wasn't happening. "I, uh, I get that all the time. It's the hair, right?" His nervous laugh wouldn't seem too out of place. Some of the men whispered around him, all saying how he looked like the Councilman. Normally, no one would notice such a small commotion, but even the tiniest ripple drew attention in the motionless waters of soldiers at attention.

General Jural approached, and Gabe ducked below the man in front of him. His heart pounded. The soldiers stopped murmuring and saluted their general. Gabe kept his head down and held his breath. He waited. Jural had to give a speech or orders or something...he had to say something. Why didn't he say anything?

"Councilman." General Jural's voice came from his side and not the front of the unit as he expected. Gabe straightened and looked to his left to see Jural at the edge of his line. "May I speak with you?" he continued.

Gabe's heart sank into his feet, and he forced his legs to carry him out of the group. Great, now one more lecture about how he was acting like an idiot. He didn't want to hear it.

"Councilman." Jural spoke without judgment in his voice. "You're not assigned to my unit. I don't think you've been assigned to the first or second waves at all, actually. You should remain and wait for the reinforcements."

It sounded like Jural hadn't heard Betil's order. At least Gabe kept his respect. He nodded. "Oh, yes. You're right. I was mistaken. I'll head right over there, thank you."

Jural gave him a firm nod and returned to the head of his unit. "Follow your unit leader's orders. Move out." He saluted, and the army broke into smaller groups before taking to the air.

Jural joined his unit in the sky, and as soon as he turned his back, Gabe ran a few feet and bounded into the air as well. He flew up to the back of the unit, and now in the air, he was home free. No one could keep him back now.

Several Seer guards engaged the first soldiers as soon as they landed. The scouts had alerted the compound, so the assault wasn't a surprise. Even though the Seers had warning and could prepare, the Winged soldiers made incredible progress toward the door. Gabe landed toward the back of the unit and saw more Seers pour out of the compound.

A small group of Seer soldiers came around the corner from behind.

Gabe held his tri-blade and turned to face the one on his side. A blade came down toward Gabe's shoulder, and he blocked with his guard before turning to counter with his blade. Afterward, the Seer's eyes glowed, concentrating as he drew the energy into his body.

Magic already, how could he stop that?

The Seer moved his hands.

Oh crap! On instinct, Gabe folded his wings in front of his face, just in time for the heat of fire to hit him. The outside slats of his wings stung. He rushed forward, opened his wings, and drove his blade into the Seer soldier.

The other men around him took out the remaining soldiers attacking the back of the group. The unit surged forward toward the doors. They must have gotten in.

Gabe followed the flow of soldiers through the doors. The others seemed to have a plan and broke off into smaller groups to clear the hallways on the first floor. Scuffles of fighting came from left and right, above and below. The men next to him motioned for him to follow.

Being one of the last to enter the building, he didn't spot any Seers. The soldiers closer to the front took care of most of the fighting. They must have done a good job, because they delved deeper into the compound with ease.

The group Gabe tailed made it to the stairwell, and with one soldier left behind to guard the entrance, the rest went ahead. The clanging of boots against the metal stairs echoed throughout the enclosed space. Gabe covered one ear to muffle the clatter. If they hadn't known they were there, they sure did now. He followed the flow of men down to the first basement level and glanced through the window on the door of the landing. It was the prison level. He recognized the area—at least he thought he did. It all looked the same. Gabe jumped back in line and continued down the next few flights.

The group of soldiers went through the doors on the fourth floor down, but he kept going. One man turned to motion for him to follow.

Gabe shook his head. "Different orders, go ahead."

The soldier nodded and went through with the rest of the group.

On the floors above Gabe, metal clanged amidst more shouting. A loud bang echoed when someone fell to the floor on the ceiling overhead. Odd, shouldn't there be more noise than that?

He continued down the stairs and checked the doors. Why weren't any of the soldiers rushing into the stairwell? He saw men run up and down hallways, but none came in. Shouldn't there be more? Maybe they were on the other side of the compound, fighting the other units. He took a breath. He needed to focus on what was ahead of him, not the others. He had to find Nor and the Stand.

He arrived on the bottom floor and looked through the doorway, empty. He readied his blade and kept his eyes open as he emerged into the hall. Through the window of the first door, he saw a small bedroom with several bunks and lockers. They must be the barracks. Gabe checked a few more rooms, all empty. The entire floor appeared deserted, and from the looks of it, they were missing a lot of soldiers.

Then, right above him, Gabe heard voices. Immediately after, the thunder of footsteps echoed from the ceiling. He tried to count the pairs of footfalls, but there were too many. That was a good sign. Where there was an army, there might be something to protect.

He squeezed the hilt of his tri-blade and ran up the flight of stairs. He cracked the door and took a look. Groups of Seer soldiers moved in both directions. Where was that area that General Betil pointed out? It was fairly deep down, so this might be it.

Gabe closed the door and leaned against the wall. *Breathe in and out.* His pulse throbbed in his neck and forearms. He couldn't hesitate, or he would lose momentum. *Focus, remember why you came.* He told the generals he needed to stop Nor to save Illirin, to do the right thing. But behind each slow blink, Lea's lifeless body lay on the floor of that cell, and his rage returned in full. Revenge. His teeth clenched and wings flared.

He threw the door wide open, leapt into the hall, and sprinted toward the group of soldiers. Gabe's unexpected arrival gave him the advantage, and he struck down the first two soldiers before they could turn. The narrow hall allowed only two at a time to reach him, turning Gabe's reckless attack on ten into a manageable fight. He fell back on his knowledge of combat from the trials at school, but most of it didn't seem to apply. He ran on intuition and luck.

He blocked two more attacks with his arm guards and slashed his tri-blade back into one soldier's arm. Most attacked with blades, but Gabe had to dodge the occasional fire blast or electric shock.

After one soldier threw a fire blast at him, Gabe bent down and charged toward him. He stabbed his blade into the man's side, and then blocked the next blow. The strikes came one after another. His body moved on its own. More men arrived out of the corner of his eye, but he pressed forward. No going back now.

He took his fair share of hits. Cuts and burns stung on places he didn't know he had. He ignored the pain and concentrated on his surroundings. With luck, his constant movement and unrelenting assault kept him alive. The Seer soldiers even seemed to notice that nothing would stop him. His new opponents had an air of hesitation and fear, which made it easier to fight as they got clumsy.

With his drive pushing him onward, Gabe barely even noticed when he cleared the hallway of soldiers. He kept going. He had to find Nor.

Around the next corner, two more soldiers rushed at him. The first cut his shoulder. He ducked, pushing him with his wings, but the Seer moved to Gabe's front.

From behind the soldiers, someone gasped loudly. A girl in a red gown had stepped out from one of the rooms.

He paused...Lea?

The soldier lunged forward, planting his tri-blade squarely in Gabe's stomach, and his own blade clattered to the metal floor. He doubled over, pain piercing through his middle. The boot kicked him in his wound, and his vision blurred. His body banging against the stairs didn't even register. The brain must have only so much room to send signals for pain.

He lay at the bottom of the stairwell clutching his stomach. It wasn't helping; nothing dulled his searing abdomen. His fingers tingled cold even with the warm blood flowing over like a blanket.

Gabe clenched his jaw, eyes squeezed shut. He failed again, but this time he wouldn't have to see the consequences for himself. It was a small consolation. Betil was right—he wasn't a soldier. At least he did what he could. He let himself believe it. Why not, he didn't have long left to think on it anyway.

Right before the guard stabbed him, Lea saw the Winged guy's face. His white hair, blue skin...he looked like Gabe. It had to be him. How many other blue Winged guys with white ponytails were there?

She moved further out of the room to see, but a guard running down the hall knocked her back inside. She cracked the door and watched the last guard take off around the corner. She took a deep breath and then ran down the stairs to find him.

Lea stifled a gasp, only because she couldn't waste her precious breath. It *was* Gabe. Red blood painted his hands and pooled on the floor. His arms gave no resistance when she moved his hands to see the damage. It was bad, very bad. The scar from his previous injury looked like a paper cut in comparison. How could she stop such terrible bleeding? She pressed her hands hard against the wound, and he grunted in reply.

"Oh, Gabe…" she whispered.

Gabe's eyelids fluttered open. After a moment, he smiled and then began to laugh. The effort pained him and cut his unnerving laughter short as he curled back in on himself. He squeezed his eyes shut again. His breathing started rapid and shallow, but then it slowed as his shoulders relaxed and he lost consciousness.

Lea shook her head and put more pressure on the wound.

Don't die. Please.

She had to do something. She exhaled and took deep, slow breaths of the crappy air. If only she could tap the aether, then she could breathe, or even think. Magic was the only way to save him, but she didn't know how.

The intense tingling on the back of her neck told her something was horribly wrong. No shit, Sherlock! She didn't need that freaking warning now, it was too late for warnings!

She thrust all her weight against Gabe's stomach, desperately trying to staunch the stream of blood. The color in his face was draining away with his life. He was bleeding out. Her mind grew fuzzy. She was running out of time.

"Don't die. Please, Gabe!" She closed her eyes and concentrated. What did that stupid journal say? It said feeling magic was instinct. Instinct? Then she'd know how already, damn it. The tingling on her neck intensified, which only annoyed her more. She didn't need that, she needed the real thing.

Her eyes popped open. That's it! She *was* trying to connect to the magic around her. She let the tingling grow, giving in to it. She asked for it, and allowed the feeling to overwhelm her. In her mind she repeated over and over, *Please heal, please don't die. Please.*

The odd sensation that started on her neck spread throughout her body. It filled her head and began to course through her, from her arms through her torso, and to her legs. A rush filled her lungs, air, glorious air. She could breathe.

The energy flowed out her hands and into Gabe's stomach.

Please heal, don't die. Stop bleeding, heal, heal!

She didn't know what to do, what to think, or whether she had to do anything special. *Please work. Please heal him.* She continued to focus the flow of energy through her body and into his. The current grew from a babbling brook into a raging river, and she nearly lost control with its power. She stopped trying, and allowed it to rush through and out of her. *Please, heal him.*

After several long minutes, the flowing energy slowed and the feeling disappeared from her body. She removed her blood-coated hands from Gabe's stomach and peeled back the flap of his shirt.

How was it possible?

She rubbed her fingers over the soft, cobalt skin, the wound completely gone—the scar too. Even the injuries on his wings and face had healed. She put her fingers by his nose, still breathing. He was okay, more than okay.

Lea couldn't stop the grin that came across her face. She did it! She saved him *and* figured out how to tap the aether. She filled her lungs, relishing the cold rush in her nose. And Gabe should wake up any second. Then, she could smack him for being a reckless ass and tell him everything that happened.

As she waited for his eyes to open, her excitement faded. He didn't wake up. Well, crap, how were they going to get out of there?

The clamor of weapons and shouts echoed down the stairwell. Even though she healed him, they weren't safe. With all the fighting, they couldn't make it out of the compound without being seen. On top of that, she'd have to carry Gabe. Yeah, did that once, no way she could drag him either far or fast. Maybe there was a thinning nearby they could use to escape to Earth. She couldn't open it from Earth, but the last time she easily went through from this side.

She exhaled and focused on the sixth sense she used to rely on without ever knowing what it really was. Now she tried with purpose to feel the direction of a thinning. The sensation came to her clearer than it had in the past. She sensed one nearby. Well, close enough. It had to be across the width of the compound. It felt about the same level they were on, so maybe she wouldn't have to climb any stairs hauling Gabe.

No point in wasting time. She knelt down, grabbed his arms, and strained to pull his dead weight onto her back. After she got him up high enough, she was able to stand, although looking like the Hunchback of Notre Dame with a pair of legs dragging behind her. He better be grateful. She was never gonna let him forget how she hoisted his heavy ass all over creation, never. At least she hoped they'd survive long enough for her to lord this over him until the end of time.

Lea elbowed the door open and shuffled into the empty halls of the barracks. The area seemed deserted, but the battles raging upstairs might come down. She could move faster if she didn't have to keep hoisting his butt from sliding off of her back. She hobbled down another hallway and sensed the thinning getting closer.

Hefting Gabe again, she turned another corner to find yet another hall. She stopped down the next corridor. The thinning was close, she could feel it, but it wasn't there. She knelt to slide Gabe off her side, and he dropped to the metal floor with a clang. She winced in sympathy and sat him against the wall, giving her back and knees a much-needed break.

Where was that damn thinning? Could she have been wrong? Maybe the it appeared just above them on the next floor. That would suck. They couldn't get there from here.

With a sigh, she leaned against the wall and glanced at Gabe. His body looked as good as new, but he slept on. Maybe he appeared whole on the outside but needed more time to heal all the way. Please wake up soon. What the hell was he doing there anyway?

Lea rolled her head to the other side and exhaled. Something looked weird about the wall over there. The corner of the wall and the floor seemed to turn translucent. She got up to get a closer look. The change happened so gradually that if she hadn't stopped there because of her feeling, she'd have never found it. At the rate the thinning moved, they had at least another half hour to wait before it came close enough to use.

Thundering footsteps above startled her. They were close, too close. Listening to her gut, she grabbed Gabe's metal shoulder pads and pulled. The armor cut into her palms, and she popped her elbow dragging him through the door into the closest room.

"The body's gone!" A voice boomed through the empty corridors.

Lea gasped and held her breath, afraid of even that small sound.

Another voice called back. "There's no trail. Double check the east wing."

She pulled Gabe to sit him up behind the door out of view of the window. Her sore elbow throbbed. He slid down, so his feet were still visible if someone looked through.

The rapid footsteps closed in on them.

He was so damn heavy, stupid metal crap. What the hell, Gabe!

She grabbed him around his waist, and used all her strength to hoist him up where she stood behind the door. Her grip slipped under his arms, and he slid down her front.

The fog of breath ballooned against the glass window. Someone peered inside. Every sound magnified, and the scrape of her shoe or the rattle of Gabe's armor were like the clang of a gong in her head.

A minute passed, and whoever was there continued on without noticing them. Lea allowed her newly breathable air back into her lungs. They made it—for now.

The half hour that followed oozed by slower than any other time in Lea's life, including her agonizing wait for Gabe outside the thinning on campus.

When the thinning crept into range, she grabbed Gabe and jumped through. Wherever they landed would be better than where they were now.

Twenty-Four

Birds chirping and a cool breeze greeted Gabe as he re-entered awareness. Shadows of leaves fluttered overhead, the only thing breaking the field of blue, cloudless sky. Soft lavender floated along the wind, the smell of spring and new beginnings. He glanced to the left to see a riverbank and the edges of a grassy slope. To his right, a castle sat on a nearby hill with a cobblestone road winding up to it. Serene and picturesque like a postcard, but not exactly what he predicted Heaven would look like.

He took a minute to relax and breathe the cleansing air, all the pain from before a distant memory. He was unhurt, perfect. He rested his hand on his stomach and felt smooth skin. Miraculous, but then again, this wasn't really his body.

Footsteps scuffed and the grass crinkled as someone knelt near him. He pushed himself up, and there sat Lea wearing a red gown, hair flowing around her shoulders and looking appropriately angelic.

She looked his way, and a wave of guilt swept through him.

Gabe moved to his knees, bowing his head. He whispered as if he were afraid to breach a sacred silence, "I'm so sorry, I, I can't say—" A sharp pain hit his ear. "Ow!"

He looked up, and Lea flicked him in his other ear even harder. "Ouch!" He grabbed his head. "What the...?"

Lea furrowed her brow. "And *that* is for almost getting killed! You scared the living crap outta me!"

"What?" Gabe sat back on his heels. "We're not dead?"

"No, and you're very lucky you're not." She still grimaced when she handed him a pear. "Don't you ever do that again."

He inspected his abdomen to see his torn uniform caked in dried blood and the flawless peach skin underneath. "And on Earth too, apparently..." he muttered. He turned back to Lea who spread a map out on the ground. "So, totally not complaining, but I'm pretty sure I know what a fatal wound looks like." He put his hand on his stomach. "And this isn't it. How is this possible?"

She bit her lip. "A lot has happened, and um...I can use magic. Or at least *now* I can." She pointed at his middle. "That was the first time. Like I said, you're lucky."

"You're a wizard?"

"Sorceress is the feminine for—"

"No." Gabe shook his head.

"Actually, it is—"

"No." He stood up and took a few steps away from her. This was a lie. How stupid did they think he was? He spoke through his teeth. "Lea is dead. Who are you?"

She scoffed. "What? I'm touched by your faith in my survival instincts. Thanks for the vote of confidence."

"Drop the act. You can't fool me again." He didn't blink. "I watched Nor slit her throat. Either she was a lie or you are. Which is it?"

Lea gasped. "No." She stood, but he backed further away. "Oh no, Gabe...you really saw that?"

She sounded like Lea, but so did Heather. Was that real concern in her face? He wasn't sure of anything. "Who *are* you?"

"It's me. I don't know what happened, but it's me, Lea."

"Prove it."

She sighed and sat back down in the grass. "I, um..." She snapped her fingers. "We were alone that day we met, remember? You took me back to the dorm pretending the whole time you didn't think I was crazy." She smirked. "I'm not, by the way."

Was she telling the truth? Gabe watched her for any sign of deception or for the magic to slip. He couldn't see a thing; she was good…very good. "Heather had a lot of details, too. More, I need something more." He wanted to believe her, but because he wanted to, he pushed back. He wouldn't be fooled again.

The corners of her eyes fell and her fingertips trembled in her lap. She sighed. "Fine. When you left me behind, I know you heard me. I love you, I do. A quasi-explanation and a goodbye was all I got. If you can't look at me and see how that still stings, then I don't know how else to prove I am who I say."

She was Lea, and she's alive. He flopped to the ground opposite her and frowned. "I'm sorry. And I'm sorry I doubted you. It's been…"

She reached over and squeezed his hand. "I understand."

"Nothing makes sense anymore." He hung his head and his shoulders rolled forward. He closed in, trying to block out everything. The light touch of hands graced his back, and arms squeezed his own to his sides. Lea's head rested on his shoulder, but she didn't say anything. She just held him, and it should've helped.

After a few minutes, she let go and lifted his head to have him look at her. "I'm okay, Gabe. I'm fine. So are you. We'll be okay."

"You're gonna have to define 'okay.'"

She held his cheek. "What did they do to you?"

Gabe waited for an answer to come to him. "Nothing, nothing to *me*. Though if you count psychological damage, I probably have a smidge of PTSD." He half-laughed. "Guess I'm the crazy one now."

"Is that why you were laughing when I found you?" Lea asked, a little more sincerely than he would have thought.

"No. That was at the cruel irony of fate. As I was dying, the angel who came to take me was the girl I got killed. What kind of sick sense of humor is that?" Gabe leaned back, holding himself up with his arms behind him.

Lea smiled. "Hate to disappoint you, but I'm not an angel."

He looked at her sitting in the grass, her dress bunched up under her knees. She was just as stunning as when he thought she was one. "You certainly look the part—beautiful."

Her face turned a color almost as dark as her dress. He cleared his throat. "It suits you, you obviously had different accommodations than mine."

"They didn't want me to stand out."

"No, I'm glad you were treated well. Sure as hell beats the alternative." He shook his head. "It's just...it doesn't make any sense. I mean, they had you there. Why didn't Nor kill you if he wanted? He didn't suddenly grow a conscience just because you're human, so why? Why the show for that matter?"

Lea picked up one of the pears and rubbed her thumb over the shiny skin. "I can guess why they didn't kill me."

He pushed up from his arms and sat up straighter. "Yeah?"

"I think Matt had something to do with it."

"Matt?" Gabe spat. "I'll wring that backstabbing little weasel's neck. He kidnapped you in the first place!"

"I don't think he's all bad. He seemed like he was honestly trying to help me in some way. I think he has a crush."

"Isn't that sweet," he said, remembering the horrible sneer on Matt's face when he took Lea from his arms. He caught his body tense up, and he tried to keep his anger in check. He didn't need it bubbling up right now.

"I'm just saying he probably saved my life."

"Well then, let's throw the kidnapping weasel a party."

She rolled her eyes. "Don't need to get jealous."

He balked. "You think that's what this is? No, it's that Matt's giving Nor the power to tear down the civilization of my world as we know it. No Council, no unity, nothing, and after Nor's in charge of Illirin, I'll bet you anything Matt's got his eye on Earth."

Lea didn't say anything, but she did have a curious look about her. She held the pear in her lap, cradling it in her hands as she lifted her eyes. Why was she looking at him like that?

She asked, "Did you help start a war?"

"What?"

"Did you start a war?"

Why did she ask that? Usually he could tell what she was feeling, but this was out of nowhere.

"No," he replied. "Nor started this war. He started it when he had my mother murdered, my father tortured and assassinated, and when he coerced the riddles from the Council. Nor wanted this war so he could take over Illirin—he told me as much. But if you're asking if the Winged attacked first, then yes, we did, but he forced my hand when he…"

"What?"

Gabe's jaw hung open. It was Nor's plan all along. How could he be so stupid? "Matt was right, I'm an idiot. I'm a stupid pawn."

"Gabe, what are you talking about?" She let the fruit roll out of her lap onto the flattened grass, her eyes on him.

He didn't look away. "That's why he killed you for me. He had what he needed to find the Stand of Unity, and he knew I'd want to stop him, but he had to be sure I'd act first. He pushed me, so that I would run straight back and get the Minster to declare war. I justified his war." He choked out a sound in between a laugh and a cry. "He made me justify his war!"

Lea stared at him a moment, and her body seemed to relax again. "No offense, but who are you to have that kind of influence?"

He reached into his belt pouch and found the Winged pin of his office. He couldn't bring himself to leave it behind. He held it out to her, not that she knew what it meant. "I'm…uh…I'm the Winged Councilman now, like my father was."

"So you had a vote in this?"

With a nervous laugh he replied, "Yeah, I guess the title does sound dumb to you, but as Councilman I represent the needs of the Winged for the Minister, who is like our president. Anything dealing with the other traits, he'll listen to me." He exhaled sharply. "Who decided *that* right? The people chose me, and I sold them out for an empty promise."

He closed his fingers over the pin. "I know it sounds overly dramatic, but it's not. I gave Nor the information he needed to find the Stand of Unity. If they activate it, Matt'll have enough power to wipe out our armies, and Nor will take over. The only hope is to stop them before then, or we have less than a fighting chance. I have to fix my mistake."

"Stand of Unity?" Lea said. "Let me guess. It heals the Schism, doesn't it?"

Gabe blinked. "How'd you know?"

She said, "Well apparently, one of the wizards who created the divide, Merlin, he was my great-great-great-great you get the idea, grandfather, and he left me a journal explaining he saw me in a prophecy."

"So you really are a wizard?"

"Sorceress."

"Whatever." He smirked.

"Anyway." Lea shot him a look. "I don't know if I believe this thing about destiny or whatever, but I don't think it was a coincidence that I met you and Matt."

"Yeah?"

"The journal said I'd have to face the descendant of Merlin's rival, and then I find out that Matt's a wizard and working with that Nor guy. If the whole prophecy deal is true, then what am I supposed to do? As soon as I learned about Matt, I had to find a way to contact you, to warn you, so I never finished the journal. I don't know how to use magic."

Gabe got up and squeezed her shoulder. "You do, you saved me." He watched her stand up and stumble a bit over the edge of her dress. She pulled up the bottom of the skirt but still caught the hem under another clumsy step.

It really was her…alive. A sense of calm came to him for the first time since his father's death, and the difference was being with her. His morning star, she guided him back to himself.

He kept watching, and after a moment she gave him a strange look, probably because he was staring. Turning serious, he said, "You know I need you, right?"

She put her hand on her hip. "I know. I'm just that awesome."

He burst out laughing. Most girls would've blushed. "The world is crumbling around me, and you still make me laugh. You have no idea how much I missed that. I'm lost without you." This time she did glance away.

He added with a grin, "Literally lost, I have no idea where we are."

She chuckled and picked up the map. "Got this from the information kiosk outside the chateau up the hill. We're in France." She pointed to the river. "That's the Loire, and I've been working on the equation, but it's hard without my notes."

"You left me lying here to go sightseeing?" He pouted his bottom lip.

"Yeah, I got us a ton of souvenirs with all the euros I have with me too. The restroom attendant gave me stink eye because I stiffed her. Well, that, or she noticed the dried blood on my hands. Either way, we should probably leave as soon as we can."

He sighed. "No money's a problem. We can't go back through Illirin. You don't have oxygen."

Lea pointed at herself. "Sorceress. I can breathe, got that covered now."

"Oh," he said. "But there isn't enough time to get you to your apartment to pick up that journal. I'll have to find someplace closer to bring you." He tapped his fingers together. How could he get her back to the States and stop Nor before it was too late? Maybe she could stay in Illirin at Concord or somewhere close by the desert.

He looked up to see Lea staring him down. "You think you're going to leave me behind somewhere? That scenario is actually firing through the synapses in your brain? *Really?*"

"Uhhh."

"Let me make this clear. I'm going with you. Period."

"But—"

"No buts."

Gabe grabbed her shoulders, and she startled. "I can't lose you again. This is dangerous, if something happens to you—"

Lea put her hand on top of his, holding her right shoulder. "That's my decision. If I get hurt or killed, it's my choice. You can't make that for me. Might be hard to believe, but I'm not a moron. I know it's dangerous, and I'm going with you. I will not leave you again."

"You just said yourself that you don't know how to use magic. I can't protect you, what can you do?" His voice waivered. He nearly lost his mind when he thought she died.

"I don't know!" she shouted. "But I healed you with instinct, and maybe that's all it takes. It's a better shot than you've got alone. Think about it, we've accomplished so much together. We rescued my parents.

We got your memory back. *We* did. And really, your track record on your own doesn't seem that great."

"Ow."

"I'm not trying to be bitchy, but don't you see that we're better together?"

He exhaled and felt his lip curl up. "Yeah."

"And didn't you just say you needed me?" She winked.

Gabe laughed. "Damn, don't need to remember everything I say." He paused and let out a breath. "Fine. I obviously can't trick you into being safe."

"You really don't have a choice. I'm stubborn."

"Alert the media."

Lea's face brightened with a real smile. "There. That's the Gabe I know."

He turned serious again almost as fast as his humor resurfaced. He experienced what it was to be with her, and all at once the fear of losing it came over him. She pulled him back together, she saved him as she always did. Without her, he'd never recover. She was right though, and there was no way he could keep her from the fight.

Time was running out. These could be their last moments together, and he wasn't going to waste them. He leaned forward and slid his hand behind her head, his fingers caught in her hair. He pressed his mouth to her warm lips and kissed her deeply.

When the kiss ended, Lea pulled back and looked at him. She took a big bite of her lower lip. "Okay, so not the Gabe I know…"

"Didn't want as many regrets if we fail." His ears burned scarlet. "I, uh, I'm not usually so bold."

She took his hand and laced her fingers between his. "I kinda like it."

"Note taken." He took a deep breath. "We need to get going. We're losing time. Are you sure?"

She kissed him on the cheek. "More than anything. Let's go."

"Then let's find a thinning and get back to Illirin."

Twenty-Five

Without her notes, Lea faced a challenge to find a thinning. Thankfully, the connection she forged with Illirin seemed to work enough to give her the nudge she needed. They tore one open and jumped through.

Lea fell, and kept falling. Below her, enormous waves crested and frothy webs spread across a turbulent ocean. She took a breath right before plunging into the icy water. Darkness spun her around, and she struggled to find the surface. She was a strong swimmer, but the current was stronger, and the stupid dress made matters worse. The wet fabric weighed her down and tangled in her legs as she kicked. Hundreds of needles pricked her lungs.

Was this it?

There! Light streamed through from her side; she turned right side up. She pulled the water with her arms, and kicking furiously, broke the surface. Gasping for air, she searched around for Gabe, but saw only the walls of the bobbing waves.

"Gabe!" she yelled and gasped for another breath. The ocean dragged her under. She surfaced and saw Gabe's white hair. She swam forward, but before she could reach him, the surf shoved them apart.

Each foot she moved, the swells pushed her back by two, the weight of her dress dragging her back with the current. It was too hard to swim. She couldn't keep it up like this much longer.

Wait, was that him? It looked like his wings flailing in the surf. She had to get to him. She kicked rapidly to push her upper body over the surface, nothing—nothing but water. She couldn't find him, let alone land.

Another wave pressed Lea back, so she swam up it, attempting to float above the water. It crested too fast and plunged her down before she could breathe. When she found air again, she gasped and choked. She took another breath as the surf pulled her under once more.

Lea choked, her lungs aching from desperately trying to expel the salty water. Her vision started to blur, and something brushed her arm. Seaweed? A shark? Did they even have those here? Oh no, it could be something worse than that. She tried kicking and moving her arms, both to tread water and to keep whatever touched her away. She felt it again before another wave pushed her under, and she blacked out.

Oh fantastic, now there was rain, too. Lea curled her fingers into the wet sand and let the grit slide under her palms. The salt from the sea stung her skin and left a film in her mouth.

She sat up to see the edge of the ocean lap at her feet and the beach stretch to a curve behind some tropical looking trees. The veins of the palms contrasted in a deep maroon, so unique. Wait…she was in Illirin. She was alive! That thing didn't eat her, and she didn't drown.

"Gabe?" She stood and her feet slipped into big divots in the wet sand. Grabbing the hem of the dress, she found sure footing. The heavy rain made it hard to see any distance down the empty beach. "Gabe!" She shouted again.

"Right here."

She spun around to see him coming from the inland area with another man, his skin a marriage of kelp and slate. Spiky fins protruded from the sides of his calves, forearms, and where his ears should have been.

"Awake, thank goodness. You scared me," Gabe said as they approached.

"Good. Now you know how I felt." Lea rolled the long sleeves up on her arms to get the wet fabric out of her way.

He gestured to the Finned man wearing only what looked like tight spandex pants. "This is Namil. We owe him our lives."

"I can't thank you enough." Lea bowed her head, partially to respect him, but also to hide her stupid blush. It might be normal for them to go around shirtless, but she sure as heck wasn't used to it.

Namil held up his palm. "No need. We protect the oceans and those who come within. It's our duty, nothing more."

"But still, thanks."

Namil nodded politely, his arms down by his sides.

Gabe raised his hand to shake and awkwardly put it down. He gave a little bow-like nod. "After things settle down, if the Finned need anything, just contact me through your councilman. I'll see to it we discuss it quickly."

Namil smiled with a closed mouth. "We don't need a lot from the other traits, though thank you for your offer." He turned toward the water, likely to head back from where he came.

Gabe looked to Lea. "We're on the mainland near the bridge to the Finned's island. Union is only a few miles away. We can get there and contact Ceru to see if the army succeeded and what's happened."

"Sounds like you've got a plan then. Let's go."

Namil glanced back. "I've heard of a commotion going on there. I don't know much, didn't really care, but I advise you to be careful."

Gabe nodded and the Finned dove back into the shallows, disappearing into the murky sea.

Lea squeezed some of the excess water from her skirt, though the rain wasn't helping. "The ocean washed off most of that dried blood. We look slightly less horrible."

His face was stern, probably considering what Namil had said. "Let's hurry."

She took his hand and followed him quietly up the beach and onto the road. Acting pensive, Gabe didn't seem in the mood for traveling conversation. His demeanor left Lea to her own thoughts as well.

After a few minutes of silent travel, something felt different. Well, *she* didn't feel different. Illirin felt different. When she first tapped the aether, the power enraptured her, filling her lungs and her body with that amazing energy, magic. Later, when she waited for the thinning in the compound, the connection had faded to a mild touch running over her skin like the static electricity in a bundle of freshly dried towels. But now the connection had strengthened. The energy flowed through her more like blood. She felt almost part of Illirin as much as she belonged to Earth.

Lea hadn't told Gabe he'd been unconscious the rest of that day and well into the next morning. She snuck a glance at her watch, and they were already approaching evening. He spoke only of running out of time or being too late. A shudder flowed down her spine into her toes. Maybe they already were.

"So." She intruded on Gabe's interior monologue. "What exactly happens if Matt and this Nor guy manage to activate the Stand of Unity? How bad is it, you know, right away?"

"When the worlds bind, the aether will begin to seep into Earth. It strengthens the force both here and especially there, and humans like Matt who can use magic, will have a greater command of the energy because of its connection with Earth. Within Illirin, they will be the most powerful, but on Earth where magic is foreign, the might is unparalleled."

He glanced at her as they continued half-jogging down the road. "Other than that, not a ton. The thinnings will be stationary, the Schism will weaken, and the worlds will be closer together for anyone to travel between. But, you know how it is for humans on our side."

"Oh, so like it just makes that possible. Nothing like explodes right away or anything, that's good."

He slowed down. "Why do you say that?"

"Making sure nothing terrible happened right away. That's a *good* thing," she said with a lopsided smile.

He stopped in the middle of the road. "You're not telling me something. What is it?"

She didn't know how else to say it. "I think they've already used the Stand."

"What do you mean? How can you know that?"

"I can feel it. I'm not sure, so maybe I'm just imagining things feeling different. I didn't want to worry you about it."

"That's all there *is* to worry about!" He grabbed the sides of his head.

She tapped him between the wings with a gentle shove. "We're almost to the city, right? We'll find out from your friend soon enough."

Gabe gazed off in the distance. "I hope you're wrong."

"Me too."

They both went faster, and pushed past their exhaustion to keep going. The fight with the ocean took a toll, but Gabe had found strength somewhere. So much that once Lea saw the skyscrapers inching over the horizon, she had a hard time keeping up with him.

"We're almost there," Gabe said between breaths. A few hundred feet from the first building, he stopped in his tracks.

Lea stumbled into him, then fell back on her heels.

"What are you stopping for?" Lea held her hand over her eyes to shield them from the piercing drops of rain, which of course fell straight into them. Always the best of luck.

A commanding voice echoed over a megaphone. "Who approaches Union. Announce yourselves and stand ready to be searched."

Lea grabbed Gabe's arm. "What's going on?"

"He's a Seer soldier. One of Nor's men," he whispered.

All the windows in the buildings had been blown out. Shattered glass coated the ground in a dazzling pattern reflecting the fading light. From where she stood, not a single pane survived. The entire city must be in the same condition.

Lea squinted. A mound rose near the building through the lessening rain. She gasped. Bodies piled one on top of another in a heap. The dead consisted of various traits wearing the same uniform, some kind of police. Someone had thrown them together like garbage. She shuddered and looked away.

She squeezed Gabe's arm. "What do we do?"

Three Seer soldiers approached from the edge of the city as the man on the bullhorn had warned.

Gabe took a step backward. "The city is occupied. We need to run. They can't find me here, or we're both dead." His voice sounded all business, but something rumbled just beneath the surface.

He grabbed Lea's wrist, jerking her to the right so fast it hurt. *"Run!"* he yelled.

They ran, and they ran hard. Traces of water in Lea's chest made her wheeze, and she strained to keep up.

Gabe's hand never left her wrist, so when she slowed, he tugged forcefully to keep her next to him. Her arm hurt, her lungs hurt, and she knew she couldn't keep running.

She glanced behind and the men were still on their tail. Gabe looked at her, and she shook her head. She couldn't keep going. She dropped to her knees, and her wrist slipped from his grasp.

He turned back and scooped her up as smooth as a choreographed routine. She was certainly easier for him to carry than vice versa. Gabe continued to run and glanced back to check on their pursuers. He took a deep breath. "I've never done this before. If we fall, get up and keep going, okay?"

"Done what?"

"Okay?"

"Okay," she said.

He spread his wings to catch the wind, and he jumped forward. Her stomach lurched. She could feel him beat his wings hard against gravity, hoisting his own weight with hers. The downward force of the rain only added to his struggle for altitude, but the world continued to drop beneath her with each labored movement. Behind them, the soldiers stopped pursuing and returned to the edge of the city. Gabe strained to keep them aloft, and they remained low to the ground despite all of his efforts.

"You can land, they went back," she said hoping he could rest.

He shook his head.

The rain slowed to a sprinkle, which seemed to make things better. After a few minutes, he stopped beating his wings so hard and they stayed spread, gliding.

"Updraft." He breathed. "We'll get higher…easier."

She nodded and let him do what he thought he had to. After riding the warm currents for a while, they got high enough, and the stiffness in his face relaxed just a bit. He now glided most of the time, giving his muscles a break.

"Are you doing okay? You don't have to talk if you can't. I just want to make sure, ya know, we won't go plunging out of the sky." Lea gripped tighter around his neck, not that it would help if they did plummet.

"Don't worry, I'll know when that's happening." He took a few more breaths and then finally seemed like he'd recovered from their takeoff.

"That's encouraging." She squeezed her wrist harder. At least she wouldn't fall without him.

He simply nodded. Severe concentration dug deep in Gabe's wrinkled brow and tight face. She'd never seen him fly before, but doing so by himself probably didn't take near as much effort. Before now, she didn't think she weighed that much.

After a couple hours, Gabe couldn't take it any longer, and he landed them in the plains to rest. The grasslands stretched for miles around, only dotted by bushes and small clumps of trees. With the rain far behind them, the sun dipped close to the horizon, but still bright enough to force Lea to squint. Gabe must be tired, because he didn't even bother to bring them near any shade, and she could see some trees in the distance.

Lea wanted to let him recover a bit before playing "twenty questions." So, her mind drifted back to the city they had fled, the dead officers, and the broken glass. The way the windows had all been blown out, it looked like wreckage from a windstorm. Matt must have been the one to damage the city with another tornado or something else.

The destruction to the buildings was one thing, but the dead were another. Did Matt do that, too?

Maybe the people died in a fight with the Seer army. The soldiers could have easily killed them. It didn't have to be Matt. Besides, how could Matt do something like that? He couldn't, could he? The way Gabe spoke of him, he easily believed Matt was capable of real evil. Lea couldn't take that leap. Matt might be misguided, or maybe Nor manipulated him.

Matt had talked about persecution, and maybe he made choices based on misinformation.

Lea looked over and saw Gabe lying on the grass, wings spread flat as if he didn't even have the energy to bother folding them. She took a seat next to him, intent on keeping her thoughts about Matt to herself for now. She wasn't looking for an argument.

"Where are we heading?" she asked once Gabe opened his eyes.

"To Wren, my hometown where we met my father. I must find Ceru, find out where the Minister and the army are. More importantly…" A different shade of worry passed across his creased forehead. "If Union is already occupied, I don't know. I hope Ceru was able to get Aime out of the city, but how would he have known? She has to be okay."

"Who's Aime?" she asked. "And Ceru, for that matter."

"My sister. Ceru is like an uncle, and the one person who's helped me though this mess. Though I don't know how much he can help now."

The worry in his face never faded. It couldn't be good to keep focusing on the bad. Maybe some small talk would help. "I didn't know you had a sister," Lea said.

"We've been reunited long enough for a fifteen-minute conversation. It didn't come up."

"You don't need to snap at me."

He rolled onto his stomach and pushed himself to a sitting position. "Sorry."

She heaved a sigh. It was like he had this whole side of him she knew nothing about, and he wasn't willing to talk about it. Yeah, now was not the time for lengthy getting-to-know-you conversations, but part of her still felt left out, if not left behind.

No time to brood about that now. They had to get to Wren, find Gabe's friend, and figure out what to do. She pinched a bit of grass between her fingers and fidgeted with it. What were they going to do?

Gabe sighed. "I don't know what to do."

Was he reading her mind? She tossed a piece of grass on the ground. "We'll do what you suggested. Find out what's happening first, then figure something out."

"What can we do? We're too late to stop them, and that was my only idea. Now the war's started." He folded his wings and breathed in and out. "All I can think is that I want to find Ceru and have him tell me what to do. I just want someone else to tell me what to do."

"Maybe Ceru will know something," she said with her confident smile. He didn't buy it.

Gabe seemed like he intentionally avoided her line of sight. He got to his feet and reached to help her up. "We have to get going. It doesn't matter how tired I am, we don't have time to waste."

"You can rest a little. These few minutes aren't going to make or break anything that isn't already broken."

He stretched his wings, rolling his shoulders. "No. I'm crawling out of my skin waiting here. Besides, I think I can find that thinning on the way to Wren and get you back home. Now that the—"

"Oh, no you don't. We settled this already, and I'm going with you. It's my choice, danger or not."

"It's not just that!"

Lea put her hand on his elbow, but he flinched away. "What is your issue?"

"What do you think I'm going to do when I find Nor?"

She could see he was worried, but why? Did it matter? She wanted to be there for him even if she couldn't actually help.

Gabe wet his lips. "I'm going to kill him, with my bare hands if that's all I have." He looked away again. "I have an immense amount of anger, and I don't want you to see that side of me. I just don't." Turning back, he took her hand. "It's selfish, so then okay I'm selfish, but I want you safe, and I don't want to scare you away."

She smiled, and he got that sweet, confused bump in his eyebrow. Didn't he see his concern for her was the important thing? She took the time to carefully form her words. "Gabe, I know you think I don't know you 'cause I don't know all you've been through, but I do. You're passionate about everything, and you act on it whether it's empathy or love. Anger is an emotion too, it's all the same." She closed her hand around his fingers. "You run on your gut, and I love that about you. The characteristics of our strengths are often our weaknesses as well. I'm not afraid to stand with you, I promise."

He stared at her a full minute before responding. "You're too damn stubborn to let me protect you."

"See, strength and weakness."

Gabe failed at stifling a smirk. "Fine. But don't say I didn't warn you."

"Fully warned." Lea grinned. "You ready to lug me all over creation for once?" He raised his eyebrow.

She chuckled. "Inside joke. Let's just go."

He picked her up and made sure he had a good grip. "Hold on tight."

She resumed her death grip around his neck. "Don't have to tell me twice." As soon as she was secure, he ran through the plain to get enough speed before taking to the air. It went a little smoother than last time but no less frightening. At least one good thing came out of this adventure. She was conquering her fear of heights, crash-course style.

Twenty-Six

Every muscle in Gabe's body burned. The flight to Wren took a toll on a normal day with calm winds, but carrying the weight of a second person was just about killing him. Gabe steeled himself and kept going because there wasn't any other option.

He flew in a trance, concentrating on wind, air pressure, and all the usually mundane things about flying. Whenever he lessened his focus, he lost altitude, but every once in awhile he'd notice Lea shift her grip. The flight had to be hard on her too, but he couldn't waste the effort to comfort her. He squeezed her tighter. He'd never drop her. She had to know that.

Behind them, the sun fell below the horizon leaving only an orange haze on the edge of the world. A similar warm glow grazed the bottoms of the wispy clouds ahead. But they were heading due east. What could cause that glow?

Gabe lost concentration, and they dropped lower. Something was wrong. Up ahead, instead of the tips of the skyline, tongues of flame curled above the city.

Lea gasped, and he looked down. Bodies littered the ground—Winged guardians and what appeared to be a remnant of the army. No, it couldn't be.

His wings went slack for an instant, and they fell several hundred feet.

Lea screeched and squeezed his neck in a choke hold.

He fought for breath at the same time he struggled to regain control. His wings trapped enough wind to stop the fall, though he stayed in a glide and didn't climb back into the air.

"Gotcha, sorry," he said, straightening them out.

He could feel Lea shake, but at least she wasn't choking him anymore. He tilted his wings and descended faster, though not as quick as he wanted. He didn't want to give her a heart attack again. He lifted up to land as softly as he could, which still pounded them both hard on the ground.

Gabe got back up in the field surrounded by the bodies of his kinsmen, some burned beyond recognition and others bloodied from close combat. He didn't have the luxury to feel the keen sorrow at the loss of life. The fires raging in his home and Nor's army were just ahead. He had to save lives, not mourn the dead. He grabbed a tri-blade from the hand of a guardian.

He turned to Lea who finished stumbling to her feet. "Sorry…" he said. He pivoted on his heel and leapt into the sky. The rush of the wind didn't muffle her protests enough. He wouldn't put her in the middle of danger, even though she'd follow. Hopefully by the time she got there, he'd be finished.

Gabe flew swiftly, and as he approached the city limits, he could see a few remaining soldiers fighting scores of the Seer army. Nor had to be leading from somewhere, maybe with the contingent of men ahead. He braced himself to endure the smoke from the fires, but the plume never came close. What the…?

The smoke billowed up and then stopped above the city without dissipating or going further. Gabe flew straight toward the fight in the city. He hit a wall of wind, throwing him back. He righted himself and was able to land at the edge of the field. He reached forward and the rushing wind wrenched his hand, forcing him to pull away.

Within the barrier, the Seers overwhelmed the few remaining Winged men fighting through suffocating ash. He could see the battle and the civilians fleeing behind them, but heard nothing except the blasting wall of wind. A woman leapt from the window of a skyscraper, and she flew up to get away from the smoke. Her lips pantomimed a coughing fit before she was thrust down from the top of the barrier back into the cloud of gray. He lost sight of her after that. The fires raged, and the smoke filled the barrier, leaving him alone with the rushing sound.

Gabe squeezed the hilt of his borrowed blade and took to the sky again to search for Nor. The barrier was a death trap, and there was no way Nor led his army from inside. He rose above the city for a better view.

To the north marched most of the Seer army. Like a falcon diving for prey, Gabe shot through the air toward the enemy. Nor stood there at the front! He readied his blade to attack from above. His eyes locked with Nor's.

The Seer pupils began to glow. Nor raised his arm and summoned a bolt of electricity.

Gabe's vision went white, a bird shot from the sky. The lightning sent his system into shock, so he couldn't feel the branches break his fall. A tingling sensation ran over his skin, and as it wore off, he began to feel again. He lay in a contorted wreck, and once the pain crashed into him, each injury sucked away the last of his endurance.

His momentum ceased, and now lying in the dirt, he couldn't imagine moving again. His wing twisted and broken under his chest seemed almost symbolic of how grounded he felt. A tear dripped down the tip of his nose and onto the ground.

The crunch of footsteps approached from behind. *Nor.* Gabe couldn't give in to his weakened state. He had to find the energy somewhere. He had to fight. He pulled his arm under him and pushed up to his knees. His broken wing bumped his arm and he grimaced, the pain shooting into his spine. He looked up as Nor arrived. Where was it? The blade was long gone.

Gabe clenched his teeth and took a step to stand, but Nor backhanded him across his jaw, driving him back to one knee. The dirt under Gabe softened, and his foot, knee, and right hand sunk down. The soft ground re-hardened, trapping him in a genuflect. He twisted his head to the side.

Nor straightened to his full height, and the glow left his eyes. "Makai Ilat. I'm pleased you survived the siege on my compound."

Gabe spat at his feet, which would have been more insulting if it wasn't tinged red from the coppery blood seeping into his mouth. Now he noticed his throbbing cheekbone.

"It would have been a shame for you to die before seeing the results of your gift to me," Nor continued. "I couldn't have done this without your help. Look, see the fruits of our efforts."

He wouldn't give him the satisfaction. He kept his head down, defying him in the only way available.

"I'm honored by your reverence to me, but I insist." Nor yanked Gabe's hair, twisting his head and forcing his view of Wren—his home. The barrier had vanished, and the black smoke billowed unrestrained, the charred smell just beginning to float his way. Gabe squeezed his eyes shut, but without the roaring winds he could hear the screams of the people trapped in their homes.

Nor pulled harder, and Gabe gritted his teeth. "Look!"

Gabe couldn't keep his eyes shut. The sound alone allowed him to imagine something worse. He stared at the horror, no, reality was more gruesome than anything in his mind. Amongst the raging flames, bodies lay strewn about the street. Some probably tried to flee, and others who attempted to fight the Seer army were closer to the border but just as dead.

With a strained voice he asked, "What did I do to you?"

Nor gave him a puzzled look and then smiled. "Oh, you think this is personal? Oh no, dear boy, you're just a convenient symbol I latched onto." He put his face close to Gabe's, Nor's breath hot against his cheek. "I hate *all* of you."

He let go of Gabe's hair and shoved his head down once more for good measure. He stood back and gestured to the top of the nearest high-rise, a bank headquarters. "Did you notice how much oomph was in that bolt? You can thank your friend, what's his name…Matthew? He gave me a little extra power just as he has the rest of my forces, and look at him, at the power he wields alone."

Against better judgment, Gabe followed Nor's hand pointing to the silhouette of someone atop the building. The air immediately around him seemed to shimmer as a fog of light. Then, the light focused into his hands forming an enormous ball of flame, which he thrust through the sky like a cannonball. It landed far out of view, probably in the suburbs.

Nor chuckled, a playful lilt in his voice. "Isn't it amazing? And to think the extra power he's charged my army with will allow each soldier to do things almost as marvelous. We're heading north to take care of the rest of your arrogant trait." He looked into Gabe's widened eyes. "You've never even been outside an integrated city, have you? You have no idea what your equality means to the non-Winged. The rest will thank me for delivering them from your control."

Nor's clenched fist hung close to Gabe's face as he stared off at the man tossing fireballs from the roof of the building. "I'd prefer to kill you myself, but I have to throw my dog a bone. He'll want his shot at you. So watch your city burn, and once you've had enough, your *friend* will come here and end your suffering."

Gabe froze, not just from the hardened mud that trapped him. Everything around him blurred, unable to deal with reality. Nor's vague form sent another running toward the city, and then he turned and shrank into the distance to join his army.

Was this really happening? He must be having a nightmare, because it was all too insane to be real. At any moment he'd wake up in his dorm room about to miss class again. Matt would laugh at him for sleeping through the alarm. They'd go get lunch together. He'd make some whiny comment about missing his memory and get on with his day.

His broken wing shifted and he winced, once more feeling the searing pain shoot throughout his body. Matt wasn't the guy from those dreams he used to think was his life. He was up there killing thousands of innocents. Tears streamed down Gabe's face. If only his fall had taken his memory again, releasing him from the guilt. He bowed his head to pray for forgiveness from the dying, not that he expected anything but silence. For him, forgiveness was impossible.

Lea yelled until her breath gave out and Gabe all but vanished in the darkness. He left her behind! And worse, he was risking his life alone. Wasn't the whole point of her coming to help him? The nausea that rose in her stomach overcame her anger. He better not get himself hurt.

She kept her eyes up and focused on her worried irritation with Gabe, because otherwise the truth of what happened would steal her attention. It got harder to ignore as she ran through the field jumping over and dodging corpses, the smell of sweat and burned flesh thickening the air. She misjudged and tripped over an outstretched arm, tumbling to the ground. A dead soldier's wing slipped under her hand with a squeak. Getting up on her knees, she couldn't hold it in and she vomited in the grass. The awful taste clung inside her cheeks. She coughed and spat trying to get it out. She couldn't erase the scene from her memory as easily.

She stood and wiped the tears from her eyes. She didn't have time to get upset. Gabe needed her help, or at the very least, she had to make sure he was okay. They needed a real plan to help with this war. Running blindly into the fight was hardly a good idea. He should have waited for her.

After a long run, she arrived close to the city limit. A scene similar to the one in the field greeted her in the street, only the remains of a battle enough to reveal the loser. Lifting her eyes, she choked on the remaining contents of her stomach. *Don't throw up. Don't cry.* She had to be stronger.

Her head still tilted skyward, she saw a ball of fire soar through the air and crash into the other side of the city. What was that—magic? The aether felt different, as if it pulled from another direction. She followed the flow, first by walking, and then jogging around the edges of the city to the origin of the energy. Another fireball soared, and she traced the source, the top of that building. She ran closer to see what it was.

No, it couldn't be. She guessed, she knew, but she didn't believe it when she saw Matt drawing the energy into himself before creating another monstrous flame. It was truly him, black cape flapping in the wind and all. She stopped breathing. One of her only friends was capable of real evil. Ignoring her personal feelings, how was she supposed to face that? She shook, now afraid he'd see her standing there.

Her old friend tingled the back of her neck to remind her of her other fear, Gabe. On impulse, she turned her head. A form hunched on the ground not far in the distance. She glanced back to check on Matt, and he had exited the building on the ground floor. There was only one place he'd go, and she had to get there first.

She ran harder than ever, unable to look behind her. She had to get to Gabe, to save him, because if Matt was able to kill all those others, then one more Winged would be nothing.

Lea found Gabe kneeling with his head hung down and one wing bent at an awkward angle. She jumped to his side and grabbed his shoulder armor. "Get up! We have to get out of here, he's coming!"

Gabe raised his head and narrowed his eyes as they made contact with the approaching figure.

Why wasn't he getting up? She yanked his arm again, and it didn't budge. Holy crap, he was embedded in the ground? The dried earth butted up against his wrist and ankle like he had dipped them underwater to test the temperature.

"Can you free me?" Gabe's voice cracked. He hadn't taken his gaze off Matt.

Lea gulped. "I have to…" What did she do the last time? She couldn't remember; nothing stuck out. She glanced up and saw Matt coming closer. No time. She put her hands on the hardened mud and concentrated on an image of it breaking. Nothing happened. She hit it with her fist. Damn it, what was she missing?

Maybe she just needed to stop trying so hard. She took a breath and relaxed to let the aether flow into her as it did naturally. The warm feeling grew. With her hands back against the mud, she released the tension in her arms and let the energy flow out into the ground. The mud cracked all around him. It worked!

Gabe gritted his teeth and ripped himself free, but he didn't stand up. He breathed hard. Lea grabbed his arm and squeaked, "Run."

She helped him to his feet, taking some of his weight, but as soon as he was standing, the pressure vanished from her shoulder. He tensed his body, and she could see his chest rise and lower with each deliberate breath. Breaking his view of Matt, he turned to her and gave her arm a gentle squeeze.

Gabe mouthed 'I love you' in one instant, and in the next, ran straight toward danger.

She could kill him. She took off after him screaming, *"Stop!"*

Bright white sparks crackled around Matt's arms, and he stopped walking to focus.

Lea was able to catch up to Gabe, and as she did, she saw Matt's eyes widen.

He was about to release the electricity, but at the last moment he swept his hands up, and a blast of wind came instead, throwing both Lea and Gabe back a hundred feet.

Lea recovered before Gabe and made it to him by the time he was ready to fight again. She got in front of him and put her hands up.

"Stop!" she said.

Matt charged up again, eyes locked in a staring match with Gabe. Gabe swept her hands down with his arm and stepped around her.

"No!" she cried again. He was going to get killed! She jumped back between them. Maybe Matt would listen to her if only Gabe wasn't trying to fight. It was their only chance of getting out of there alive.

Gabe's hand moved to sweep her to the side, but she wouldn't let him.

She clenched her fist and forced the flow of energy into her arm. She threw an uppercut to Gabe's chin. The powerful punch dropped him, and compounded with his other injuries, knocked him out cold. Lea spun around, spreading her arms protectively, acting as a human shield between him and Matt.

Lightning sparkled around Matt, his raised fist shaking violently. His cold glare sent ice into her veins, stopping her heart, but she stood still. She wouldn't leave Gabe. She searched Matt's face for hope, and through the anger she saw something else. Maybe she could reach him.

"Why?" she asked. He had killed so many. Wet trails swept down her cheeks and she cried again, "Why!"

Matt gritted his teeth, his fist shaking harder with the buildup of power. He stared at her for a full minute, seething in electricity. Then the sparks vanished, and he dropped his arm to his side. He breathed in and out once. "Go."

She blinked, unmoving.

Matt yelled, *"Now! Before I change my mind!"*

"Matt…" Lea stammered. She backed up a step.

He inhaled and looked through her. "You chose your side and you lost. Never come back here." He turned and walked away, leaving her behind.

What just happened? She touched her face. Real. Alive. Next to her, Gabe lay unconscious and wounded. That woke her up. She had to get him to safety, and the only safe place for him now was Earth. She knelt to pick up her charge, but this time had no humor in her heart to joke about it.

The dim lighting in the motel room did nothing for Lea's mood. Gabe hadn't spoken since he regained consciousness. Underneath him, the scratchy bedspread lay neatly made, a stark contrast to his body bandaged in strips of crimson fabric. He leaned against the headboard staring at nothing, and when he happened to catch her eye, he looked away.

Lea never felt this lost before. She always had a clear goal, and now she didn't even know if there was one. The journal said she'd have to face Matt…how? She wasn't a warrior, and even if she could learn to use magic, she couldn't fight someone, especially him. She'd never be able to face Matt alone, but could Gabe recover from this?

She glanced at him again and this time he glared at her with a hardened stare. She shuddered. So that was what it's like to be on the receiving end of his anger. She'd give anything to never see him look at her like that again, anything. She grasped the seat of the desk chair.

Gabe inhaled slowly though his nose. "You stopped me from killing him."

"I stopped *him* from killing *you*," she replied. She saved his life, both their lives. She regretted how, but not that she did.

He jumped off the bed yelling, "You had *no* right to interfere!" His rash movement made him cringe from unhealed injuries.

She stood up and replied just as loud, "You didn't have a chance against him. What were you gonna do, throw him a right hook? The man burned down a city!"

Gabe winced like she punched him in the stomach.

She didn't mean to say it like that. "I'm sorry...I'm sorry," she said meekly.

He sank back onto the bed shaking his head. His shoulders rose and fell. "And he won't stop with one." He turned to her, so much pain written on his face it hurt to look at it. "I deserved to die fighting him. It was my last chance to redeem myself, because now, not only is my legacy the genocide of my trait, but I am also a coward." He dropped his face into his hands, his shoulders curving over as if he wrapped his intangible wing around himself. Although she couldn't see his wings, he moved his body like he could feel them, evidence of the changes the Stand brought to Earth.

"What have I done?" he said into his palms.

"*You* didn't do it...you saw who did," Lea replied. What else could she say? It wasn't just one death, it was the eradication of his people. It's not like there's a Hallmark card for that sorta thing. She couldn't do anything for him. Worse than useless.

Gabe shuddered and lifted his head slightly. "Nor was right. I was arrogant. I thought if he started a war, somehow I could end it. I don't know, war seemed abstract...doable, but I never imagined, never..." Tears streamed down his strong jaw, dripping onto the floor. "Who was *I* to decide that? Who was *I* to trade one life for so many, *many* others? They die, and I live. How is that right?" He trembled and dropped his head once more.

Was it possible to physically hurt from empathy? Lea's chest stabbed answering her question. He always seemed unbreakable, like a pillar she would lean on. Now she had to hold him up, if she could even carry the dust in her arms. She wanted to take his pain for herself or blow it away into the wind. Though he probably thought there was only one way out of it, and she'd never let him. She saved his life. She'd never allow him to throw it away. She needed him. Gabe was more to her than someone she loved.

Kneeling, she brushed his wing away with the back of her fingers. She couldn't touch it, but it affected how the aether flowed, and in that way she could tell where it was.

"I'm sorry," she said. "I'm sorry this happened, and I'm sorry you blame yourself. But I'm not sorry I saved your life. I need you."

"No, you don't." His voice rang hollow, so much worse than somber.

She hesitated before touching his hand and then resting hers on top. "I do, and I don't mean because of how I feel. I need your help."

"Lea…"

"Let me finish." She returned to her quiet speech. "Now I truly believe that prophecy is real, and I'll have to face Matt. I survived because I have to save those left behind in Illirin and protect Earth. But even though I saw what evil he's capable of, I still don't think I could actually fight him. I don't have that in me. I'm not a warrior or sorceress. I'm just a regular girl. I can't hurt someone…I don't know how to fight." She paused. "I need you to teach me."

"I can't teach you magic," Gabe replied.

If only he'd look at her. She sighed and squeezed his knuckles. "The journal can teach me that. I need you to teach me to fight, to have the drive. I need you to give me your anger."

He looked up; his bloodshot eyes lacked the spark he used to have. His hurt resonated in her bones.

She breathed through her nose to keep her own tears at bay. "I need you. I need you to pull yourself together for me. Can you?"

After a few seconds, he put his other hand on top of hers and swallowed. "Always…I'll do anything for you."

"Even live?"

He took a slow breath and nodded. "Even live."

She lunged onto him, holding him tight. She wouldn't let him carry the burden of her feelings as well, so she hid them in his shoulder. They say that the greatest demonstration of love is to give up your life for another, but Lea could tell Gabe's sacrifice was greater.

Gnarled branches and some fallen rocks disguised the opening of the cave entrance from a distance. Ceru finished putting some last-minute touches on the camouflage before heading back through the twisted corridors to the cavern in the back. The tunnels had been carved out long ago by underground tributaries, leaving an elaborate network through the rock.

Ceru traced his hand along the cold stone on the edge of the cavern opening. A slick dampness seemed to coat the uneven rock face, making it hard to warm enough, and a mossy smell stuck to the inside of his nose. The fire roared in the center of a makeshift pit to heat and light the refugee dwelling. He sighed as he took in the rough accommodations. He hoped this would be a short-term stay, not really for his own comfort, but for Aime's.

Aime sat near the fire on a pile of long grasses intended to soften the ground, but really only made it itchy. Clumsily whittling the ends of some sticks, she looked completely out of her element, thin, pinkish arms holding a blade and hacking away in the glow of the firelight. She belonged at her home, comfortable and bored, not hiding in a cave making parts for traps. His best friend's daughter, always an outcast, was now a refugee. It made him sick. How much adversity had she already faced to now have more heaped on top of her? There had to be a way to make things right.

"Uncle Ceru?" Aime asked, "You're sure you want me to call you that?"

"Please, I insist. I was like a brother to your father."

She changed positions on the grass pile. "Of course. I'm not used to it is all."

He smiled. "Neither am I, but I'd like to get used to it." He spread out some more of the scratchy grass and took a seat next to her. It was mildly better than the cold stone. He held out his hand. "Here, let me take that over. You don't need to be doing it."

"I want to do something to help." She gripped the knife tighter. "I can't make the traps or anything. I can at least do this."

"If you want to, that's fine." He grabbed and extra-long twig and stirred the fire. Red sparks danced above the pit.

They sat for a while and listened to the crackling flames, Aime sharpening the sticks and Ceru tying them up in bundles. The tasks kept only their hands busy. What was Aime thinking about? The worry lines in her brow creased as she worked on shaving off little pieces of wood.

More than concentration, her intense gaze seemed as if she pondered something deeper than her mundane task.

Ceru cleared his throat and asked, "Are you okay?"

She whetted her lips and hesitated at first. "Yeah, I'm…" She dropped her hands into her lap. "I was thinking about Mak…about Gabe."

He nodded. "Yeah, me too."

"You really think he's still alive? Didn't you say the generals never found him at the Seer compound?"

"Oh yeah, he's alive." He tapped his chest. "He made me his riddle keeper. The magic would have alerted me if I was needed, and it hasn't. He's still around…somewhere."

"But the riddles were used to retrieve the Stand of Unity, so why would the magic continue to bind the riddle keeper? I'm not sure that's enough to go on."

Ceru finished tying a bundle and set it down. "Maybe you're right, but I still think he's alive."

"How do you know?"

"I just do. I know that boy. As much as he denies, he's like your father and nothing would stop him either. I've got faith in him."

She smiled a little. "I'm glad you do. I'd like to think he's out there, that he'll come back and bring the Winged survivors together."

"He left an impression on you, didn't he?"

"Not just me, on Illirin." She stared out into the distance. "He's charismatic, and I think because he doesn't realize it, people like him even more. I was uncertain when he said he was running for Councilman, but what I heard of it, I think you were right to suggest him."

Ceru heaved a small sigh. "Not sure he'd agree, but maybe I could convince him. I hope I get the chance."

"Me too." She picked up one of her sharpened sticks. "How long do you think we'll have to hide in here?"

He looked away. Why did she have to ask that? "Honestly, I have no idea. I'll keep trying to find out more information, but what I've heard so far isn't promising. There isn't a lot of answer from anywhere in the Winged territories. I think…" He paused. "I'll be preparing a stockpile for when winter comes. We'll prepare to house as many survivors as we can find."

Aime nodded and kept working. "Yes, of course."

"Your nurse?"

"When I left, Leena said she could blend in with the Tailed sympathizers, no problem. She's a tough little woman. She'll get by."

"Good, I'm glad," he said.

As she resumed her work, she became even quieter than before. Ceru cleared his throat. "And so will we."

Focused on her work, she nodded. He wished he could promise her more, promise her something. He wouldn't disrespect her with platitudes of what could be. He gave her the truth, which was a less-than-uncertain future. Things were likely to become a great deal harder than even now, and it was better to prepare for that than to waste time on wishful thinking. The only wishful thinking he'd allow himself was that his heart was right—Gabe was alive.

Coming Soon

UNITY

Illirin Book Two

To overcome *his* grief

To face *her* destiny

To find redemption

They'll need faith in unity, or they'll have to sever the worlds forever.

Acknowledgements

Special thanks to my mom for naming me after an author which marked my destiny, and to my dad who would have loved Lea's analytical nature and engineer personality. To Beth and Gene who are the most excited in-laws ever, cheering me on from that not-Texas state over there.

A million more thanks to my loving hubby who helped me go to zillions of hours of critique groups, who supported my crazy dream, and who I love the mostest-est. Of course thanks to my daughter and her own amazing imagination.

I could get into the whole "it takes a village" metaphor, but we all know how that goes. I'd like to thank my village members, including my first beta readers Amy, Jason, Katie, and Grandma Maisano. My in-depth beta Travis, and all the advice from the North Texas Speculative Fiction Workshop and North Branch Writer's Critique Group. And to my special village chieftains, Keely and Louis, who spent hours typing random stories with me honing dialogue into my finest weapon of choice. To Tex who helped me navigate the perilous waters of promotion and networking, and to Kara who helped me get this puppy published.

Thank you Jane for being my Obi-Wan Kenobi and mentoring this fledgling writer in the mysterious ways of publishing and reading some very bad first drafts (my sincerest apologies ☺).

And of course the village members at the MuseItUp team including my lovely editor Lisa who wasn't afraid to quibble about commas with me. And a big thanks to Lea who believed in Gabe and Lea enough to give them life. Thank you everyone for all your hard work making my little book shine.

Note from the Author

I hope you enjoyed reading SCHISM, and I promise the sequel UNITY isn't far behind. Word of mouth and reviews are the lifeblood for an author, and if you liked the book, please tell a friend. Or five friends, or every person you know. If you post a review to Amazon, Barnes and Nobel and/or Goodreads, I'll appreciate every one.

Thank you ☺

About the Author

Laura's debut novel SCHISM is a YA Fantasy to be followed by the sequel UNITY. She has an MA in Technical writing and is a Senior Editor at Anaiah Press for their YA/NA Christian Fiction.

Her gamer husband and amazing daughter give support and inspiration every day. Their cats, Talyn and Moya, provide entertainment through living room battles and phantom-dust-mote hunting. Somehow, they all manage to survive living in Texas where it is hotter than any human being should have to endure. You can find updates about writing and the random stuff in her life on her blog www.LauraMaisano.blogspot.com or follow her on twitter @MaisanoLaura. If you're more interested in just the professional angle, check out her website www.RayhaStudios.com.

CPSIA information can be obtained at www.ICGtesting.com
Printed in the USA
LVOW07s1813160715

446498LV00007B/953/P